A STORY OF PASSION AND INTRIGUE INVOLVING ONE OF ENGLAND'S GREAT FAMILIES!

Lord Edward Falcon—the tyrannical patriarch of Kingsmead, whose wealth, power, cunning, and greed make him one of the most feared men in England.

Lady Falcon—his adoring wife, who is driven to despair and suicide by her husband's insensitivity and neglect.

Helen—his eldest daughter, who awakes from a dream of love to a nightmare of horror when the man she loves is destroyed by her father's obsessive quest.

Nathan—the handsome and carefree youngest son. When he threatens to defy his father's command and marry his childhood sweetheart, Lord Falcon has him drafted into the army. He is killed at Bunker's Hill.

THE FALCON SAGA by Catherine Darby

A FALCON FOR A WITCH
THE KING'S FALCON
FORTUNE FOR A FALCON
SEASON OF THE FALCON
FALCON ROYAL
THE FALCON TREE
THE FALCON AND THE MOON

All exclusively in Popular Library editions

Catherine Darby's
The Falcon Saga - 4
Season Of The Falcon

POPULAR LIBRARY · TORONTO

FALCON FAMILY DYNASTY

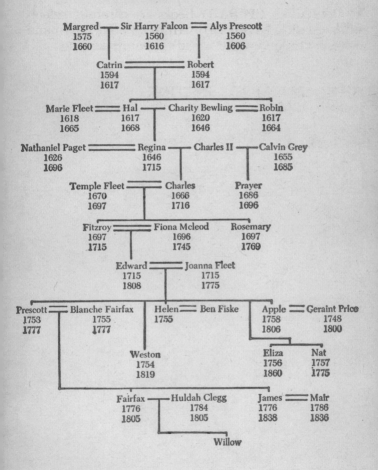

Margred 1575–1660 — Sir Harry Falcon 1560–1616 = Alys Prescott 1560–1606

Catrin 1594–1617 — Robert 1594–1617

Marie Fleet 1618–1665 = Hal 1617–1668 — Charity Bewling 1620–1646 = Robin 1617–1664

Nathaniel Paget 1626–1696 = Regina 1646–1715 — Charles II — Calvin Grey 1655–1685

Temple Fleet 1670–1697 = Charles 1666–1716 — Prayer 1686–1696

Fitzroy 1697–1715 = Fiona Mcleod 1696–1745 — Rosemary 1697–1769

Edward 1715–1808 = Joanna Fleet 1715–1775

Prescott 1753–1777 = Blanche Fairfax 1755–1777 — Helen 1755 = Ben Fiske — Apple 1758–1806 = Geraint Price 1748–1800

Weston 1754–1819 — Eliza 1756–1860 — Nat 1757–1775

Fairfax 1776–1805 — Huldah Clegg 1784–1805 — James 1776–1838 = Mair 1786–1836

Willow

PROLOGUE

1746

Having decided to propose marriage that evening, Lord Edward Falcon had dressed himself with particular care. The cream silk stockings and black velvet breeches fitted his muscular legs without a wrinkle; the silver-buckled black shoes shone without blemish. Over the long waistcoat of pearl satin, the stiff-skirted coat of blue and silver brocade displayed to advantage broad shoulders and long, lean torso. Frilled white shirt bordered with black velvet, an ivory-headed cane, doeskin gloves, and low-crowned black tricorne completed a picture that, in his own estimation, was extremely handsome. He smoothed the curled white wig that hid his own cropped black hair and showed his excellent teeth in a brief smile of self-congratulation.

At thirty, Edward Falcon could look back on a placid childhood and boyhood, enlivened by a year's tour of Europe with a tame tutor who had been quite content to fall in with his pupil's plans. For the past ten years Edward had stayed at home, concentrating upon improving his property. He thought of *Kingsmead* as his own creation, though the stone manor house had stood ever since the monks had been driven from their land by Cromwell's agents. Originally it had been a simple two-storey building, with a high-raftered central hall out of which wide stairs led up to a broad, railed gallery. In the time of Edward's great-grandmother Regina, a wing had been added to transform the original house into the fashionable L-shape. Edward had added an adjacent wing, knocking down the stables in order to accommodate the extra rooms.

On this fine spring afternoon *Kingsmead* stood, proudly complete, its wings sweeping back into the green turf, its façade enclosed within the high walls of the courtyard. Beyond the courtyard a drive bordered with sentinel oaks and elms wound between pasture and orchard to the main London road.

This was the Falcon kingdom, stretching down to the river, bounded by road and deer-park. As a small boy Edward had ridden his pony through the long grass with his mother mounted close behind on her own bay mare. He had never known his father, for Fitzroy Falcon had been killed, fighting against the Old Pretender in the first Jacobite rebellion. His childhood had been dominated by the stiff, upright figure of his Scottish mother, Fiona. He had only to close his eyes to shrink down again into a child, gazing up at his mother's plain, freckled face under its crown of red hair, hearing again her voice.

"This is Falcon land, my son. *Your* land! Hold fast to it. Extend it if you can. Work it well. Land endures long after the people who trod upon it are gone."

Fiona had been a soldier's daughter, following the drum from one barrack town to the next, and land had meant a great deal to her. After her young husband's death, she had travelled south to claim *Kingsmead* for her child, and she had spent the rest of her life impressing upon Edward the necessity of improving heritage.

Although she knew nothing of the countryside she h.. set herself to learn, to such good effect that within five years she had doubled the profits on hops and corn. She made herself respected in the village, even if not much liked, for she had a reputation for being "close" and no talent for making friends.

Between herself and her son there had been a close bond of shared interests and mutual aims unclouded by any demonstrations of affection. Her death the previous winter had caused Edward the only grief of his life. Yet even in dying, Fiona Falcon had displayed a firm and quiet tact. The new wing was complete, the harvest gathered and sold, the garden replanted, and the new carriage horses broken to harness.

"You must marry," Fiona had told Edward. "A man needs an heir."

He had nodded thoughtfully, and she had closed her eyes, settled her head more comfortably on the pillow, and slipped peacefully out of life a few days later. The physician might write "kidney trouble" on the certificate if he pleased, but Edward was certain that his mother had simply decided it was time to make way for another mistress.

The problem of finding a wife was simple. At the other side of the river the smaller estate of the Fleet family sloped down from the manor house where Astons and Fleets had lived for more than two hundred years. Fleets and Falcons were not only neighbors, but also blood-kin. Edward's grandmother Temple was a Fleet, and the present owner was her niece, which made Edward and Joanna kissing-cousins. Joanna was last of the line, and her marriage to Edward would secure all the land on one side of the road to the Falcons.

as nearly six months his senior and not
or little against the land. She was a
man, rather addicted to church-going,
, pleasant manners. Edward's brief, infrequent visits to London had afforded him some experience
in the arts of seduction, and he was certain that she
would prove an excellent wife.

Satisfied with his appearance, he turned from the long
mirror and walked briskly through the adjoining
dressing-room to the broad, railed gallery which looked
down into the central hall. The hall had remained
unchanged since the sixteenth century, its stone walls
hung with faded arras, its stone floor swept bare now of
rushes, its few pieces of heavy furniture dark and smooth
with age. Except on the hottest days fires blazed in the
twin hearths at each side of the stone staircase, flames
throwing their quivering reflections on the silver, pewter,
and copper dishes which crowded the shelves of the
towering dresser.

The kitchen and stillroom and servants' quarters were
on the left, with four sleeping chambers above them. On
the right, a door led into the parlor which separated the
drawing room in the new wing from the solar, whose
windows looked out into the courtyard. Edward's own
rooms were over the solar and parlor. Until her death, his
mother had slept in the big room over the drawing room.
That apartment would later serve, he decided, as a nursery.

Standing at the head of the staircase, he was struck
afresh by the timeless quality of his surroundings. Generations of Falcons had stood here before him, looking
down into the heart of the house. He felt himself to be
the greatest in a long line of owners. That his only living
relative was an aunt, sister of his dead father, caused him
no regret.

Aunt Rosemary occupied a small cottage near the river bank, where she enjoyed her reputation as local witch. Edward had no idea if she was a genuine witch or not. His training and temperament inclined him to the belief that she was no more than a vinegary spinster with some knowledge of herbs, but at times he surprised in her amber eyes an expression which made him feel cold.

Now that he was older he enjoyed visiting her occasionally, but he had never felt the lack of brothers or sisters. Brothers might have expected some share of the harvest profits, and sisters would require dowries. It was infinitely more preferable to be the sole master of *Kingsmead,* to stand alone at the head of a prospective dynasty.

A servant passed across the hall, braided head bent over a tray, black skirt rustling. Edward, who had put off his own mourning that day, watched her with approval. His mother had taken it upon herself, shortly after her arrival at *Kingsmead,* to dismiss the servants then employed there and engage young ones from Maidstone who could be trained up to her ways. There were only three of them, apart from the cook, and two footmen, for Fiona considered it a scandalous waste to keep an army of domestics "eating their heads off." The maids were expected not only to keep the house clean but also to help in dairy and cowshed, and both footmen doubled as grooms when occasion demanded.

There would be, Edward thought, very little for Joanna to do when he installed her as mistress of *Kingsmead.* The household, thanks to Fiona's good management, ran very smoothly, and with the estate affairs in the capable hands of an excellent bailiff, Edward had time to spare for hunting and for the improvement of the house. He had already purchased a considerable number of handsomely bound volumes to display in the drawing room, and the new stables, built at some distance from the main building, were good enough for people, let alone four-legged beasts.

He walked slowly down the stairs, his cane tapping the stone lightly, possessively. The main door was open, and the faint breeze of a silver afternoon stirred the patched and faded tapestries. Walls now were beginning to be hung with paper, but Edward liked the softly blurred outlines of the dim figures in the hanging cloths.

In the cobbled yard Diamond, the gentlest of his mares, waited patiently, coat and saddle gleaming. He mounted without aid, and she responded at once to the slight pressure of his unspurred heels and ambled toward the arched opening in the wall. Just outside, spreading rust-colored, purple-veined leaves against the stone, a tree reared from the ground. There was some tale about the tree which Aunt Rosemary had attempted to explain to him once, but he had cut her short, having no patience with legends. Yet he reached out as he rode beneath the branches and plucked a leaf, crushing it in his long fingers and inhaling the sharp, vinegary fragrance.

At the main road he turned left, riding slowly, for it was no part of his plan to arrive looking hot and bothered. On the right, below the level of the high ground, a path slanted down toward the village. Marie Regina had grown up at the foot of the grass-grown tor crowned by the ruins of the monastery from which it had taken its name. Small cottages meandered down both sides of the twisting street toward the village green with its pond and stocks. The church stood back from the houses, its graveyard fanning out over the hillside.

The main road swerved toward a bridge beneath which the river gurgled, separating Falcon land from Fleet land, the village from the ruins on the tor. A small figure, clad in black, sat on the parapet. Edward, seeing his aunt, cursed softly under his breath. If she wished to see him there was nothing to prevent her from coming up to the house, but she preferred to make what he considered to be a spectacle of herself by sitting like a gargoyle on the bridge.

Under the brim of her old-fashioned black hat black hair straggled in elf-locks and her little, pointed face glowed in welcome. He supposed that she had once been a very pretty girl, but now she was close on fifty and looked older, her skin sun-yellowed, her mouth drawn up tightly, her hands twig-thin.

"Aunt Rosemary." He drew rein politely.

"I was waiting for you," she said primly. "I knew you'd be riding this way."

"You ought to have come up to the house," he said patiently.

"Why trouble my legs, when you were bound to come anyway?" she asked reasonably.

"What did you want?"

He frowned slightly, putting on the face that sent his grooms scurrying to their work. Aunt Rosemary, however, put her head on one side and squinted up at him.

"Are you going to ask Joanna Fleet to wed you?" she enquired.

"I might," Edward said cautiously.

"You should. She's been waiting for years to have you ask the question, and she's a good woman. Dull, but good."

"The two estates can be worked together," he said.

"Joanna owns the old Wittle farm and the house in Maidstone where that silly mother of hers used to live," she reminded him.

"They can be leased out," he told her. "And it's not seemly to speak ill of the dead."

"Who? Barbara Kingston? She was an exceedingly silly

woman," Aunt Rosemary said calmly. "All eyes and curls and fainting spells. I don't imagine her intellect has improved since her demise. Now, Joanna's grandmother, Mistress Abigail, was a different kettle of fish. Hard as nails was Abigail. She ruled the roost until her death, and kept that estate solvent even in the bad seasons. She died when you were a little lad, but she had the sense to put a good man in to make sure that her flighty daughter-in-law didn't squander the profit on every bushel of corn."

Edward stifled a yawn, having heard similar sentiments from his aunt ever since he could remember.

"Your grandfather always wanted that Fleet land," she said now. "He wed Temple Fleet to get it, but *her* father upped and married Abigail and got himself a male heir, so your grandfather didn't get what he wanted after all. And now their grandchildren will wed and the estates be joined together in the end." She laughed, with something bitter in her face, as if she had expected wine and tasted vinegar instead.

"Did you wait here to wish me luck in my wooing?" he enquired.

"Luck? Falcons make their own luck in the best way they can!" she exclaimed. "No, I have a cowslip posy for Joanna. I spent most of the day making it, and you may carry it to her."

"Cowslips!" He looked in amused dismay at the petalled ball on its loop of green ribbon. "Those are country manners."

"And we are country folk, for all your fine education and your year in Europe. Take it to her."

She urged the bauble into his hand and slipped from her perch, adjusting her hat. He wondered if the gossip he had heard in the village was true. They said there that Rosemary Falcon had once loved Joanna's father and been jilted by him. Certainly there had been a duel between Grey Fleet and his own father. It had ended with Grey lying dead and Fitzroy Falcon, his sister's honor avenged, riding off to fight the Old Pretender. It was odd, Edward reflected, that both he and Joanna were posthumous children, and odder still that Aunt Rosemary should live to see the land her father had craved gained by his grandson.

He half-turned in the saddle to wave, but his aunt was already descending the steep bridle path into the green-tipped woods which clustered along the river bank and hid the small cottage where she lived. Edward's frown darkened as he thought of that cottage, for it was not part of the main estate, but could be bequeathed as its owner wished.

Aunt Rosemary had inherited the place from her grandmother, Regina Falcon, and was forever hinting that one day she would leave it out of the family alto-gether. The thought irritated him so much that he put the image of Aunt Rosemary into the back of his mind, and turned in at the gates of the manor, looking about him with deliberate pleasure at the trimly clipped hedges and lawns that bordered the curving drive.

The manor house, although of the same age as *Kingsmead*, was a much smaller building, set like a jewel in a garden which in summer was heavy with roses. On this afternoon the borders were bright with daffodils and nodding jonquils, and the mingled scents of various herbs rose to Edward's nostrils as he rode up to the main door.

He had sent word of his coming, and a groom hurried to take Diamond while a small maidservant took his hat, gloves, and cane and ushered him across the wide hall to the parlor on the left.

As usual the long, narrow room was warm and bright

and faintly untidy, with a straw basket spilling colored wools over the surface of a rosewood table, petals lying unheeded near a bowl of primroses, a music case open on the windowseat, a scarf tossed carelessly over the back of a chair. A pretty, feminine, miscellaneous clutter in the midst of which Mistress Joanna Fleet sat, nervously waiting.

In contrast to her surroundings Joanna was a big-boned woman with a flat, quiet face and no trace of her mother's beauty, though in a soft light she had a certain tranquillity which had its own charm.

On this day she had chosen to wear a dress of turquoise silk patterned with cream rosebuds, its laced bodice displaying an undershift of white lace. Her light brown hair was drawn back smoothly into a heavy knot at the nape of her neck and confined there with a knot of turquoise ribbon. The outift had been made for her by a dressmaker in Maidstone and its style was some two years out of date, a fact that neither Joanna nor her dressmaker knew.

Edward's quick, flicking glance as he came into the parlor made her uncomfortably aware that she was no fine London lady but a simple squire's daughter who had never been more than a few miles beyond the village in her life. In her own sphere Joanna moved with assurance, but Edward Falcon always made her feel inadequate and inferior.

That he intended to ask her to marry him one day was a fact she had known for years; that he had delayed until the time when he began to feel the need of an heir had caused her very little pain. Under her placid exterior burned no passionate fires. Joanna's life had moved smoothly from childhood to girlhood until, looking at herself in the glass, she saw the face of a mature woman.

Edward and she had been friendly ever since she had

been considered old enough to ride alone in the woods and fields around the manor. Her grandmother had disapproved of the friendship and had seemed relieved when Edward went off to Europe, but by the time he returned Abigail had died and Joanna's mother was too indolent to care that Edward came visiting once or twice a month.

Since her mother's death his calls had become more frequent, and the warmth of his manner made her quite certain that he would soon propose marriage. Despite her tranquillity she could not help a quiver of nervous excitement as he bowed over her hand.

"I hope I don't come at an inconvenient time?" he questioned.

"I'm happy to see you," she said, looking up at him trustfully.

"And I think you know why I have come." He released her hand and sat down on the chair she indicated. "We have known each other too long for formality, and we have known for a long time that we would eventually marry. We are both of full age and in good health, and the joining of our two estates would be most profitable."

"Where would we live?"

"At *Kingsmead,* of course. It is much larger and more convenient for a family, and I see no reason why you should not have several children."

His tone was pleasant, his expression kindly, yet inexplicably her eyes filled with tears. She had been waiting for so long for Edward to propose, and she had expected something a little more romantic, more in the style of the poems her mother had enjoyed reading.

"With our respective mothers passed away," he was continuing, "I can see no reason why the marriage should not take place very soon. It would be convenient to wed before the early harvest, don't you think?"

"Most convenient," she said, and blinked rapidly.

"My aunt will be pleased." He grinned wryly, looking younger. "She looks upon our marriage as a reconciliation between our two families."

"Mistress Rosemary has always been very kind," she said stiffly.

"She gave me this, for you."

A trifle awkwardly, he handed her the cowslip ball, and nodded in satisfaction as she smiled her thanks.

"Ladies like such things, so my aunt tells me," he observed. "She's always enjoyed making bits and pieces out of flowers and leaves and such like."

"It's very pretty," she said, and turned the petalled ball gently between her palms.

"Quite useless, save as an ornament," he commented, amused.

"But very pretty," she said again, and bent her head over it because her eyes had filled with tears again.

"Then I take it your answer is favorable," he said briskly.

She nodded, her wet lashes brushing the pale tips of blossom.

"We will suit together very well," Edward said. "I think it would be an excellent notion if this manor were leased out when you have taken up residence in *Kingsmead.* The rents would be most useful, and tenants would keep the house aired and sweetened. Later on we might consider giving it to our son as a wedding present."

"Our son?" She looked at him in surprise, but his face remained calm and interested, as if he were discussing the price of apples.

"You are young and in good health," he said, "so I see no reason why you should not bear a healthy son. He will inherit a sizeable property when I am dead, not to mention the peerage conferred upon my family by the King in recognition of my father's services to the Crown during the first Jacobite rebellion."

"I know the Falcons were always an important family," Joanna said humbly.

"We will be happy together," he informed her, and leaned forward to pat her hand, as if it had dawned on him that some tactile gesture was appropriate.

"I'll get some wine."

She rose, still clutching the cowslip ball, and could not avoid seeing his glance of irritation. A lady expecting a gentleman ought to have had the decanter set out ready and not have to go hurrying across the hall to the kitchen in order to find a bottle. She read his thought in his look and felt the ready color flush up in her cheeks.

In the hall she paused for a moment, striving to regain her composure. Edward had never been a demonstrative man, and she had never been beautiful. It was her great good fortune that he had chosen to marry her, and after they were wed he would become warmer, more affectionate. Certainly she would strive with everything in her nature to please him, and be a good wife.

She buried her face in the flower ball and gave a sudden cry of pain as something seared her cheek. It was buried deep in the heart of the tiny, closely packed blossoms, and she drew it out cautiously, holding it between finger and thumb. A sharp-spined thistle, its tiny leaves pointed and malicious, its stem hard as bone. Aunt Rosemary must have woven it most carefully into the innocent bauble.

Into her mind there echoed something her grandmother had once said. Joanna had ushered Edward to the door after one of his early, infrequent visits, and turned to see old Abigail regarding her from the foot of the staircase.

"You think yourself in love, don't you?" the old woman had said. "You think that one day Edward Falcon will come riding up on a white horse and snatch you away to eternal bliss."

"I think he will marry me one day," Joanna had replied, with all the confidence of seventeen.

"No doubt he will," Abigail had said sourly, "but have the goodness to wait until I am under the ground. I have no love for the Falcons, not that that's any business of yours. But you're my grand-daughter and I don't want to see you tied for life to a member of that family."

"The Falcons are an important family," she had said, impatiently.

"There is bad blood in them," her grandmother had said. "Oh, they're handsome. Handsome and proud and good at enriching themselves, but there is something in that family . . . something dark and twisted, to be glimpsed by moonlight and never brought into the light of day!"

Joanna had wanted to ask more, but old Abigail had gone back up the stairs, a thin, upright figure in her grey dress, and soon afterward Edward had gone to Europe. The forgotten words came back now, mingling with the pain in her cheek.

She threw the thistle to the floor and rubbed the bruised flowers against the weal on her face. A thin trickle of blood stained the pale yellow of the cowslips, like a dark threat on a golden morning. For an instant the world was darker than she had known it, and then she shook away her fancy and went sedately into the kitchen to find wine in which to toast her forthcoming marriage.

1774

CHAPTER ONE

Apple Falcon was casting a spell. She had not much hope that it would work, for she had been casting the same spell for years and she was still, in her own estimation, distressingly plain. No other girl in Marie Regina had red hair, freckles, and a turned-up nose. That no other girl had her swift, slim grace or clear hazel eyes was a fact that had never entered Apple's head.

Frowning, she sat back on her heels and contemplated the little piles of grass and flowers laid in a semicircle before her. If she remembered the words correctly, something wonderful might happen. There was no harm, after all, in being optimistic. Aunt Rosemary had taught her carefully, but her small niece had not always listened as diligently as she might. It was a great pity that the old lady had not lived a few years longer, but she had died in Apple's twelfth year, and month by month her image became fainter.

"You would not be afraid if I came back to see you?" she had questioned, and Apple had shaken her head truthfully.

Aunt Rosemary, however, had not come back, though Apple had lived in the daily expectation that she might. That the dead could return she knew, for once or twice, in the silence of the wood, she had glanced up and seen a young girl watching her, a girl with hair as red as her own but with a far more beautiful face. The girl had been gone before Apple had fully realized she was there, and only a silver birch whispered, sad and mocking. Once, too, when she was near the cottage, she had seen a shambling creature which stared at her out of little red eyes and then broke into a little, shuffling dance.

"A bear? Don't be ridiculous!" her father had said, amused.

"I remember hearing, when I was a girl," Aunt Rosemary said, "that one of the early Falcons, the one who came from Wales, had a little dancing bear. A tame pet, child. It won't hurt you, so there's no need to be afraid of it, living or dead."

Apple had had no thought of fear and had often waited afterward to catch sight of the little dancing bear, but not even the shadow of its ghost troubled the solitude.

But Aunt Rosemary had never come back, and there were moments when Apple found it hard to recall the old woman's face with its slanting yellow eyes and locks of white hair.

Now, biting her lip as she gazed at the little heaps of greenery, Apple tried desperately to remember the words of the spell.

The man riding over the brow of the hill checked his mount as he saw the girl crouched beyond the low wall of the cemetery. His keen, dark eyes took in the scene while his mind drew about it an oval frame. The rain-washed blue sky, the mellow stone and blue-shadowed grass enclosed the figure in the wide-brimmed straw hat and flaring skirts of dark mulberry.

She heard his approach and sprang up, twisting to face him. A shaft of sunshine beamed upon her young face and struck fire from the braids of red hair that hung almost to her knees. The planes of her face had a flat, stolid quality like the faces of the women he had seen in Amsterdam, but there was a mobility in her wide mouth and a flash of gaiety in the clear hazel eyes turned up to him.

"Good-day, sir."

She dropped a neat curtsey and showed blunt white teeth in a polite smile.

"Good-day, mistress."

He dismounted and swept off his tricorne with a gesture that had in it something vaguely foreign. In appearance he was not the conventional Englishman, but dark-haired and sallow, his hands long and thin, his voice quick and soft and lilting.

"Are you looking for someone?" she enquired, tilting her head to one side. Speaking to strangers was a habit about which she had frequently been warned, but there was, she thought, no harm in showing friendliness to a man who looked as if he were lost.

"For anyone who will tell me the best place to find lodgings in this district," he returned.

"There is an inn which has a very good reputation," she informed him. "If you go back to the main road and take the steep path to the right it will bring you into the village. Or you can take a short-cut through the graveyard."

"Were you on your way to the village, mistress . . ." he hinted.

"Apple. Apple Falcon."

"That's an unusual name."

"It's Abigail, really. I was named for my great-grand-mother, but when I was young I couldn't pronounce it correctly, so now everyone, even my father, calls me Apple."

"You are, of course, elderly now."

"I will be sixteen in September," she dimpled suddenly.

" 'Sweet sixteen and never been kissed?' " He read her thought. "I am six-and-twenty, mistress. Does that seem old to you?"

"Oh, no. My father and mother are nearly sixty," she assured him.

"Do your parents live in the village?" he enquired.

"We all live at *Kingsmead*. We are the Falcons," Apple said, surprised.

"I am not acquainted with any Falcons," he told her, "but then I have not been in this part of the country before. I am from Wales, from the south."

"And do Welsh gentlemen have names?"

"A thousand pardons! I forgot my manners in the contemplation of your beauty. Geraint Price, and your most humble servant."

He put his hand on his heart and bowed deeply, with something that was not quite teasing in his face.

"We Falcons are descended from the Welsh!" she said eagerly. "Long ago a woman came from the north of that country and married her daughter to a Falcon. Look! that is the daughter's grave."

She pointed to a headstone sunk deep into the surrounding turf.

"Outside the churchyard?" he queried.

"She was a witch and was swum as a witch, and died," Apple told him.

He went closer, bending to read the letters cut into the stone.

HERE LIES CATRIN FALCON
BORN DECEMBER 1594
DROWNED JUNE 1617

"She was young," he said in pity.

"They say she does not rest," Apple said, coming to stand beside him, "but that she walks down by the river with her long red hair loose about her shoulders and her hands open, beseeching mercy."

"Not a comfortable ancestress," he said lightly, abruptly conscious of the chill breeze.

"She wouldn't hurt you," Abigail said earnestly. "The dead cannot hurt."

"But the living can?"

He had thought her all sunshine, but there were faint shadows under the big hazel eyes and a droop to the slim shoulders as if she had remembered burdens.

"I suppose so. But we are a very happy family," she said, quickly and defensively.

"Is that why you spend your afternoons brooding over graves?" he enquired.

"I was working a spell," she said.

"A spell! I thought the witch was swum years ago!"

"As to that." Apple hesitated, drawing the end of her braid through her teeth. "From time to time, in our family, one is born who bears the mark. A crescent moon, purple-black, on the leg. My aunt bore the mark and I bear it, too, and so the power is passed down."

The sophisticated part of him, the part that had travelled through the great cities of Europe, wanted to smile, but the dark undercurrent of Celtic superstition inherited from generations of his forebears stilled his amusement. Half-unconsciously he rounded thumb and forefinger in the ancient sign against the evil eye.

"I just thought of something!" she exclaimed. "You said you wanted lodgings."

"And you said there was an inn."

"Oh, an exceedingly respectable inn," she said earnestly. "But not many gentlemen come to Marie Regina, and it might be more comfortable if you took lodgings—if you intended staying here longer than a night or two, I mean."

He had not intended to stay longer than a night, but now, looking at her as she stood gazing up at him, he knew that he would stay for as long as he could.

"I came to paint," he said. "I'll stay for as long as it takes to finish the work I intend to do."

"You're an artist? Do you paint people?" she asked.

"Sometimes," he said cautiously.

"But that's better than anything!" she exclaimed. "My father has been talking for months of having all our portraits painted in order to celebrate Prescott's birthday."

"Prescott?"

"My brother Prescott. He is twenty-one next week and we're having a dinner, a late dinner at seven o'clock. I'm sure my father would be very pleased to have you paint all our pictures."

"All? How many of you are there?" he exclaimed.

"There's Prescott, the eldest, and then Weston. He's twenty. Helen is nineteen." She enumerated them on her fingers. "Eliza is eighteen. Nat is seventeen; and then there's me. Six of us."

"And you all live at *Kingsmead*?"

"It's the biggest house in the district," Apple said proudly. "My father owns all the land on the other side of the highway, and it will be Prescott's one day. There's another manor on the property, too. It used to be my mother's home, but now the Fairfaxes are tenants. Blanche is to marry Prescott next year."

"And where am I supposed to lodge?" he demanded, bewildered by her chatter.

"There's a small cottage near to the river," she said. "It used to belong to my Aunt Rosemary, and when she died she left it to me. That, and a piece of land up in Wales, only none of us has ever been there. I look after the cottage myself, and it's very private. My father would allow me to rent it to you, I'm certain."

"I think we had better consult your father," he said.

"He'll probably be at home now," Apple said.

"And his name is—"

"Lord Edward Falcon. The title will go to Prescott one day. He and my father are very much alike." She heaved a small sigh, then brightened again. "We don't have very far to go," she assured him.

"Shall we ride together?"

She nodded, her smile breaking out again like sunshine. Helping her to the saddle he was conscious of excitement deep within him. If the rest of the Falcons had the charm of this girl, he would enjoy painting them very much.

They cantered back across the fields to the broad road which stretched like a dusty ribbon to the bridge beyond.

"These are the main gates. They are kept open out of habit," she told him.

"To welcome strangers?"

Under his arm her slight body tensed. Then she said in a low, hurried voice, "You must not mind if my family, some of them, appear a little . . . odd. We have never been away from Marie Regina, you see. My father does not approve of folk moving about from place to place."

"Then he will scarcely approve of me," he commented.

"You paint pictures, so he will expect you to be restless," Apple said cheerfully. "This is the courtyard wall. You can see the roof of the main wing over the top of it."

He was staring instead at the tree which arched rust-leaved branches against the stone. The pointed leaves with their tracery of purple quivered in the breeze which sprang from nowhere, ruffling the horse's mane.

"That's the luck-tree," Apple told him, wriggling about to catch the question in his face. "There's a story that it was once cursed, but we call it the luck-tree. Its leaves smell of vinegar when you crush them."

They were in a cobbled yard now, with the walls bending at left and right to hold between them a stone house with windows deep-set in ivied mullions, and a door that was propped open by an iron weight.

Apple slipped nimbly to the ground and straightened her hat as a groom came around the corner of the building.

"Sykes, take this gentleman's horse to the stables and see if you can find my father," she ordered briskly.

"Lord Falcon is in the drawing room, mistress," the man informed her, giving Geraint and the horse a frank, inquisitive look.

"Then I'll see him myself."

She ran up the shallow steps into the dim interior while Geraint Price followed more slowly.

The hall, reaching up through two storeys and hung with faded tapestries, catapulted him into a bygone age. On the left an immense table was set about with carved benches and two high-backed chairs; on the right a dresser stretched upward, its shelves gleaming with silver, pewter, and copper. Twin hearths glowed at each side of a stone staircase that rose to a railed gallery above.

"This is the old part of the house," Apple volunteered. "If you will wait here, I'll find my father."

She vanished through a carved door on the left and he

was alone in the echoing hall. He walked the length of it, absorbing the silence, feeling the centuries press down upon him. In such an apartment ruffs and farthingales and peascod doublets would have been more in keeping than cravats and tricorne hats.

Somebody was watching him through the rails of the gallery. He stepped back a pace, raising his head slightly, and the figure of a woman drifted into view. As she began to descend the stairs he had a sudden, eerie feeling that the vanished Apple had grown old, her young face creased into resignation, her darting glance bowed and thickened by the passage of time.

"Lady Falcon?" His voice sounded too loud in his own ears.

"I am Joanna Falcon, yes." She had reached the bottom step and leaned against the stone balustrade, frowning a little.

"I am Geraint Price, your ladyship. A—a friend of Mistress Apple."

"Don't be foolish," the woman said. "Falcons have no friends."

"Mistress Apple seems most cordial," he said.

"She is not yet beaten down," Joanna said, and moving toward him laid a beringed hand on his arm. "She and Nat are the ones who struggle against their chains. The others have already ceased from battle. And I . . . I have forgotten what freedom ever was. Oh, I was warned, you know, in a cowslip bell many years ago. I took no heed, but I have learned better since. A noose can be woven of silk as well as hemp."

He wondered uneasily if she were a trifle crazed, but her faded eyes held a terrible sanity, as if she had pierced through to the reality of things.

From the side door Apple said, "Mother, I see you have met the gentleman who is to paint our portraits."

"An artist?" The faded eyes surveyed him. "Do not make your price too low, sir. My husband never values anything unless it has cost a very great deal of money."

"My father will see you," Apple told him.

She was darting back through the doorway again, and he turned to make his bow to her mother, but Lady Falcon was drifting up to the gallery again, her full skirts whispering over the stone.

The door at the left led into a small, panelled chamber with another door on the left and a curtained archway on the right. Following the girl, he found himself in a long, light apartment furnished in pale shades of apricot. Rugs lay on the polished floor and mirrors set into the panelled walls reflected the sprays of flowers arranged in narrow vases on the small tables down one side of the room.

The gentleman lounging at his ease in a wing-armed chair watched his approach from eyes as dark as his own. Under a full-bottomed wig the face was impassive, the features regular.

"Father, this is Geraint Price, the gentleman I was telling you about," Apple said eagerly.

"My dear, I did not imagine you would describe one gentleman and then introduce another," her father said drily. "You must forgive my daughter's manners, sir. We are a trifle rustic here, and Apple is in the habit of bringing home stray animals."

"How fortunate she can feel confident of their receiving a welcome," Geraint said pleasantly.

"You paint pictures, she tells me." Edward Falcon leaned back, lids drooping over the dark eyes. "I cannot pretend to be familiar with your name."

"I have studied on the continent for some years, sir. In Paris, Rome, Amsterdam."

"How very restless of you," Edward Falcon remarked.

"To be restless is a privilege of the artist, sir."

"So I am given to understand. But your native country is Wales, is it not?"

"The south, sir."

"Ah! that accounts for your swarthiness. In South Wales there were, I believe, many Spaniards at one time, blown off course when their armada was scattered. They took refuge there and left many bastards behind."

"The bastards of one generation become the gentlemen of the next," Geraint said levelly.

"So they tell me." A white hand was flicked as if its owner was bored. "And what exactly is your business in Marie Regina?"

"To paint what pleases me, and to lodge where it is comfortable," Geraint said promptly.

"Which means that you hope to paint my family's likenesses and lodge on my daughter's property, eh?"

"I have not yet seen the cottage," Geraint told him, "and I fear that it might not be practical to attempt to capture any likenesses of your relatives. My prices are expensive."

"Do you think I am unable to meet them?" Edward Falcon demanded.

"Perhaps."

"I am a wealthy man, an extremely wealthy man. Name your price, sir!"

"You have not yet seen any examples of my work, sir."

"I did not suppose that even a Welshman would be fool enough to ride around the countryside seeking commissions if he could not paint," Edward Falcon said. "Your price!"

"Fifty guineas."

"I will give you a hundred," Edward Falcon said calmly. "Sit down for a moment. Apple, find your sister Helen, and tell her to pour out two glasses of port."

"I can pour it, Father," Apple began.

"No doubt you can. However, I wish Helen to pour it. You will retire to your room and attempt to render yourself respectable in time for supper."

"And the cottage, Father? I have no objections to a lodger."

"Your approval or disapproval is not of the slightest consequence," her father said serenely. "Run along and find your sister."

Apple gave an impatient little curtsey and sped toward the door, almost colliding with a taller girl on her way in.

"Ah! Helen, my dear! I wish you to pour two glasses of port for this gentleman and myself." Edward Falcon raised his voice as the girl glided toward them. "This is Geraint Price, out of Wales and sundry other places. He is to paint our portraits and to lodge in the cottage until his task is completed. Try to pour the liquid without spilling it, my love! Shy, feminine grace is very pleasing in a woman. The clumsiness of a carthorse is not."

The girl, pouring with shaking hands, was as thin and pale as old crystal. Her hair, of a light amber hue, was drawn in a chignon to the back of her head, and against the panelled walls her profile had the delicacy of a cameo.

"Helen is the eldest of my three daughters." Edward said as the glasses were handed. "I am training them to be a comfort to me in my old age. My sons will marry, of course. Prescott is already betrothed to Mistress Blanche Fairfax. Her father is a tenant of mine at the old manor, but a sound man of healthy stock, and plump in the pocket. We are having a dinner next week to celebrate Prescott's majority. You might care to join us, sir."

"I would be interested to meet the rest of your family," Geraint said truthfully.

"I have six children," Edward said. "You may not credit it, sir, but I was married to my wife for seven years before she succeeded in carrying a living child to its full term. And then, overwhelmed, I assume, by my reproaches, she presented me with six infants in as many years. She was forty-three when Apple was born, after which she had the good taste to cease her pregnancies."

"I met Lady Falcon."

"Not a pretty woman, I fear, but a good breeder, after an initially bad start." Lord Falcon handed the glass to his daughter without looking at her. "And you have thoughts of lodging in the cottage? It was left to my daughter by my aunt, but as Apple is under age, in strictly legal terms it belongs to me. However, I have neither use nor liking for the place, so you are welcome to stay there."

"I am ready to pay, sir."

"Of course you are. Even a Welshman would not expect lodgings for nothing," Edward smiled. "However, I am a man who is not averse to a small gamble. You may lodge in the cottage for as long as you get commissions in the district. You will naturally complete the portrait of my family first, at the agreed fee. After that, I will claim twenty-five per cent of any payment you receive for any other paintings."

"I may decide not to accept any other commissions," Geraint said.

"In which case I lose the gamble. Do you agree?"

The artist nodded slowly.

"Then the bargain is sealed. Helen! take our visitor's glass and show him to the stables. Sykes will guide him to the cottage. You will have privacy there. The place is known locally as Witch's Dower and is avoided by the villagers. Helen! have you forgotten the way to the door?"

The girl started violently, her face paling even further until the ivory skin stretched like a mask over the exquis-

ite cheekbones. Geraint made his bow, but the older
man had leaned back, his eyes half-closed.

The hall was deserted as they came into it again,
though he had the impression of watching eyes, as if the
figures in the tapestries had a strange, hidden life of their
own. As he drew level with the girl she began to speak in
a low, rapid voice.

"It would be better if you did not stay. Believe me, it
would be better if you rode away now."

"You think your father dislikes me?"

"He likes you," Helen said. "If he had disliked you he
would have had you thrown out. But you amuse him,
and so he will keep you here. He keeps us all here. We
are part of the estate, you see, part of *Kingsmead*. He
will keep you here forever."

"For a few months, perhaps. I am not a man to be
tied."

"You think that now," Helen whispered. "But he will
bind you here, and the day will come when you will forget you ever wanted to leave. You run a terrible risk by
lingering."

He would have answered her, questioned her, but they
had reached the front door and the groom was in the
courtyard. As she hurried toward the servant, Geraint
paused, hearing as if in echo Lady Falcon's words. "A
noose can be woven of silk as well as hemp."

CHAPTER TWO

The cottage of white-washed stone stood in a small clearing near the banks of the river, and could be reached either by riding across the fields from *Kingsmead* or by taking the steep bridle path that plunged sharply down from the main road just before the bridge.

Invisible from the highway in its cocoon of trees and bushes and tangled ivy, it had a private, waiting aspect. Its small windows peered out from beneath tufts of overhanging creeper, and its chimneys poked inquisitively from the slated roof. The door led directly into a low-ceilinged apartment out of which a narrow staircase spiralled up into two small bedchambers. A door at the foot of the staircase led into a narrow room in which squat jars and narrow bottles crowded the shelves. There were dried leaves and grasses in some of the containers, liquids and syrups in others. On a trestle table were pestle and mortar and measuring scales, and a chest against one wall held bags of lavender.

This, Geraint presumed, was the room that had given the cottage its reputation. He wondered what the aunt had been like who had left the place to Apple. It was useless to make enquiry in the village, for though the landlord of the inn served him politely and expressed the desire that his stay in Marie Regina would be comfortable, it was obvious that no gossip would be forthcoming.

One afternoon he strolled into the churchyard and amused himself by reading some of the inscriptions on the tilted headstones. It was said that the history of a place could be traced among its tombstones, in which case Marie Regina must have slept the centuries away. The same names occurred again and again. Fiske, Temple, Aston, Cuthbert, Wittle. There were the usual number of young wives dead in childbirth and the customary small graves for children who had not survived the tender years. A joint grave enclosed the bones of Mistress Eleanor Aston and her son William Aston, 'perished by grievous accident, October 1592.'

The Falcon tomb was the largest and most ornate, shaped like a house and high enough to admit a human being. Its stone door boasted three padlocks and the figure of an angel with a sword, though whether this was to prevent the living from breaking in or the dead from breaking out was uncertain. A tablet at the side scrolled the names of those within, and Geraint ran his eye rapidly down the list, murmuring low.

" 'Here lie the mortal remains of Sir Harry Falcon. Born 1510. Died 1582.'

" 'And of his relict, Lady Elizabeth Falcon, née Weston. Born 1517. Died 1588.' "

He supposed they were the first Falcons, granted land stolen from the monks, building the original *Kingsmead*. Below them he read,

" 'Lady Alys Falcon, née Prescott. Born 1560. Died 1606.'

" 'Sir Harry Falcon, relict of the above. Born 1560. Died 1616.'

" 'Sir Robert Falcon, their son. Born 1594. Drowned 1617.' "

That was odd. The girl named Catrin Falcon who lay outside the cemetery wall had also drowned in 1617.

As his forefinger hesitated at Robert's name, a voice behind him said, "Trying to puzzle out our family, are you?"

He swung round, blinking in the sunshine, to confront a tall girl with yellow hair and boldly patterned riding habit cut like a man's. The girl was beautiful in a voluptuous, Junoesque fashion, and her blue eyes sparkled as she gripped his hand bruisingly.

"I am Eliza Falcon. You must be the artist that Apple found. I've been meaning to ride down to the cottage and pay my respects, but with the birthday dinner tomorrow night and the entire household given over to chaos, I've had no time to breathe. What do you think of the Falcons, then?"

He evaded the question by pointing again to the name. "Is there some connection with the witch buried outside the graveyard?" he enquired.

"You've been listening to Apple's nonsense!" Eliza exclaimed.

"Then she wasn't a witch?"

"The villagers thought her one," she shrugged. "The crops failed that year and then part of the river bank was washed away in a freak storm. Robert Falcon was drowned in a rescue attempt. Folk had to blame somebody so they took his widow and swum her. She was drowned, too, which made them think she must be innocent, but they buried her outside the churchyard to be on the safe side. She left twin sons. This is the wife of the

younger." She indicated the name. " 'Mistress Charity
Falcon, née Bewling. Born 1622. Died 1646.' "

Geraint read the name beneath with interest. " 'Mistress
Margred Prys. Born 1575. Died 1660.' Was that the
Welsh one?"

"The mother of the witch," Eliza nodded. "She reared
her grandsons. There is one with his wife beneath. See
it? 'Lady Marie Falcon, née Fleet. Born 1618. Died 1665.
Relict of the above, Sir Hal Falcon. Born 1617. Died
1668.' He was a great drunkard, they say. And there is
his daughter Regina. She buried a daughter, a husband
and a daughter-in-law before she died."

He bent again to read the names.

" 'Mistress Prayer Paget. Born 1686. Died 1696.'

" 'Master Nathaniel Paget. Born 1626. Died 1696.'

" 'Lady Temple Falcon, née Fleet. Born 1660. Died
1697.'

" 'Mistress Regina Paget, née Falcon. Born 1646. Died
1715.' "

"This was Regina's son, my great-grandfather," Eliza
told Geraint, moving to the line beneath. "He was born
years before she wed Nathaniel Paget, and she always
gave out that his father was King Charles II. It was
probably true. The King certainly granted him a peerage, and he always used his mother's name. Temple
Fleet was his wife."

'Lord Charles Falcon. Born 1666. Died 1716' glowed
against the stone. Below it only two names remained.

" 'Lady Fiona Falcon, née Maclean. Born 1686. Died
1745.'

" 'Mistress Rosemary Falcon. Born 1697. Died 1769.' "

"My grandmother and my aunt," Eliza said cheerfully.
"My grandfather Fitzroy is buried up in Scotland somewhere and another of the Falcons, Robin, the twin who

married Charity Bewling, died in London. Their names are at the back."

She urged him around to the back of the tomb where he read, cut in identical gold.

" 'Sacred to the memory of Master Robin Falcon. Born 1617. Died of plague 1665.'

" 'Lord Fitzroy Falcon. Born 1697. Died Prestonpans 1715.'

"They all used to be in separate graves," Eliza explained. "Nathaniel Paget had this big tomb built, and my father had the tablets set into the sides and all the names written down. This blank tablet is for us one day."

"You know more about your family than I do about mine," Geraint said ruefully. "My own mother died when I was small and my father reared me. Reared is not the right word. He was an actor and he took me along with him. At one time he had a small company of his own, and he hoped I'd take over when he died. But I had no talent save for drawing and painting, and after he died the company split up and I took to the road as an artist."

He paused, for she was not truly listening but stood running her hand over the carved names with an odd, listening expression on her rosy face.

"Did you notice the door is triple-locked?" she asked.

"Yes, I noticed."

"Charles Falcon had that done," Eliza said, "but nobody ever knew why. He was a strange man, they say. We are all strange, we Falcons. There is nobody in the district as strange as we are."

He could think of no answer so stood looking at her in silence, as the tomb threw its shadow between them.

"You'll meet the rest of us when you come to dinner," Eliza said. "We have all had new gowns from London. Helen and Apple are pleased about that. They like pretty dresses."

"Don't you?"

"Lord, no! I cannot abide fuss and frippery!" Laughter
rippled from her full, red lips. "I am happier in my
brother's breeches than in a skirt! There is no sense in
any of us making ourselves beautiful, for my father will
never allow us to marry."

"And don't you wish to be married?"

"Not if I can possibly avoid such a fate," Eliza said.
"No! it is better to have a father than a husband! And after my father is dead, I shall be virtually independent. I
shall breed horses and dogs and tramp mud into the
drawing room."

She clapped him on the shoulder in boyish fashion and
sped away, twisting and turning between the headstones.
There was, he thought, something a little desperate in
her gaiety, a false note in her hearty young voice. There
was more pity in him for her than for the nervous and
gentle Helen or Apple with her unawakened sweetness.

He turned toward the golden list of names again, but
they told him nothing beyond the bare facts of birth and
death. Yet tumbled in this stone were the bones of a
woman whose daughter might have been a witch, a
woman who had been the mistress of a King, and the
strange man who, according to Eliza, had ordered the
tomb to be triple-locked.

And out of all this conglomeration of ancestors had
come this family, these Falcons whom he had been commissioned to paint. From what he had seen of them already he had a feeling that they would burst out of any
frame in which they were depicted.

He left the cemetery slowly, remounted his horse, and
trotted back up the village street. One or two people
glanced at him incuriously as he passed them, but already he had been—no, not accepted, but ignored, rele-
gated to the background, a part of the scenery. In a few

weeks or months, when he rode away again, he would leave behind no more impression than that of a feather thrown into a whirlpool.

On the main highway again he rode across the bridge. At the other side of the river the road wound upward toward the green-clad hill upon which the stark tracery of the old monastery ruins reared against the sky. On the left, open gates led to the old manor house where the Fairfaxes lodged. He had not yet visited the house, but he had glimpsed a plump lady driving toward the village green in a pony trap, and had heard a man on the street call out to her.

"Good-day to you, Mistress Fairfax."

The ruined monastery, etched against the sky, attracted him. The landlord of the inn had told him that the village had taken its name from the monastery. It must have been a very handsome building, he thought, until the agents of a greedy Tudor King had seized and sacked it, smashing the stained glass, tearing down the statues, burning the vestments, melting down the gold and silver ornaments until the beauty was violated. And when the King's agents had gone, driving the dispossessed monks before them, Nature had raged in, covering the cloisters with bindweed, forcing apart the crumbling walls with the savage winds of winter.

Orchards, extravagant with blossom, covered the slopes beneath the ruins. He dismounted and strolled up toward the roofless skeleton of grey stone, appreciating the mingled greens, blues, purples, pinks, and white of the landscape. This picture was one he would hold in his mind, and splash it later onto canvas.

He debated within himself whether or not to introduce a figure into the pastoral scene, and as if in obedience to his imagination, a tall, slim figure in a green cloak appeared briefly ahead of him among the trees.

He recognized her at once, for the hood of the cloak
had slipped back, and loops of amber hair gleamed
around the delicate, spun-glass profile. For an instant he
was minded to call out to her, but another figure in shirt
and breeches had already stepped forward from the
shadow of the ruins, and stood with arms outstretched.
Helen Falcon paused in her upward flight, her head
raised, her hands clasped before her. Then the young
man ran down the hill toward her and the two figures
met, merged, and fused into an embrace which held all
the enchantment of a late spring.

Geraint stopped, unwilling to intrude upon the moment.
But the lovers had not seen or sensed him. Hand-in-hand
they were moving slowly up the last few yards, the boy's
head bent a little toward his companion as if he wished
to shield her from the harshness of the sun.

For a brief moment the Welshman substituted himself
for the boy and Apple for her sister. Then he smiled
wryly, for he was past five-and-twenty and had never
been in love for longer than three days at a time.

His impulse to explore the ruins had faded, and he
turned back, riding at a leisurely pace down the bridle
path to the woods. This was evidently an afternoon for
lovers; ducking beneath a low-hanging branch he came
upon a young couple, both tall and fair-haired, locked in
a close embrace under a tree. His arrival evidently disturbed them, for they sprang apart, revealing flushed and
frightened faces, and then scrambled deeper into the
green foliage.

He grinned to himself as he rode on into the clearing,
wondering if they expected him to rush to Lord Falcon
with a report of trespassers. In a way, he himself was a
trespasser, for he had no business to speculate about the
family nor to delve into their lives. He was here to paint
a portrait, and in his mind's eye the composition of the

painting was beginning to take shape. Letting himself into the cottage, he was struck afresh by the feeling that it awaited him, watched him, and suspended judgment.

At *Kingsmead*, Eliza Falcon cursed under her breath as she wriggled out of her habit into a dress. There were grass stains on her jacket and the hem of her skirt was dragging, accidents which she considered were of no consequence but which her mother shook her head over.

"What your father would say if he were to come in!" Joanna Falcon mourned.

"Father is scarcely likely to come in and catch me in my corsets," Eliza said. "Do stop fussing, Mother. It will bring on one of your headaches and then you will look a perfect fright at the dinner-party."

"I wish it were over. I am certain the gown I chose is too young for me," Joanna fretted.

"Nonsense, it suits you admirably. Mistress Fairfax will not be able to hold a candle to you." Eliza tugged at her mane of blonde hair and made a critical face at herself in the mirror.

She and her mother were in the large apartment over the drawing room. It had been the nursery, and now served as bedchamber for the three girls. Weston and Nat had bedrooms over the servants' quarters. Prescott, as eldest and favorite, had the privilege of two rooms over the kitchen and storeroom.

This bedchamber was panelled in walnut and hung with a silvery-grey material that in some lights had a hint of pink. The rugs on the floor were of a deeper coral, and flowers were arranged in silver vases on the low shelves between the vanity tables.

Eliza, flinging her discarded habit on the floor, submitted to the hairbrush.

"You must wear powder tomorrow," Joanna said, beginning to untangle the curly strands. "Your father will expect it."

"Powder and patches to greet the Fairfaxes, whom we've known all our lives!"

"It's an important occasion."

"Prescott's coming-of-age and the official announcement of his bethrothal—as if he were a royal prince!"

"He is the great-great-grandson of a King," Joanna reproved.

"Ancestors!" Eliza snorted, jerking away from the brush. "Oh! I forgot to tell you. I met Apple's artist in the graveyard today."

"The Welsh gentleman?" In the mirror Joanna's face was suddenly bleak, as if something had been glimpsed and withdrawn. "I wish he had not come here."

"Wish who had not come here?" Apple enquired from the doorway.

"Your handsome artist," Eliza mocked. "I met him in the graveyard, studying the names on the family tomb."

"He is not my artist," Apple said carefully. "I met him and thought that father might care to engage him, that's all."

"I wish he had not come," Joanna repeated. "He will be destroyed as we have all been destroyed."

"I would like to see anyone try to destroy *me*!" Eliza exclaimed.

"What do you mean, Mother?" Apple questioned. "How destroyed?"

"Swallowed up," Joanna said. "The Falcons are birds of prey, diving and grasping and tearing with claws and beaks. They are destroyers, and in the end they turn and destroy themselves."

"I don't understand," Apple said uncertainly.

"Of course you don't, because mother is talking nonsense!" Eliza said crossly. "You ought not to fill the child's head with moonshine. You and Helen are the same, forever seeing hobgoblins."

Apple had gone over to the window where she stood, looking out at the quiet lawns which sloped to the fringe of the deerpark. "But Father will not allow us to marry, will he?" she said, without turning.

"Who wants to be married?" Eliza exclaimed. "If Mother and Father are an example of a typical married couple, then I shall be happy to remain a spinster."

"It would be nice to have babies," Apple said wistfully.

"And wear yourself out before you're forty? That's enough, Mother! You are brushing my scalp raw!"

Joanna put down the brush and fiddled with the ribbons at her waist. Half-turning, Apple glimpsed the twisting fingers. She had never seen her mother's hands at rest, neither had she ever seen them finish a task. Bits of half-finished knitting and sewing, discarded watercolor sketches, dying sprays of unwatered flowers littered her progress from room to room. Into the girl's mind came the lean, dark hands of the Welshman. Those were quiet hands, with latent power in the slightly spatulate fingers. She had longed to go down to the cottage, but her father had forbidden it.

"You must not give our visitor the impression we are all completely uncivilized," he had said pleasantly.

"But the cottage is my property."

"And he is not likely to pick it up and walk away with it under his arm," Edward had told her. "So I really must insist that you confine yourself to the house and garden for a few days. I am not certain that it's wise of you to wander about unaccompanied."

"Eliza and Helen do!" she had protested.

"Eliza and Helen are sensible girls who do not chatter to every stranger they chance to meet," Edward had returned. "In any event, the young man will be coming to the dinner, so you may make yourself agreeable to him then. I wished to give him the opportunity of observing us *en famille* before he begins work on the portrait."

So Apple had confined herself obediently to the house and garden, dutifully dabbing lemon juice on her freckles, trying to banish from her mind the tall, dark man with the quiet hands.

"I must go down and check that everything is in order in the kitchen," Joanna said now, and fretted herself out of the room.

Her daughters, knowing that everything in the kitchen would be proceeding smoothly, for Edward Falcon would not have tolerated a household run with less than perfect efficiency, watched her going in silence. Then Eliza flung herself on her bed, hooking her arms behind her head.

"The artist seems a decent sort of man, I admit. I wonder how he will paint us. Father in the middle, I suppose. When I think of us I think of you and me in sunshine, and Helen and Mother in shadow. Where is Helen, by-the-bye?"

"She went out for a walk."

"Making garlands of flowers and hanging them on bushes for the fairies to find, I suppose. It is Helen who should have been the witch in the family, not you! You know, I used to wish I was the one with the mark." Eliza rolled over onto her stomach and gave Apple an oddly pleading look. "I used to wish I had the power to change things, to make unhappiness go away. But that was the foolishness of a child. I wouldn't want to change anything now."

"Wouldn't you, Eliza?" Apple looked at her sister inquisitively.

"Why should I?" Eliza demanded. "*Kingsmead* is the most beautiful house in the district, and we have everything we need. Father spent a small fortune on those wretched gowns we have to wear tomorrow."

"I know."

Apple went over to the dresses that hung limply under chiffon wraps, free of the canvas-covered whalebone hoops that would plump them into panniers.

Helen's new gown was of peach silk, its underskirt embroidered with gold tissue, coffee-shaded lace frothing the elbow-length sleeves and deep, square neckline. In such a dress she would float, insubstantial as a partly remembered dream, her eyes gentle, her hair hidden under the new white wig with its three shoulder curls.

Eliza's dress was of a deeper pink with panels of green set into the wide skirt, each panel embroidered with sprays of seed-pearls. She had flatly refused to wear a wig, which meant that at least two hours of the following day would be spent in coaxing her unruly yellow curls into a high pompadour and whitening it. But when it was done Eliza would be beautiful, even more beautiful than she was on an ordinary day.

Apple's clear hazel eyes moved to her own dress. She had looked at it so often that she knew every flounce by heart. The overskirt was of primrose yellow decorated with tiny bows of dark green velvet, the fichu of creamy lace. Such a dress deserved a lovely wearer, not a freckled red-head with a nose that turned up at the end. Perhaps the wig would improve matters, for though she was really too young her father had decreed she was to be allowed to wear one.

"We can only hope that the color of your hair will fade a trifle as you grow older, my dear," Edward had said ruefully. "I believe that red hair does break out from time to time in our family, but I don't think it has ever taken such a *violent* hue before!"

"I would change many things!" Apple cried to Eliza. "I

would make myself beautiful, and Helen less shy, and Mother more at peace—"

"And Prescott less pompous and Weston more manly and Nat cleverer!" Eliza joined in, scrambling to a sitting position.

"And you able to wear breeches all day if you wanted," Apple said.

"Fill the stables with horses for me," Eliza ordered. "And make a law stating that all young ladies should ride astride."

"And shoot guns and drink port after dinner," Apple finished.

"Father would not approve," Eliza said. "Or would you change him, too?"

"Father is perfect," Apple retorted. "He buys us lovely dresses and invites us to Prescott's birthday dinner and never expects us to do anything except live at *Kingsmead* for the rest of our lives."

"You wouldn't want to leave, would you?" Eliza questioned. "Would you, Apple?"

The younger girl was silent, her eyes moving to the window where a small, white moth beat unavailingly against the pane. After a moment she went over and opened the casement, brushing the frantic insect toward the aperture. Grey dust rose from the panic fluttering wings and then the moth fell, exhausted, its milky sheen bruised and lifeless. As she scooped up the fragile shell, she saw Helen hurrying toward the back door. Her sister wore a green cloak and as she raised her face within the ribboned hood some finger of early shadow touched her cheek, making it seem bruised like the wings of the dead moth.

CHAPTER THREE

Kingsmead was dazzling with hundreds of candles, the little pointed flames reflecting themselves in the brightest silver and pewter. Fires blazed in the twin fireplaces and greenery was looped over the beams and balustrade. The great hall wore a faintly surprised air, as if it were not accustomed to being dressed up for company. The evening being warm and light, the front door was open wide and the tapestry screens folded back to facilitate the entrance of the ladies in their swinging hoops.

Edward Falcon, somber in dark blue with a silver-threaded waistcoat, stood near the door to greet the guests. At his side Joanna, nervously playing with the knots of lilac ribbon on her black gown, hoped that her wig would not tilt askew, that the new diamond-buckled shoes would cease pinching her toes, that Eliza would remember to curtsey prettily instead of shaking hands like a boy, that the cream had not curdled nor the cheese soufflé been put to bake too soon. So seldom did the Falcons entertain that a thousand imaginary catastrophes whirled through her head.

Geraint Price, arriving on horseback, was greeted with a bow and a genial word.

"You must wander where you please and observe everyone. The artist must not be limited, eh? Oh, this is my lady-wife."

"Lady Falcon."

Bowing over her hand Geraint noticed the shine of sweat on her brow under the tightly fitting wig. Her eyes were dull, as if she had no recollection of him or of her whispered warning on the day he had arrived.

"My son, Prescott," Edward said.

He spoke, thought Geraint, as if he had only the one son.

A young man, who was a younger edition of his father, shook hands briskly, but whatever he had intended to say was interrupted by a plump, fair-haired youngster in bottle-green trimmed extravagantly with gold braid.

"You must be the artist whom my younger sister abducted and hid away in my Aunt Rosemary's cottage. My late-lamented Aunt Rosemary! I have been longing to skip down and have a cosy chat, but dear Father considered—quite rightly—that dashing about in the spring dampness would be too precarious for my health. I am Weston Falcon. My youngest brother, Nat, is about somewhere. My sisters, too, though females are of little consequence, save for breeding. But to create a work of art! To feel the onset of inspiration, to lose all sense of time and place, that must be the most sublime achievement of all!"

"Do you paint?" Geraint asked politely.

"My dear, I am one of those mortals who appreciate to the full what others can do," Weston said airily. "An artist, be he painter, sculptor, or musician, must have an audience."

"Sometimes he may create for himself alone," Geraint said.

"You must not say such a thing," Weston said, "or you will quite take away my excuse for existence."

"Talking fustian again?" Eliza enquired, joining them. "Good evening, sir. I'm happy to see you again. Are you still studying tombstones?"

"I intend to study faces this evening," Geraint smiled.

"For the portrait?" Prescott had turned from greeting a broad-shouldered young man in dark blue. "I understand Father has employed you to paint one of us all."

" 'Commissioned,' my dear brother!" Weston protested. "You must excuse my relative, sir. He is a complete philistine in matters of the intellect. Land and wealth are all that concern Prescott."

"You, I suppose, have a soul above such things," Prescott said expressionlessly. "Will you take a glass of wine, sir, while we wait to sit down to table? We are quite a small party, no more than twenty in all."

"I must congratulate you on attaining your majority," Geraint remembered.

"Thank you." Prescott bowed, raising his eyebrows slightly as if he were surprised to discover a Welshman capable of civilized enquiry.

"You must congratulate him on his betrothal, too," Weston interposed. "Is it not fortunate that my father's rich tenant has a daughter of marriageable age?"

"Blanche is a very healthy and attractive young lady," Prescott said coldly.

"And the match is suitable in every respect," Weston murmured and raised his glass.

Geraint drifted aside, moving until he stood near to the tapestries and could watch the guests as they arrived, were greeted, and mingled under the flaring candles.

Lord Falcon was, it seemed, a perfect host. He had a

smile, a bow, a few words for each one. At his side Lady
Falcon sweated a little more and endlessly twisted the
loops of ribbon on her gown. She must have been a plain
young woman, and age had brought no tranquillity. Edward Falcon could scarcely have married for love. There
was a coldness about him despite his smile and the obvious pleasure he took in this occasion.

Studying them, Geraint frowned a little. This couple,
the lady with the twisting hands and the gentleman with
the smiling face, had between them produced five—no,
six originals. He had not yet seen the third son.

Apple had ventured close to him, or as close as her
hoops would permit. For a moment he did not recognize
the girl from the meadow in the slender, white-wigged
creature who smiled at him, her face tilted upward in
unconscious coquetry.

"Are you comfortable in the cottage?" she asked. "I
have kept it aired and sweetened ever since my aunt
died."

"You must be very happy, mistress, to own such a
place," he told her.

"But the light is not good enough for painting?"

"Good enough for preliminary sketches," he reassured
her.

"And how will you paint us?" she asked. "Do we all
have to stand absolutely still for hours and hours?"

"I will make separate crayon portraits," he explained,
"and scale them down for the finished picture."

"And if the group portrait is good, then father will
recommend you to other people," she chattered. It was
the wrong thing to say. She sensed a withdrawal in him,
a tightening of the muscles along his lean jaw.

In confusion she said, "My father has always taken an
interest in the arts. You know he is the great-grandson of
King Charles II?"

"So your sister told me."

"Oh, here comes Nat with the Fairfaxes!" Apple exclaimed. "Now we can begin the meal!"

She was nodding and smiling toward a small group who had just arrived. The elderly couple were obviously Lord Falcon's tenants. He remembered the lady he had seen down in the village. Geraint's eyes shifted to the younger couple. The boy was fair-haired and tall, the girl almost as tall as he and with similar coloring. He had seen them both before, in the woods near to the cottage when they had scrambled away in panic.

"The Fairfaxes have been tenants of ours for years," Apple said. "John Fairfax has his own house in London, but he wished his daughter to be reared in the country. Blanche was practically brought up with us all."

Brought up to become Mistress Prescott Falcon, the future Lady Falcon. But it was Nat whom she had been kissing down in the woods. Geraint watched them with particular interest as they came in, the ladies divesting themselves of their cloaks and wraps, Nat's voice rising in excitement.

"I rode escort, to protect them from footpads!"

"The road between the manor and *Kingsmead* being absolutely infested with them, I suppose," his father remarked.

"The lad was being gallant," Mistress Fairfax excused.

"And who can blame him when one sees such fair visitors?" Edward Falcon bowed over her plump, ringed hand.

"At the last moment we were afraid we might have to send our excuses," she said. "Blanche has been off-color all day. We positively dreaded the advent of a megrim!"

"I hope you are quite well now, Blanche," Prescott said.

The girl nodded, her eyes downcast.

"You must meet my protégé," Edward said, beckoning Geraint forward. "Master Price is an artist of considerable reputation on the continent. It was only by the greatest good fortune that I prevailed upon him to lodge among us and accept my commission."

"Perhaps you would paint our likenesses, sir," Mistress Fairfax hinted.

"He is expensive," said Edward.

"Of course, when it is a matter of taste, of investing in the future, money is not the first consideration."

"Anyone can tell, simply from looking about at *Kingsmead*, that good taste has always been your primary consideration, dear Lord Falcon," Mistress Fairfax gushed.

"Let us hope that this evening's meal does not spoil your good opinion of us," Edward said pleasantly. "If it is unpalatable you will have to scold Lady Falcon. My wife chooses the menus."

"There is a soufflé," Joanna Falcon said unhappily.

"Then we must begin at once." Her husband gave her an archly reproving look. "You must know by now that a soufflé cannot be kept waiting. If you will take your seats, ladies and gentlemen. You will find your names at your places. Weston illustrated the cards."

"To parade my tiny talent before an artist of international caliber! It's too shaming," Weston cried.

"I did not say that you had illustrated them well," his father said smoothly.

The long table, its top worn shiny with age, was set down its length with damask napkins twisted into roses, silver cutlery and dishes, glasses of crystal, ivory-handled cups of almost transparent china, sprays of jonquil and ivy looping the candlesticks.

Lord and Lady Falcon took their seats in the high-backed chairs at the head of the table as the others arranged themselves more or less comfortably along the benches down both sides.

From his place near the end of the table Geraint was able to observe all the Falcon children for, defying convention, they were seated in a row opposite the other guests, with the Fairfaxes and an elderly gentleman whom Geraint had heard referred to as "Doctor" further down on the same side.

Next to her father, Helen drooped a little in her place, her cheeks as pale as her wig. It was difficult to imagine her running to meet a lover with sunshine gleaming on her hair. She gave the impression of being trapped between Edward Falcon and Prescott, who was tasting the game soup with a slightly critical air, as if he expected to find something wrong with it.

Eliza was tucking in heartily, her face flushed, her hair already untwisting from the thick powder with which it was coated. At her other side Weston picked his teeth with a delicate gold pick, waved away the soup with a perceptible shudder and nibbled water biscuits with an air of doing the company a great favor.

Apple, who was almost opposite Geraint, seemed afflicted by sudden shyness, for she had ducked her head and was eating with great rapidity. In contrast, Nat was eating very little, and his plain, pleasant face bore a dreamy expression as if, in spirit, he still rambled in the woods. He was separated from Blanche by the solid figures of her parents, but to the artist it seemed that an intangible cord roped boy and girl together, though neither looked at the other.

"My friends, if I may be permitted the indulgence of a few words on this occasion?"

Edward Falcon had risen, cutting into the murmur of conversation. Profiles were averted, heads inclined in polite, listening attitudes.

"This is a celebration," Edward said, "for today my eldest son is twenty-one years of age, and on this day his betrothal to Mistress Blanche Fairfax is announced, though I cannot believe the news comes as a complete surprise. All of you must be aware of the close friendship that has existed between our two families. I am indeed happy to have as tenants two people for whom I feel both respect and liking, and very happy to welcome such a charming young lady into our family."

Pausing, he inclined his head in Blanche's direction, raising his glass slightly. The girl swallowed convulsively, the muscles of her throat working painfully.

"I am not ashamed to say," Edward continued, "that the Falcons began in a humble capacity, as Knights of a Tudor King. This land was granted to Sir Harry Falcon in 1536, but it was his grandson Robert who was further honored by having as godmother Her Majesty Queen Elizabeth I. The stirrup-cup on the dresser was a personal gift from the Queen to the babe. And that babe was, in a sense, honored also in his dying, for in the great storm of 1617 which swept away the banks of the river he gave his life in trying to save the villagers.

"His son Hal further distinguished the family by fighting for the Royalist Cause as one of Prince Rupert's ablest officers. It was this Falcon's daughter Regina who served the Crown in a different manner by bearing a son to King Charles II. That son, Charles, was the first Lord Falcon. Unhappily, his own son Fitzroy did not live to inherit the title. As you all know, he was killed while fighting against the Jacobite rebels. I was brought here to *Kingsmead* by my late mother when I was no more than a babe, and I have not left it since save for the most pressing business reasons.

"One day, but not, I hope, too soon, my eldest son will take upon his shoulders the mantle of the peerage, the joys and responsibilities of this estate. I do not think, Master Fairfax, that you need have any qualms about allowing your only child to wed the heir of *Kingsmead*, for Prescott has been moulded in my image, and I think I may say, without vanity, that I have a certain standing in this community."

There were approving murmurs and nods around the table. Nat's hand was clenched about the handle of his knife.

"My friends, I ask you to rise and drink the health of my son," Edward said, "coupling that with the name of Mistress Blanche Fairfax, whom he has honored with a proposal of marriage."

Geraint, rising with the rest, met Apple's eyes and was filled with a sudden desire to protect her, for in their clear hazel depths was a puzzled, seeking look, as if she tried to strip the words from her father's speech and divine the meaning beneath.

The meal proceeded through its separate courses. Darkness closed in as the front door was barred and more tapers lit. Geraint watched the candlelight play over the features of Lord Falcon's children, giving Helen's skin an ivory sheen, exaggerating the shadows under Apple's eyes, the plump contours of Weston's face. Nat and Blanche Fairfax still sat silent, not looking at each other.

"There are tables set up in the drawing room for faro and backgammon," Edward Falcon announced. "My daughter Apple will amuse us on the spinet while we play, and Eliza will sing. I fear that poor Helen has no accomplishments, but she may be trusted to supervise the clearing of the table. Come, my love." He was arming his wife out of her chair, as the others rose, silken panniers swinging free of their confinement as the benches scraped back.

Apple gave Geraint a swift, pleading look and followed Eliza through the door at the left of the stairs.

"Do you care to play, sir?" the doctor was enquiring.

Geraint shook his head.

Over his shoulder Edward Falcon said, "Master Price will wish to wander about, to absorb the atmosphere. Do feel free, my dear sir. The profession of artist confers its own privileges."

And its responsibilities, Geraint thought. If I am to portray this family honestly, then I must paint a portrait that Edward Falcon will hate. I must reveal the egotism of the man, the trembling nervousness of his wife, the trapped expression in Helen's eyes, the defiance of Eliza's hearty manner.

The great hall had emptied save for a couple of domestics, who began to cover the remnants of the dinner. He strolled through into the small, panelled parlor. It was only partially illuminated by a low fire in the hearth, but a silk curtain hung across the wide arch of the drawing room glowed rosily from the lights within.

Geraint held back the thin folds of material and stood for a few minutes, observing the guests as they moved about in the long, pale-hued apartment. The doctor and a gentleman, who had been briefly introduced as Master Gideon and looked like a member of the legal profession, were arguing amicably over the advantages of a fireside chair compared to one further away from the heat. Apple's white-wigged head was bent over the instrument and a few notes of melody stole into the air. Weston was exclaiming over the embroidery on Mistress Fairfax's dress. Nat had drawn aside from the rest and was drinking port as if it were water and he were parched with thirst. Edward Falcon had taken up his stance between the two fireplaces where, hands behind his back, he surveyed his family and his guests with a benign and level gaze.

"So you did not leave," Helen said.

He had not heard her approach, and started slightly as he dropped the curtain and turned to face her slender, glimmering form. In the half-light she had an insubstantial quality, as if one of the tapestry figures had stepped down from its place to join the living.

"I am interested in painting the portrait," he said.

"To capture us on canvas, imprison us in oils? We are captured already," she said, low and bitter.

"Only if you allow yourself to be captured," Geraint said.

"We were bred to it," Helen said. "Ever since we were little, as long as I can remember, we have been told that we are the Falcons; the great, powerful, beautiful Falcons; the petty Kings of Marie Regina."

There was such an intensity of despair in her soft voice that he gripped her hand, and felt his own fingers held tightly in return. The music and chatter from the other room had grown louder, and Eliza had begun to sing in a clear, high, untrained voice.

"Your father is proud of the family name," Geraint said soothingly. "There is nothing wrong in that."

"You heard the speech," Helen said. "You listened to Father's version of the family history."

"Your sister Eliza gave me a slightly different version."

"Eliza mocks what she fears and Apple trusts where she cannot understand," Helen said. "But I can show you my ancestors! Their portraits hang on the walls here, for you are not the first artist who has ever locked a Falcon into a frame. Look!"

She snatched a candlestick from the mantelpiece and held it high above her head. The walls of the room were

lined with portraits of varying sizes, each one flickering
in the light.

"This is the old parlor," Helen said. "Through there is
the solar. Mother uses it now as a sewing room. The portraits are all hung here. Father intends to have them
cleaned and reframed and hung along the back of the
gallery. But for the present they wait here, as they wait
in the tomb down in the churchyard. Look at them, Master Price."

The candlestick shook so violently in her hand that he
took it from her and leaned forward himself to study the
pictures. Two stiff and stylized faces stared back at him
out of their separate frames.

"That is the Knight of the King who was granted the
land the monks were driven from," Helen said.

"The next one is his son?"

"Another Harry Falcon. He sued for court favor and
was granted a monopoly on the cider made in this district. And that is Robert Falcon, who died in the flood. I
know nothing evil about him."

"And this?"

His candle had illumined the face of a very young girl
with red hair hanging straight as rain about her shoulders. The picture was badly executed, but the eyes were
alive, yellow as amber, slanting like a cat's.

"She was the witch-girl." He answered his own question, shivering as the eyes met his.

"I believe she was good." Helen said. "The evil came
from her mother, I think, from the dark woman who
planted the luck-tree and cursed it as she planted, and
the evil grew and grew and overshadowed us all."

"You speak of evil."

"In the hearts of every Falcon. Those who are not evil
themselves are destroyed by the wickedness in those
about them. Look at this one. Sir Hal Falcon! The brave

cavalier who fought with Prince Rupert? They say he seduced his brother's wife, that he drank the estate dry. And this is Regina Falcon, the King's mistress! Anybody's mistress, perhaps."

"She was very lovely," Geraint said, studying the handsome, passionate face with its cascade of auburn curls, the sleepy green eyes.

"And this is her royal bastard," Helen said, moving on. "There are tales whispered about him. Terrible tales! My Aunt Rosemary was his daughter. Oh, she was my father's aunt really, but she was a part of my childhood."

"You see evil in too many things, mistress," Geraint said. "That can be a sickness."

"Sickness? We are all sick," Helen said. "All destroyed, by ourselves perhaps, for we are all Falcons. Nat is in love with Blanche and she with him. I saw the way you watched them at dinner. Nat is two years younger than she is, but they are equally foolish. Blanche is intended for Prescott. Her parents are father's tenants and will do as he bids. Weston and Eliza have no lovers. They are twisted, both of them, but neither knows it."

He thought that she was a little twisted herself, and a feeling of sadness swept over him. This beautiful house had surely known great happiness as well as misery, but the frail girl with the cameo profile thought only of the dark days.

"Paint us truly," Helen said. "And when you have painted us, then leave Marie Regina. Don't stay, Master Price!"

The curtain across the archway was swished aside and Nat Falcon came into the dim parlor. "Alone with a member of the opposite sex, dear sister? What will Father say!" the boy exclaimed.

"You have been drinking too much," Helen said coldly.

"An excellent way of passing the evening," Nat said.

"My father tells me that you are going to lodge at the cottage for quite a while and accept other commissions. You will soon be a part of the estate."

"Master Price does not intend to remain here longer than is absolutely necessary," Helen began.

"Surely that is for Master Price to decide, my dear," Edward said from the archway. "It would be very foolish of him to hurry away without taking full advantage of any opportunities that might present themselves. Helen, if you can contrive to cross the drawing room without tripping over your skirt, will you turn the music for Apple?"

The slim wraith had become a creature of flesh and blood, moving on leaden feet into the drawing room.

"I see you have been examining some of the portraits, sir," Edward said genially. "I intend to have them cleaned and reframed and hung along the back of the gallery. They will look effective there, I think. Nat, instead of pouring that liquid down yourself at such an alarming rate, will you kindly see that our guests are sufficiently provided? Master Price, will you not join the rest of us? I am certain that you have several interesting travellers' tales to whet our rustic curiosity!"

Smiling, he held open the curtain and allowed them to precede him into the long drawing room.

CHAPTER FOUR

Geraint had been at Marie Regina for a month and the
delicate tints of spring had warmed into the passionate
shades of summer. Since the dinner party he had visited
Kingsmead upon several occasions and had a considerable pile of sketches from which to make the finished
composition. His suggestion that separate portraits be
made, for the same price, had met with a chill reception.

"We must leave space in the gallery for Prescott's son
and those who will come after him, sir. And what would
my children do in frames of their own? We are a united
family, Master Price. That is our strength," Edward said.
"When you begin to work in oils, you may use the
drawing room as studio. The light is excellent there, and
I shall give orders you are not to be disturbed during the
hours you are working. You may buy all you need in
Maidstone and charge it to my account."

His visits to the house had fallen into a pattern. The
family dined at twelve after the old country custom, and
Geraint arrived soon afterward, entering through the

long windows at the back of the drawing room where his easel was set.

"Cover it when you leave each day, and rest assured no hand shall lift one corner of the sheet," Edward had said.

The canvas, with outlines sketched upon it, stood in the corner. He had already decided that the central figure would have to be Lord Falcon himself, with his shadow falling over Lady Falcon. The others would be ranged in a semicircle. It would be the kind of conventional group portrait that his patron would expect. Only a discerning eye would be able to pick out the small touches he intended to introduce.

His fingers tingled a little as they usually did when he was about to begin a new composition. Later, when the varnish had dried upon the paint, the disappointment would come, when he was forced to admit that he had failed to realize to perfection the ideas that had seeded in his mind.

He had seen a great deal of the Falcons, but they had not continued to reveal themselves so openly as at the first. Lady Falcon flitted through the rooms, her smile vague, her hands ceaselessly moving. Weston and Prescott occasionally looked in to bow and smile, Eliza trailed earth on her skirts from forays into the gardens, Helen drifted past with no more than a gently reproachful look. Apple came more often, obediently keeping her eyes averted from sketches and canvas, her round face earnest and friendly, her voice chattering on, until she seemed to realize that he was listening with attention, when a confusion of shyness would overcome her and she would hurry away, her small feet tapping the echoing floor, her hair a beacon in which the afternoon sun was captured.

He was in the drawing room one afternoon, working

on the first, subtle brush strokes when the sound of raised voices beyond the window disturbed his concentration.

"But you *shall* listen to me, Father! This once you shall listen, or I swear I'll shout it from the village green! I'll shout it until every soul in Kent knows."

"Do keep your voice low, Nat," came Edward's deeper tone. "I am very willing to listen to anything you have to say."

They were stepping through the long windows, the boy flushed and excited, the man smiling still. As they caught sight of the artist Edward Falcon frowned slightly.

"We will go up to the study," he began, but Nat interrupted him.

"We will talk here and Master Price may listen. Then you will not be able to deny what I have said."

"If you insist, my son."

The master of *Kingsmead* shrugged elegant shoulders and sat down in a wing chair.

"Blanche and I are in love and mean to wed!" Nat burst out.

"I am aware that you are fond of her," Edward said calmly. "We are all fond of her. You may imagine your own feelings are warmer than the sentiments of friendship. Young men frequently do, but these feelings usually burn themselves out fairly quickly."

"I love Blanche," Nat repeated. "We love each other."

"The young lady is betrothed to your brother," Edward reminded him. "It is not long since that betrothal was announced publicly."

"Prescott would not wish to marry a girl who didn't care for him."

"Prescott is far too sensible to be swayed by romantic considerations," Edward said. "And Blanche is a good, dutiful girl who will obey her parents. They are extremely happy about the proposed match."

"Then they will want Blanche to be happy, too," Nat argued.

"Blanche will be Lady Falcon one day. That is sufficient reason for happiness."

"And if she wanted more?"

"More than *Kingsmead*?" Edward looked astonished. "I cannot imagine either Blanche or her parents would look higher than *Kingsmead*. If she were to wed you she would have considerably less."

"I could earn a living," Nat said defiantly.

"At what, pray? You are not trained to any profession."

"Is that my fault?" Nat cried angrily. "We were none of us ever sent to school or to college. We were none of us reared to any life save that of gentlemen."

"I considered myself quite capable of instructing my own sons," Edward said. "As for a profession—I am, thank Heaven, not in a state where it is yet necessary for me to send my own children out to earn their bread."

"Does it mean nothing to you that I love Blanche?" Nat asked in a low, shaking voice.

"Calf-love," his father told him. "It affects all of us at one time or another. I have every sympathy with its victims, for the symptoms are exceedingly painful. Fortunately, cure is inevitable and instantaneous. Blanche is the only young woman, apart from your sisters, with whom you have been in close contact. She is two years your senior as it is. More important, she is betrothed to Prescott. May I suggest that we cease this discussion and leave Master Price to get on with his work?" Edward had risen, flicking out his lace cuffs, his expression bored.

"It will not end here," Nat said, and there was dignity in his young face. "We were wrong to let the betrothal be announced, but it was impossible to speak out in front of all the guests. But Blanche will be of age next year, free to marry where she chooses. Her parents would not disown or disinherit her. And I do not care what you choose to do."

Geraint, sucking the end of his brush thoughtfully, waited for the explosion. It did not, however, erupt. Edward Falcon merely gazed at his son for a few seconds.

"It begins to look as if I have underestimated the strength of this attachment. You must not fancy me completely unsympathetic, my dear Nat. Has Blanche spoken to her parents yet?"

"No. We agreed that I would talk to you first."

"I cannot approve of your attempt to supplant your brother," Edward said coldy. "I am disappointed that family loyalty should count for so little, and a little ashamed that any child of mine should stoop to deception. However, if you are certain this is more than a passing infatuation, then something must be contrived. But we must move slowly. Prescott's feelings have to be considered, and the last thing we must have is an open scandal in the village."

"Couldn't Prescott marry someone else?" Nat pleaded.

"Undoubtedly he will have to, but one cannot reach up to pluck an heiress out of the skies," Edward said, with a wry glance at the artist. "You will have to be patient for a week or two, until I have thought this matter over."

"I did not expect you to take it this way," Nat said, bewildered.

"You thought I would fall into a tremendous rage and forbid you to darken my doors again, did you?" Edward looked amused. "I am not in the habit of falling into rages, nor of making stupid threats. But you must leave me to deal with the matter in the kindest and most tactful manner I can devise. And now we must leave Master Price to continue his work before the light changes too

much. I am sure, sir, that both Nat and I can rely on
your complete discretion."

Geraint bowed silently. The ease with which Nat had
won his case, the complete lack of temper with which
Edward Falcon had behaved, aroused in him the liveliest
disquiet. At all events his concentration was broken, and
having covered the canvas with its sheet he left the
house and rode slowly back to the cottage.

The last rays of sunshine were filtering through the
green leaves as he sat on the step of the cottage,
munching the bread, cheese, and sliced onions that com-
prised his supper. It was pleasant to be alone, with nothing save the occasional scurrying of a small animal in
the undergrowth to disturb his tranquillity. The cross-
currents of feeling that stretched between the various
members of the Falcon family had no reality here.

Apple, guiding her mare skillfully down the twisting,
uneven bridle path, paused at the edge of the clearing to
watch his dark and dreaming profile. Everything about
the artist fascinated her. To engage him in conversation,
to draw from him some positive response, had become a
kind of private game. Yet when he did look at her she
could think of nothing interesting to say.

"Mistress Apple!" He had noticed her now and was on
his feet.

"Do finish your meal!"

She dismounted and came toward him, her gown of
green dimity with its yellow flower pattern blending
with the sunlit trees.

"I rode over to see that you have everything you need.
I usually look after the cottage myself, for Father will
not spare servants from the house, and folk from the village avoid it."

"Because of the witch-girl?"

"Because of the witch-girl's mother, I think. Aunt

Rosemary told me that long ago a Falcon offended the Welshwoman, and so she planted the tree outside the courtyard and cursed it. The curse is told to those who bear the mark. Margred—that was the Welshwoman—told it to Regina Falcon, and she told it to Aunt Rosemary, and Aunt Rosemary told me."

"And you will pass it?"

"To the next one who bears the mark," Apple said solemnly. "It will be one of Prescott's daughters, I suppose. Weston does not wish to marry, and Nat is too young, and Helen, and Eliza, and I are to be spinsters."

"Is that what you want?" he asked bluntly.

The puzzled look crept into her eyes again, and she tugged at the end of one of her thick red braids.

"I never thought about it," she said slowly, "until recently. We took it for granted, just as we took it for granted that we would always live at *Kingsmead*. But these past weeks I have begun to wonder how it would be to leave Marie Regina, to travel a little. My father says it is a mark of instability to be restless."

"Did he give you permission to come here to enquire after my welfare?" he asked teasingly.

Apple's face flushed as red as her hair. "My father thinks it unladylike to ride about in the woods," she said. "Oh, except for Eliza, of course, but she has always liked to do boys' things. But Father is not here. He and Nat rode over to Maidstone on some business, and won't be home until tomorrow night. So we may all do exactly as we please for a little while."

"Did your father say what business?" Geraint enquired casually.

"Something about a new plough, I think. Ben Fiske is bailiff at the old Wittle farm on the far side of the monastery and he is forever wanting to make improvements. The farm belongs to father. It was part of my mother's dowry. There is a house in Maidstone, too. My father rents that out to short-term tenants."

"But this is yours." He indicated the cottage behind them.

"This, and the land I told you about in Wales. None of us has ever seen it, but I have the original deed. I keep it in a drawer in the herb-room here. It's written in Welsh, so none of us can read it. Would you like to see it?"

"I would indeed."

She darted past him into the room at the right and tugged at a drawer set in the table. Geraint followed and bent over her shoulder as she spread a yellowing parchment out.

"Read it aloud," Apple said.

He read it carefully and slowly. *"Ewyllys a thestament Olaf Prys ap Prys, Saron ger Caernarfon. Yr wyf yn gadael fy farm, Saron, ye tir, y cropiau a'r holl stoe ar celfi i Margred, unig ferch fy ddiweddar fab, Teuan ap Prys.*

"Prys ap Prys. Tystion:—Ioan ap Robert. Owain ap Ianto. Degfed o awst, yn y flwyddyn, unmil, pump cant, wyth deg a naw."

"The words sound like music," Apple said dreamily. "Do all the Welsh people speak like that?"

"There are differences in dialect from region to region," he explained.

"Can you teach me to speak it?"

"If it were necessary," he said cautiously.

"And these words? What exactly do they mean?"

He translated them. " 'This is the testament of me, Prys son of Prys, Saron, near Caernarvon. I bequeath my farm Saron, the land, the crops, and all the stock to my granddaughter, Margred, only daughter of my late son, Teuan. Prys son of Prys. Witnesses:—Ioan son of Robert. Owain son of Ianto. On the tenth day of August, in the year fifteen hundred and eighty-nine.'"

"Prys, son of Prys," she repeated thoughtfully. "Isn't it strange to think that long ago that man willed his land to his grand-daughter, and she left Wales and came into Kent, and became my great-great—how many greats?—grandmother? And none of us has ever seen that land!"

"You may see it one day."

"I would like to see it!" Eyes shining, she turned to him. "I would like to travel there and see my land."

Before he had considered the implications he had bent his head and kissed her full on the lips. For an instant she gasped, and then her arms went about his neck, and she was responding eagerly. As they drew apart she gave a small, embarrassed giggle and made a great business of returning the document to the drawer. When she looked at him again her young face was serious.

"You are the first gentleman who ever kissed me," she said tremulously. "I sometimes wondered how it would be, if such a thing ever happened to me. I never truly thought it would."

"A kiss," he said awkwardly, "is not as rare as you would seem to believe."

"It is for me," Apple said breathlessly. "But it will do no good to approach my father. He would never tolerate one of us having a sweetheart."

"I was not," said Geraint truthfully, "thinking of approaching your father."

"And I must go home now." But she lingered still in the room, her eyes and lips hungry.

"I will come up to *Kingsmead* tomorrow," he said, and took her firmly by the shoulders. Her mouth was tempting, but he contented himself with a light kiss on her cheek and led her out into the clearing again.

As she mounted the pony, she said shyly, "When I first

met you, by the witch-girl's grave, I was working a spell to make me beautiful like my sisters. I never finished the spell, and now I feel that I don't need it any more."

She had ridden into the trees before he could frame a reply, and the silence of the summer evening closed round him again.

For some reason he did not analyze, the cottage looked lonely now that she was no longer there. For the first time he became aware of the long years of living the little stone building had witnessed; for the first time felt, deep in his bones, that he was a stranger with no right to be here.

He went slowly across the clearing and pushed his way between the bushes toward the river that ran full and sparkling, dividing the estate into two. At the edge of the water reeds grew thick and wild, and the first moths of evening dived and swooped above the glinting ripples.

One day he would paint the river as it was now, in its secret murmuring and brief flashes of brilliance. He would introduce only one living creature, a deer, perhaps, come to think of it, drinking at the water's edge. He imagined the neat, proud head, the pricked ears and liquid eyes, the dainty legs and hoofs.

In his mind the eyes of the deer were Apple's eyes with their puzzled, searching expression. Another figure hovered on the edge of the picture, a frail, slender girl with amber loops of hair. He shook his head to clear it of the image, forcing himself to think only of the gentle, seeking deer. But the figure of the girl hovered still on the edge of his imagination and would not go away.

The next afternoon he rode back to *Kingsmead*, with deer and girl sheeted in the canvas of his mind. The house was, as usual, quiet, as if, even when its master was away, each member of the family lived a separate existence within its walls. He let himself into the drawing room and began work on the canvas. Today his fingers worked fluently, obeying his ideas. The background was taking shape rapidly and soon the figures would begin to emerge, each in its separate color. Black for Edward Falcon, shot with paler tints of blue and silver-grey. Silver-grey for Joanna Falcon, muted by the brown shadow of her husband. Eye and hand, mind and brush worked in conjunction, snatching colors from the palette.

The scream echoed shrilly from the great hall. For a moment it seemed to hang on the air and was succeeded by the pattering of feet as people ran from all parts of the house. Voices rose in frantic, questioning tones.

Geraint put down palette and brush and hurried out into the hall. They were gathered there, as if they had posed for some portrait of their own.

Edward Falcon, still in travelling cloak and boots, was the center of the group, as he would always be the center of any group. Joanna Falcon, her mouth still open, sagged on Prescott's arm. The others clustered about their parents but, as Geraint walked into the hall, Apple broke away.

"Oh, Master Price, what are we to do? For here's Nat taken by the press gang and my poor mother like to die of shock!"

"Your mother is simply exhibiting the slight hysteria peculiar to her sex and appropriate to the occasion," Edward said. "And your brother has not been taken by the press gang. He has joined the army; not, I agree, entirely of his own free will, but they say there are excellent opportunities for advancement in a military career."

"But what happened, sir?" Prescott asked.

"It's lamentably simple," Edward said. "We arrived in Maidstone and transacted our business. I was tired and went upstairs early. Nat stayed in the taproom drinking with a group of army officers. I was not at that time aware that one of them was a recruiting sergeant."

"But what could have induced Nat to take the King's shilling?" Eliza demanded.

"Nat swore the coin was left at the bottom of his tankard and that he accepted a drink unsuspectingly. I am of the opinion that he was by then too foxed to know what was going on. He was still three-quarters drunk when I saw him this morning."

"But couldn't you have bought him out?" Eliza persisted.

"That possibility did occur to me," Edward said. "But on reflection I decided to let matters take their course. After all, it hardly sets a good example to the lower classes if they see their own sons being dragged off while a peer's son is simply bought out."

"I didn't know you took such a close interest in the welfare of the lower classes," Weston remarked.

"There was also Nat himself to be considered." Edward ignored his son. "The boy has been restless for a long time. It's a natural phase at his age, very natural. Marie Regina began to appear dull and provincial to him. I am very sure that he will regard this as a splendid adventure in years to come."

"But where is Nat now?" Apple demanded.

"The regiment marched out this morning," Edward said blandly. "They are to embark for the Americas, I understand."

"But that's the other side of the world!" Joanna cried, and began to sob feebly.

"My dear, you speak as if we were still living in the days of Drake and Hawkins," Edward said patiently. "The world is growing smaller as trade increases."

"But there is war in the Americas! Nat will be going into battle," Joanna said.

"We can scarcely dignify by the name of war a few colonists who protest about paying their due taxes," Edward said. "A warship or two, a regiment, firm diplomatic handling—it will probably all be over by the time Nat arrives, and he will be sadly disappointed to miss the excitement."

"Nat never said anything to me about wanting to leave Marie Regina," Eliza said.

"Brothers do not invariably confide in their sisters," Edward said quellingly.

"I did not even say good-bye to him," Joanna mourned.

"Eliza, take your mother upstairs and administer hartshorn and vinegar or whatever females administer at times of stress," Edward commanded. "My dear, if a woman cannot weep prettily, she is wiser not to weep at all. Your nose is quite abominably red. Prescott, I think you ought to ride over to the manor and acquaint the Fairfaxes with the news. Poor Blanche will be very upset, I fear. She has always had a particular fondness for Nat, and he, for his part, fancied himself half-in-love with her! Were you going to say something, Helen?"

"No, Father," the girl said.

"Then you should not stand with your mouth open. It gives the impression of half-wittedness. Master Price, this family business must be most uninteresting."

"It interests me very much," Geraint said.

"How very civil of you, my dear sir. I trust that Nat's departure is not going to spoil the portrait."

"I can work from the crayon drawings."

"Of course! I had forgot the ingenuity of the true artist! You should take heed, Weston, and one day you may produce something worthy to hang upon a wall."

The hall was emptying. Between Eliza and Apple, Joanna Falcon slowly mounted the stairs. Eliza's voice floated back to them.

"We will be receiving a letter from Nat in no time at all. Mother. And they say that social life in the regiments is splendid. You know how Nat likes a touch of gaiety."

Prescott, looking anxious, had hurried away, presumably to inform the Fairfaxes.

Edward unfastened his travelling cloak and, flinging it to Weston, remarked, "Nobody in this household seems to realize that I have just had a most fatiguing ride, and I shall have to send word to Ben Wittle that the new-fangled plough he's been craving for will be here in a few days. I tell you Master Price, there is nobody in the world more importunate than a bailiff with modern ideas! Be thankful that you do not bear the responsibility of a large estate." Putting his hand on his son's plump shoulder he moved heavily toward the parlor.

At the foot of the stairs Helen watched them go. Of all the Falcons she was the one who fitted into this ancient hall, and her loose sacque gown of brown tissue heightened her other-worldly quality.

Geraint could not read the expression on her face, but he saw her slender hand clench upon the stone balustrade and heard her swift, sobbing intake of breath.

CHAPTER FIVE

Geraint had been over to Maidstone to buy fresh paints and a new sable brush. On this second visit to the town he had stayed overnight, with some idea in his mind of shaking off the influence of *Kingsmead*. Gradually he was being drawn into the life of the Falcons, becoming part of their strange, enclosed world. He was forced to remind himself constantly that one day he would move on again, that his life would not be spent in this rustic backwater.

Yet, even when he was riding along the highway, pictures of the family darted through his mind. Nat, drinking too much, his pleasant young face flushed and unhappy. Apple, her mouth pouted into a kiss, reaching up to embrace him. Joanna Falcon, her eyes red-rimmed and weary, stumbling up to her room between her daughters. Of Helen he deliberately did not think.

And in Maidstone the affairs of the family intruded again. He had decided to lodge overnight in a modest inn, but the glittering sign outside a larger establishment coupled with the tempting aroma of pie redirected his steps.

"Travelled far, sir?" The landlord smiled genially as he served the tankard of port that Geraint had ordered.

"From Marie Regina."

"But you're not from these parts, sir?"

"I'm staying in the district a while," Geraint said cautiously.

He knew from experience that artists were not usually regarded with much favor by the landlords of expensive hostelries. He had often been required to settle his account before being shown to a room.

"We had some folk from Marie Regina staying here a week or more back," the landlord volunteered. "Lord Falcon of *Kingsmead*—you'll have heard of him if you're staying in the village. The Falcons are the most important family there, but they keep themselves to themselves. Lord Falcon usually stays at his own property at Paget Place, but this time he stayed here. Brought his son, too. Pleasant young fellow, ready to drink with anyone, God save him!"

"God save him?" Geraint cocked an enquiring eyebrow.

"Why, sir, the military were in Maidstone, seeking recruits. There were more than a dozen lads took the King's shilling, and wasn't Lord Falcon's son one of them! *Drunk* as a lord he was! Mind, his own father did nothing to prevent it. Urged him on, he did. And when the shilling turned up at the bottom of the tankard, why the recruiting sergeant swore he'd never put it there! But Lord Falcon would not have it so. 'My son is as worthy as any man's son to march with the King's regiment. No Falcon ever broke his word nor diminished his honor.' That's what he said, plain as plain. Mind, there's some could tell you odd tales about that family! Not that I credit all that I hear, sir, but one cannot help the listening."

Geraint had agreed that one could not, indeed, help the listening. Then some other customers had come in and the landlord's attention was engaged elsewhere. Geraint had eaten his meal and slept peacefully in a bed pleasantly free of lice, and had ridden back to *Kingsmead* with much to occupy his mind.

It was with faint surprise that he saw a mounted figure waiting at the manor gates—obviously waiting for him, for she trotted to meet him.

"Mistress Fairfax?" He took off his tricorne and inclined his head.

"Apple told me that you had gone to Maidstone and would be returning today," Blanche said. "I have been waiting these two hours."

"What service can I render you?" he asked formally.

"I wondered if you might have heard—" For a moment she hesitated, biting her lip, and then burst out, "Oh, sir! Master Price, can you tell me if you have heard anything of Nat? You're almost a stranger and I ought not to ask, but I need to know. He could not have taken the King's shilling of his own free will, but I cannot believe they would force a lord's son into the regiment."

"You are concerned about Nat? Forgive me, mistress, but isn't Prescott Falcon your betrothed?" He spoke harshly because pity threatened to overwhelm him, and pity was useless.

"Prescott is a very worthy gentleman," Blanche said unhappily, "and I would have no wish to hurt him. But Nat and I—we told nobody, though I think Helen guesses. But you saw us down in the woods that day. We feared you might tell, but you said nothing and we were grateful for that. Oh, sir, if Nat left any message for me, if he left one word, I will wait for him. I will tell Prescott that I cannot wed him. If you could only give me a little hope!"

Geraint hesitated, his eyes searching her haggard young face. It was an attractive face, but not a strong or a passionate one. This girl would never, he was certain, have the courage to defy the pressures that would be brought to bear upon her.

"He left no message," he said briefly. "He left no word for you, mistress."

Blanche began to weep softly, her curly blonde hair falling over her face.

She is like Lady Falcon in her helplessness, Geraint thought. In twenty years' time Prescott will be like his father and Blanche will be another Joanna, vague and untidy with twisting hands. She is formed in the same mould and cannot change.

"It would be useless to wait, mistress," he said gently. "Better not to waste your life in fruitless hoping. If Nat had truly loved you, would he not have found the courage to speak out? Would he not have found the means to leave one word for you?"

If she has any spirit at all, he thought, she will tell me to keep my opinions to myself, and then she will ride after Nat, demand to know where the regiment has gone. But she sits there, weeping, and will not go.

"I thank you, Master Price," Blanche said, at last, and rubbed her hand across her eyes. "I think I knew all the time that it was useless. My betrothal was arranged so long ago and my parents are anxious for me to marry well."

She urged her mount back through the gates of the manor, and he was left with the dubious consolation of knowing himself to be right. Nat was too young and Blanche too fearful, and their love, though sweet, had been shallowly rooted.

In the weeks that followed he worked steadily on the portrait. It was taking shape under his hands, becoming almost what he had envisaged in his mind. Edward Falcon smiled benignly, one arm stretched along the back of the chair in which his wife sat with a piece of embroidery in her hands. Weston sat on the arm of the chair, admiring his reflection in a small mirror that Apple held. Prescott and Eliza, clad in riding clothes, inclined toward Nat who sat on a footstool with his face turned up to them in conversation. A little apart from the rest Helen stood watching, loops of hair obscuring her cheeks, one hand lightly clenched. He believed that he had caught the likenesses, but he was not certain that he had captured the inner spirit that animated each one of them.

He saw little of the family. Weston stayed in close attendance on his mother whose reddened lids and vague, meaningless gestures told Geraint more plainly than words that no letter had come from Nat. Prescott, perhaps at his father's suggestion, spent much time at the manor. Eliza was usually out-of-doors, often with her father, with whom she spent a considerable amount of time discussing the quality of horseflesh. Apple came and went, chattering shyly with hopeful questions in her eyes. Of Helen he saw nothing beyond an occassional brief glimpse as she flitted across the lawn at the back of the house on her way to some secret assignation of her own.

The last touches to the canvas, the final, searching look at each painted fold and ruffle, and it was done. Geraint stepped back, conscious that to add more would be to diminish it. In a few weeks it would be ready for varnish and frame. For the present his fingers ached and he wanted to wash the smell of paint out of his hair.

"Is it finished, Master Price?" Edward Falcon had come into the drawing room.

"Finished. Soon I need trespass on your hospitality no further, sir."

"But we made a bargain," Edward said genially. "Twenty-five per cent of any other commissions you accept from now on belongs to me. The Fairfaxes have told me they wish to have their likenesses immortalized. I told them you would not accept less than two hundred guineas."

"It's very good of you to accept commissions on my behalf," Geraint said icily.

"Not in the least. I consider myself to be, in a manner of speaking, your patron," Edward told him. "Now, are we to see this portrait? You must admit we have been models of patience."

"You may see it now, though it is still wet. After you have seen it you may regret having called yourself patron."

"You are very modest," Edward said. "Strange in an artist! However, with your permission, I will call down the rest of the family."

He went out again into the hall where Geraint heard his voice raised in clear tones that rang up to the rafters like the chimes of some soulless bell.

The familiar panic gripped him, the clench of fear deep in his guts that attacked him when the moment came to display his work. He swallowed hard, composing his face into the indifferent expression that would hide pain and pleasure.

"We are all here, save Helen," Edward said, returning, "and I doubt if Helen's opinion is of much value. But the rest of us are eager to admire!"

It no longer mattered what they thought. He stood back silently and let them crowd about the easel.

"But it is excellent!" Edward cried in tones of unflattering surprise. "I declare you have caught us exactly."

"It is very much like Nat," Joanna Falcon said in a low voice.

"It is very like all of us," Weston said, raising an eyeglass to study the painting more closely. "How clever of you to portray me gazing at my own reflection. It is the one thing in the world that fascinates me above all else."

"It is very good," Prescott said critically, "but the outline of my own figure seems less clear than the others."

"Because you are only a copy of Father," Weston said with malicious perception.

"And only Father is smiling," Apple said. "Only Father is really smiling."

"A man with such a handsome clutch of sons has the right to look pleased," Edward Falcon said.

"And daughters!" Eliza said. "You have as many daughters as sons."

"And you balance the composition beautifully," Edward said pleasantly.

"It is very good," Joanna Falcon said.

"That is most agreeable of you, my dear," her husband said, "but I cannot believe that Master Price relies too heavily upon your good opinion of his work."

"I am grateful for your opinion, Lady Falcon," Geraint said.

"And you are entitled to express it, my dear," Edward said promptly. "Do not imagine for an instant I was trying to prevent you from expressing yourself. What is it that pleases you so much? The flesh-tints, perhaps? They are most lifelike, most delicate. Was it the placing of the figures? Have you, unknown to any of us, an eye for design and symmetry?"

"It is very like Nat," she repeated faintly.

"Very like Nat as we recall him," Edward corrected. "By now, tossing on the ocean waves may have imparted

a greenish tinge to his complexion. Weston, you are supposed to be the expert of the family in artistic matters.
Have you no pearls of wisdom to fling before us?"

"It's good," Weston said with unusual brevity. "Better
than we know, perhaps."

"It is a great pity that, despite my efforts, you are
quite incapable of expressing yourself coherently," Edward said. "Master Price, we are most satisfied with the
work. Most satisfied. I do pride myself on having an in-
stinct in these matters. The portrait will have an honored place in the gallery, sir."

"I thank you."

Even as he bowed formally the taste of defeat was in
his mouth. Only Apple, and possibly Weston, had seen
beyond the externals of the painting. To the others it
was no more than another acquisition to the treasures of
Kingsmead.

"Father, may he not stay to supper?" Apple was
pleading.

"Another evening, if I may. I have nothing in my
mind now beyond sleep," Geraint said swiftly.

"The exhaustion that follows creation, no doubt. We
will expect you tomorrow, or the day after that, if it
please you. No need to stand on ceremony," Edward
said.

As Geraint left the drawing room they had begun to
discuss the painting again. He mounted his horse, spur-
ring it with unusual haste down the long drive. In
painting the family he had hoped to escape from the
strange fascination they exerted over him, but he was
beginning to realize that he had simply bound himself
more closely to the inhabitants of *Kingsmead.*

He rode toward the ruins, his eyes fixed upon the
greens and golds and scarlets of early autumn. Spring
and summer had gone in the painting of one picture.

Greater than his need for sleep was his sudden hunger for a woman. It was a familiar hunger that attacked him when a particular work was finished. Perhaps there would be a girl in Maidstone willing to trade her body for a gold coin. He decided that he would ride over the next morning and choose a girl. And when he touched her he would close his eyes and pretend that her hair was amber.

The trees on the slopes were heavy with apples. He reached up and pulled one down, biting through the rust skin to the white flesh beneath. The long grass beckoned him as he rode slowly to the tracery of frozen stone that arched against the sky.

Despite himself he was swallowed in sleepiness as he tethered the horse and flung himself down in the shadow cast by the angle of two crumbling walls. His eyes closed, his arms crossed beneath his head, he allowed himself to drift over the threshold of oblivion.

The sound of voices roused him from a deep and dreamless sleep. For an instant he was confused, the walls assuming in the fading light a sinister, tilting aspect. The voices came from the other side of the wall, and for a few seconds their words were muffled. Then Helen's voice sounded clearly.

"Oh, my dear love, there must be something we can do! There must be somewhere we can go!"

"Why cannot we speak to your father?" The man's voice was deep and pleasant, with a faint country burr.

"He would never permit it. He has always made it clear that he wouldn't allow any of us to wed. My sisters and I, I mean."

"But that's insane! A woman has the right to be married."

"Not a daughter of Lord Falcon. There would be no dowry."

"Then I will take you without dowry. I never cared for you because of the money in your family."

Geraint had scrambled into a sitting position and now, through a gap where the walls did not quite meet, he could see the two of them framed in the stone. The young man held her gently as if he feared she might break. In her green cloak, with her hair looped in shining coils, Helen was the girl the artist had followed in a hundred fragments of dream, the creature he had seen a thousand times in the eye of his imagination.

"I have saved carefully these two years," the young man was saying. "I've worked hard, done without everything, never taken a wife—"

"I never stopped you from taking a wife," she interrupted. "I begged you to find another girl, Ben."

So it was Ben Fiske whom she loved. The bailiff from the Wittle farm which was also part of the Falcon property. Geraint had not seen him about in the village at all, but assumed that his duties kept him close to the farm.

"I never wanted another wife. I never wanted anyone but you," Ben said. "When I first saw you, on the day you rode over to the farm with your father, I knew then that no other girl would ever catch my heart. I would have gone to Lord Falcon long since, but you said we must wait. We can't wait forever. I'm not of your class, but I know my work and none better, and your father knows my value for he pays me well and leaves me alone to manage the farm as I deem best."

"It would be a very different matter if he ever learned that you loved one of his daughters," Helen said wryly. "He would dismiss you."

"There are other farms."

"He would use his influence to make sure you never

worked as a bailiff again. He would hound you from the county."

"You talk as if he were a monster," Ben reproved. "Your father is one of the most respected gentlemen in the whole district. I cannot believe him capable—"

"Because you are good, Ben. You are good and kind and cannot see evil in another, but I know him. I know him through and through. Ben, listen to me!" She had moved closer, her hands at each side of his face, her voice intense and passionate. "Dear love, you know my brother was tricked into accepting the King's shilling. I can tell you something about Nat, but you must never speak about it, not to a living soul. Nat loved Blanche Fairfax and she loved him. I knew about it but nobody else does, though my father guessed it, I think. I am sure he guessed it, because Nat went with him to Maidstone and never came home. I think he guessed."

"You cannot be sure."

"No, I cannot be sure, and that is why I am afraid. My father never punishes us, never loses his temper. In his way he is very generous. He likes us to be prettily dressed, to do justice to *Kingsmead*. He allows us to wander where we choose, because it never enters his head that any of us might disobey him."

Geraint heard the quiet despair in her voice and felt his own nerves quiver in sympathy. This girl needed to be loved. He craved to love her. But a wall and darkness and the arms of another man stood between her and his desire.

He wanted to leave, to go away as swiftly as possible and not to intrude upon their private talk, but if he moved now they might hear him. And he wanted to go on looking at her for as long as he could before darkness completely hid her from view.

"So must we wait forever, until we are so old that love

no longer matters?" Ben asked. "I will not do it. I will not let your fear spoil what we have. I'm not in your class, but the Fiskes have lived in these parts for centuries and are well-respected, too. There was never a Fiske hanged or sat in the stocks for wife-beating. I had a good education at the grammar school in Maidstone and I can coax crops from sand. You'd have no call to be shamed by me."

"Oh, love, I could never be shamed by you," Helen said. "But it would make no difference if you were a duke. We may none of us wed."

"Then we must run away," Ben Fiske said.

"Elope! We could not—my father would discover it and drag me back!"

"If we had left the country he could not," the young man said.

"But where could we go?" she whispered. "Farming is the only life you know."

"There are farms in France and in the Low Countries. In Scandinavia, too. We could take ship for the Continent. If we planned it carefully—would you leave *Kingsmead* and risk your fortunes for me?"

There was silence for the space of a heartbeat, and then she laughed aloud into the darkness.

"Dear heart, I will risk my whole life for you! We will go away together, soon, soon! And now I must go home. I have missed supper and will have to invent a tale."

She had broken away, was lost from view behind the wall. And then, through the gap, the two figures met and merged under the first, faint powdering of stars.

Geraint watched her as she left her sweetheart for the second time, and ran past the angled wall against which he crouched, stiff and uncomfortable. He had tethered his horse lower down, under the trees, but she took a different path, sure-footed over the tussocks of grass.

He had never wanted to follow anyone so much in his life. His bones ached with the wanting, but Helen had no thought in her mind for any man but the young bailiff.

Ben Fiske was walking away, down to the little farm at the other side of the old monastery. Helen would grace such a house like a princess. Helen would grace any house.

Geraint judged that it was safe to move. Helen would be speeding along the road now, running fleet as a deer to where her own mount was tethered. There was a rustling in the long grass not many yards from where he crouched. As he turned his head a figure rose from the concealment of bush and fern and stretched cramped limbs. The first rays of the moon shone full on the white wig and regular features. Edward Falcon had not noticed him. He yawned, white teeth visible in the darkness, wrapped his cloak more tightly around him, and went steadily down the hill.

He will find some way to prevent it, Geraint thought with a queer mixture of foreboding and excitement. He dreaded the thought of Helen's misery if her romance were shattered, yet there was the possibility that in her unhappiness she might seek a friend.

In one respect, Ben Fiske had spoken truly. He was not of her class. No man could be of Helen's class. Her sweetheart was young and handsome and, no doubt, he loved her dearly after his own fashion. But young women like Helen were not framed by Nature to be farmers' wives. The artist pictured her thickened by childbearing, coarsened by hard work. She would never survive such a life. Better that she should remain unwed, perfect and inviolate as the girl in his dream.

The moon was fully out when he reached the cottage. It hung like a pearl over the white building, draining the color out of the surrounding trees. The river was black ink, the branches and twigs of the willows stretched out like the bleached bones of murdered brides. Even the night creatures were still, as if others walked the woods who had more right there than the living.

For the first time, as he opened the door, Geraint felt himself to be not merely a stranger, but a stranger to whom the very place where he lodged was hostile.

CHAPTER SIX

Apple had waited all day in the hope that Geraint would come for supper, but the meal had passed with no sign of the lean, dark man. Since the day he had kissed her she had been half-fearful, half-hopeful that he would kiss her again. That he had not she attributed to his delicacy of feeling. Both Helen and her father had missed the evening meal on the previous day. Helen had complained that a headache had stolen her appetite. Her father had ridden down into the village on business.

The days were drawing shorter, the twilight rushing into darkness. It would be full autumn soon and then winter, and by spring the artist might have gone. She was sixteen now and believed herself a woman.

"If you are born with the mark," Aunt Rosemary had said, "you may choose to use your power or not to use it, to use it for good or for ill, to be witch or wanton. Nobody can teach you how to choose. You will find that answer in your own heart."

Apple pulled up her skirt and examined the purple crescent on her thigh. All her life when she had looked at the mark she had been struck by a sense of her own unique identity. Youngest of the children, plainest of the girls, she bore in her own flesh the proof that she was special. Now, remembering the kiss, she was no longer certain that she wanted to be a creature set apart.

Geraint Price did not appear at supper, and it was hard to keep tears of disappointment from her eyes. Had anyone noticed them she would have said she was crying at the thought of Nat so far from home, but as the family did not notice Apple, except when her hair was looking particularly red, she got through the meal without comment.

The Falcons generally retired early except on the rare occasions when there was company. Apple, who had never completely overcome her childish fear of the dark, liked to be asleep before her father had extinguished the last of the tapers in the great hall. Her sisters stayed up a little later, Eliza considering a visit to the stables an absolute necessity, Helen brushing her long hair dreamily.

Apple fell asleep almost at once, being one of those fortunate beings whose problems diminish with the coming of night. Geraint would be sure to come on the next evening, and she might have the opportunity of speaking to him for a few moments. She yearned to speak to him, to watch him, to touch him. The prospect of this had its own enchantment, for she was at the age when to dream of love was almost as exciting as to experience it.

To wake in the middle of the night was so unusual that her first reaction was one of astonishment. The room was quiet, save for the steady breathing of Eliza and Helen. Apple raised herself on one elbow and listened. She could hear nothing untoward in the apartment or beyond it, yet her nerves tingled.

After a moment she pushed back the bedcovers and

padded softly across the room. Opening the door a little way she slipped out to the gallery and stood there for a moment irresolutely. There was a faint light in the great hall below, which meant that her father was not yet abed.

She moved forward cautiously to the rail and looked down. The low murmur of voices drifted up to her as two figures moved out from the shadows. A slight frown creased her brow. She knew Ben Fiske, though not well, for as bailiff he was a cut above the villagers, but not on terms of social equality with the gentry. Yet her father appeared to be on the most neighborly terms, resting one hand on the younger man's shoulder as he conferred with him. Ben Fiske was nodding and touching his forelock, shifting the bag he carried to his other hand as Edward Falcon opened the front door.

They passed through and stood for a few seconds on the step, then Edward Falcon turned and came back inside, closing the door and sliding across the huge bolts. As he moved toward the stairs Apple stepped back hastily. There was no reason in the world why her hands should tremble nor her heart hammer, because her father had not seen her. He stood smiling, not glancing in her direction, and then reached up to extinguish the tapers.

Back in her own bed, with the covers pulled tightly over her head, Apple told herself it was the darkness, and the lateness of the hour, that had frightened her so badly. It was a long time before she slept again, and then she dreamed of Helen running through the long grass beyond the graveyard with her hair about her face. In the dream, Apple called to her, over and over, but her sister never answered nor turned her head.

The clock on the table in the corner was chiming eight when the girl woke. The family usually breakfasted at seven, Edward Falcon having been reared in the discipline of early rising, but this morning there was an unusual stir and bustle throughout the house.

She jumped out of bed and began to pull off her nightshift. Usually one of the maids came to help lace her into the tight corset that pinched in her waist and pushed up her small breasts into tempting globes. This morning, however, when she rang the silver bell which hung by her bed, the sounds of raised voices continued. The door was flung open, not by a servant with some interesting titbit of domestic disaster, but by an excited and vociferous Eliza.

"How can you be such a slug-a-bed when all hell is breaking loose?" she cried. "We've had a robbery and Father has gone off to Maidstone to swear a warrant, and he is sure to be hanged—"

"Who? Father?"

"Not Father, stupid. Here, be still while I pull your laces. Ben Fiske will be hanged, for they caught him with it in his saddlebags."

"With what?"

"The stirrup cup that Queen Bess gave to Robert Falcon when she was godmother at his baptism."

"Ben Fiske took it? But why would he do such a thing?"

"To sell it, I suppose. It was very foolish of him, for the cup is engraved. 'Robert Falcon. 1594.' You remember."

"But why would—Ben Fiske was here last night!"

"Yes, he was." Mistaking the exclamation for a question, Eliza nodded energetically. "Father asked him to come over to talk about the new plough. It seems it is much heavier to drive than they expected, and Father wished to discuss means of making it easier to handle before the spring season. Ben Fiske let himself out and when Father went to lock up he never noticed it was missing. But he woke early and decided to take a gallop. Amber's leg has been very sore, and the liniment I used doesn't seem to help."

"Never mind Amber's leg. Go on!"

"I was telling you. Father thought exercise might loosen the muscles, so he came down early and saw the cup was gone. He remembered that Ben Fiske was the last person to leave the house, so he roused the men and sent two of them over to the Wittle farm and the others along the highway. And Ben Fiske was caught, on his way to Maidstone, with the cup in his saddlebags. Father rode out as soon as the news was brought. They're holding Ben Fiske in the town gaol, but he's certain to be hanged."

For some reason she could not understand, Apple said, "And Helen? Where is Helen?"

"That's why everything is at sixes and sevens!" Eliza cried. "And how you contrived to sleep through it I cannot imagine, for we have been rushing about like ducks in a thunderstorm. Helen came down early, too. You know how she wanders around as if she were in a dream half the time. Father was just setting off to swear the warrant, and she suddenly flew at him, saying he was a monster and Ben Fiske would never do such a thing. And then, if you please, she fainted dead away. I never knew Helen to faint before. And then, of course, Mother fainted, too, and Weston couldn't find the vinegar bottle and nobody has made a bite of breakfast, which is a great pity for I am absolutely starving!"

Apple, struggling into her gown, was silent. The scene of the previous night returned to her. Her father, his hand on the bailiff's shoulder, ushering his visitor to the front step. Her father closing the door, sliding the bolts,

moving to extinguish the tapers, smiling as if something
had amused him very much.

"You'd better come downstairs," Eliza said. "We'll find
out what has happened when father gets back from
Maidstone this evening."

In the drawing room Lady Falcon was moving rest-
lessly from one table to the next, picking up objects, putting them down again. Helen lay on the sofa, her face
turned from them, her whole attitude a rejection of any
intended sympathy. Weston, his plump face a mixture of
excitement and curiosity, was sipping madeira.

As Eliza and Apple came in, their mother exclaimed,
"I knew this would be an unlucky year. First Nat, and
now poor Ben Fiske! I always thought him such a
pleasant, honest fellow. And capable at his work! Not
many men are bailiffs before they are five-and-twenty."

"There must be some mistake," Apple began.

"None at all," Weston interrupted. "Apparently he was
found with the cup in his saddlebag. Father and Prescott will have the truth of it, I suppose. I wish somebody
would tell *me* why Helen fainted. After all, the cup is
safe, and it's not as if it's a member of the family who is
to be hanged!"

"You talk too much and nothing to the purpose," Eliza
said levelly. "Apple, come with me to the kitchen and
help me set the maids to their work. They will gossip
the day away, otherwise. We may as well behave as if
this was a normal day. Weston, cannot you think of anything to do but drink? You would be better employed in
helping Helen to her room. Mother, there is a bad rip in
my dimity gown. Your stitches are so neat, will you not
see to it for me?"

Eliza, thought Apple, obediently trotting after her sister, was sometimes quite splendid.

The day returned to a semblance of normality. Helen

remained upstairs, not coming down for dinner, and when Apple took her something on a tray the older girl seemed to be asleep. Weston had occupied himself with the writing of a sonnet, frequently raising his head to declaim lines to his mother who hunched in a chair, made an occasional stitch in Eliza's skirt.

"If only Nat were here! If only there were some word of Nat!" she murmured.

Nobody mentioned the bailiff or the cup. It was as if so many questions waited to be asked that nobody cared to begin the asking.

Toward evening Apple slipped outside for a breath of air. Her head ached and she felt hot and scratchy. That her father had lied, that Ben Fiske was honest, that Helen had fainted, these things jumbled in her mind, formed into a pattern. She closed her eyes and shook her head as if to shake suspicion out of it. Hoofbeats pounded the drive and she opened her eyes as Geraint Price swung to the ground before her.

"Mistress, is it true?" he asked urgently. "I met one of your hands on the road and he tells me that your bailiff is taken for theft. Is it true?"

"Yes." She nodded, puzzled at the wildness in his eyes.

"And there is no mistake?"

"It seems not, but we are waiting for my father to return from Maidstone."

"I suppose—this must have been a great shock to the family? To your sisters? To find a trusted servant dishonest?"

She wondered why on earth he was stammering, but she answered him politely.

"We are all very upset, but my father will do everything he can. You will stay for supper? We expected you last night."

"I went fishing," he said briefly, and began to walk his horse into the courtyard.

"At night!" she exclaimed, but he was walking rapidly and she had to run to catch up with him.

They were assembled in the great hall, where their meals were still taken, when Edward Falcon and his eldest son arrived. Joanna had returned Geraint's greeting helplessly.

"This is an unlucky house. It is very foolish of you to venture here."

Weston had launched into a reading of his sonnet, interrupted by Eliza, who declared she had never heard such fustian in her life and shaken hands briskly with Geraint.

"You must think us quite mad to set such store by a cup, but 'tis a family heirloom. Excuse the smell! I have been doctoring Amber and the liniment is pungent."

Helen was not there. One swift glance around had told him that, and lacking the right to enquire why, he accepted a glass of port and listened with half an ear as Weston rambled on.

"To restore these old tapestries would be a real labor of love. They are of Flemish workmanship, but sadly faded. Tell me, my dear sir, is it possible for a work of art to regain its former glory if touched upon by different hands?"

"If the restorer remained faithful to the spirit of the original," Geraint said.

"Then the spirit of the original would have to be most strongly conveyed, don't you think? What do you think, Mother?"

"You are too clever for me, Weston," Joanna said helplessly.

"So clever that I sometimes cannot understand myself," Weston said airily.

"We had better begin supper," Eliza said with a grim look at her brother.

"Your father might not like—"

Joanna broke off as the door was thrust open and her husband and eldest son came in. Looking at them, Geraint was struck afresh by the resemblance between them. They were of the same height and coloring, but the ruthless strength of the older man's features was muted in Prescott's face. The son was a pale copy of the father, his tragedy was that he had no idea of it.

"Master Price, how very civil of you to take up my invitation to supper!" Edward Falcon advanced cordially. "You find us sadly disorganized, I fear. You will have heard of the excitement we have had here. It will be a nine days' wonder, I believe, but in this rustic corner of the world—where is Helen? Surely she has recovered from this morning's indisposition."

"Helen is not well," Eliza said.

"The shock of discovering that our most prized possession had almost been stolen, no doubt!" Edward smiled. "But the cup is recovered, so she has every reason to feel well now. Do call her down to join us."

"She is not well," Eliza repeated.

From the gallery above, Helen called, "I am quite well now. Do excuse me for being late for supper."

For the first time she dominated the scene instead of standing at the side, watching the others. She had dressed herself carefully as if she were going to a ball in a gown of amber taffeta, banded with pale turquoise, laced with cream velvet ribbon. Above the deep fichu, her exquisite face, crowned with its loops of pale hair, stared down at them with perfect composure.

"My dear Helen, you look quite charming!" Edward exclaimed. "A brief indisposition evidently suits your constitution."

"I am recovered now," Helen said calmly and began to descend the stairs.

"Then we will have supper. I am vastly hungry," he began, but she interrupted him, a smile lifting her mouth.

"Surely you are more anxious to give us the news of your visit to Maidstone. Isn't that why you wished me to be present?"

"What did happen, Father?" Weston asked.

"Nothing of any great moment." Edward tossed his cloak across the back of a chair and poured himself a glass of wine. "I went to the justices and swore my statement. It was as I told you this morning. Last night I invited Ben Fiske here to talk over the merits and demerits of the new plough. We sat in the parlor together until near midnight. Then he bade me goodnight and left. I got up a little later and bolted the doors. I did not notice the cup was missing until I came down this morning. None of the locks had been forced, nor the windows opened, so I concluded that Ben had taken the cup. I sent some of my hands over to Wittle Farm and some along the highway. He was apprehended and the cup found in his saddlebag."

"And what did Ben say?" Helen asked. "What did he say to the charge?"

"A fantastic story," Edward said. "A tale not worth the telling."

"I would like to hear it," Helen said, and the very gentleness of her voice had the strength of steel.

"He declares that I gave him the cup and told him to take it to the silversmith's in Maidstone so that the design on the rim could be re-chased."

"That doesn't sound very fantastic," Eliza said stoutly.

"The silver needs no rechasing, either on the rim or

anywhere else," Edward said. "If it did need doing, why would I send a bailiff to Maidstone with the cup?"

"Ben Fiske told the justices that Father asked him as a particular favor, because he had a touch of gout," Prescott said.

"You all know that I have never suffered a twinge of gout in my life," Edward said. "Would a man suffering from gout rise early in order to go for a gallop? I'm afraid there is no doubt that Ben Fiske took the cup, that he hoped to sell it, probably have the inscription erased."

"May I ask, sir, what will happen now—to Master Fiske?" It was Geraint who asked the question.

"He will be tried and hanged," Edward said.

"In Maidstone?"

"In London," Prescott said. "Father felt that as he is himself a justice and the Falcons a leading family in Kent, it would be fairer if Ben Fiske were tried in London."

"I shall not, of course, attend," Edward said. "My sworn statement will be read out in court. As a peer of the realm it would scarcely be fitting for me to undergo cross-examination in so trivial a case."

"It means a man's life!" Apple said, shocked.

"I am not indifferent to that!" her father conceded. "I have already written to the Lord Chief Justice, detailing my bailiff's former excellent character and recommending that the death sentence be commuted to transportation. Ah! I see we have a cold collation this evening. How intelligent of you to order it, Joanna!"

"Eliza saw to the supper," his wife said faintly.

"It seems I overestimated you as usual, my dear," Edward said. "But it's pleasant to discover that Eliza has a soul above bran mash and oats. Master Price, be good enough to take a seat. These family troubles must be very boring for you."

"If Master Price will excuse me for a very little while," Helen said loudly, "there is something I would like to say."

Joanna Falcon put her hands to her mouth with a little, gasping sound.

"I love Ben," Helen said, and there was pride in her face. "I have loved him for a long time and he loves me. He wanted to come to you openly, Father, and ask your permission to wed me. I told him that it was useless, that you would never permit any of your daughters to marry. So he begged me to elope with him, to start a new life together in some place where you could never find us. And I said that I would. For a whole day I really believed it was possible. But you found out about it, didn't you, Father? Somehow you found out, and now there is no more Ben Fiske, just as there is no more Nat."

"What has Nat to do with it?" demanded Weston.

"Nat was in love with Blanche Fairfax," Helen said, "but Blanche has always been intended for Prescott, so Nat suddenly found himself pressed into the army, on his way to the American colonies. Why, Father, that's almost as effective as transportation!"

Prescott, his mouth working, stepped forward and clutched at his sister's arm. "You lie!" he said hoarsely. "Blanche is older than Nat."

A curious look of pity came into Helen's face. "I said that Nat loved Blanche," she said gently, "but she thought of him as a brother."

"You talk as if Nat were dead!" Apple cried.

"As good as dead," Helen said with brutal gentleness. "It will be months—years—before he comes home again. And Ben Fiske will never come home again. You made certain of that, didn't you, Father? I don't know how you found out, but you did, didn't you? Ben won't tell anybody how he loves me. He'd not have my name dragged through a public court."

"You seem quite ready to scream out this preposterous tale in front of a stranger," Edward said coldly. "I must apologize, Master Price, for my daughter's lack of breeding. It is unworthy of—"

"Of the Falcons? Of the high and mighty Falcons of *Kingsmead*? That's it, isn't it?" Helen said bitterly. "This house, this land, it means everything to you, doesn't it? Everything else comes second. *Everyone* else! We are here like—like that silver cup that the old Queen gave to Robert Falcon. Ornaments! Pretty ornaments!"

"I've been very patient," Edward said heavily, "but I feel we have endured your nonsense too long already. You may go to your room, Helen, and we will all endeavor to put this unfortunate episode out of our minds."

"You would find it very easy to do that, wouldn't you?" Helen said. "But I do not intend any of you to forget. I do not intend to be an ornament in this house any longer."

"If you have any notions of leaving home," Edward began.

Helen laughed, and her laughter was like chips of glass tinkling together.

"I intend to stay," she said, and her slim hand flashed toward the table, seized one of the sharp supper knives and drew its point deeply down the side of her face. Her laughter changed to a scream of pain that rose up and hung on the air, and blood spurted from the torn flesh and gushed scarlet down the side of her neck. The others were frozen, as if a sculptor had modelled them and placed them in some eternal tableau of horror.

"I intend to stay," Helen said again, wincing with pain as she moved her lips. "I will be the one whom you will not be able to forget, Father. I will be here every single day of your life."

Apple began to sob, her eyes wide with terror and shock. Joanna was rocking to and fro, her own face convulsed.

"Send for the physician," Eliza said in a voice from which all emotion had been banished. "For the love of God, Father, send for the physician."

Edward moved then. Slowly he crossed the room to where Helen stood and looked down at her.

"The scar will fade in time," he said, "but by that time you will be too old for any man to love."

CHAPTER SEVEN

It had been the longest winter and the coldest spring
that Apple had ever known. Sometimes it seemed to her
that her heart was frozen, too. Geraint had never kissed
her again, never touched her. There were times when
she thought it might have been better if he had gone
away, but he had stayed on in the cottage, accepting the
commission to paint three separate portraits of the Fairfaxes, coming up to *Kingsmead* once or twice a month
for supper.

And at those times it was sufficient, just for a little
while, to be near him, to listen to his voice, to watch the
dark eyes and long hands and hold them in her memory
until he came again. Often she went down into the
woods, intending to come upon him by chance, but
shyness always held her back. It was, after all, for a
gentleman to speak, and, even if he did, what hope
could there possibly be? Helen with the fiery scar on her
cheek was living proof that the daughters of *Kingsmead*
would never leave it.

There had been word of Nat. Prescott, for once acting

without his father's permission, had made enquiry in London.

"Nat is with General Sir William Howe's regiment," he had reported back. "A small expeditionary force sailed to the colonies to make preliminary investigation of the situation there. Nat was among them."

"And there has been no word?"

It was Apple who enquired, for her mother had begun to weep again. Joanna spent much of her time in tears these days.

"There is not likely to be, until he is home again," Prescott had said.

But he could have contrived to send word, Apple thought. Other soldiers must send letters to their families. But Nat is too angry to write. Perhaps he thinks we should have prevented it, made Father buy him out of the regiment. As if any of us ever influenced Father in the smallest degree!

As she grew older it seemed to her that she saw some things more clearly and others not at all. She could discern in her father's smile not only ruthlessness but the anxiety of a man who needs to possess in order to feel safe. And in her mother's constant weeping there was an element of malice, as if Joanna punished those around her for her own weakness. Yet Apple no longer glimpsed the shadow figures in the wood. They had withdrawn from her as she grew out of childhood, and sometimes she looked at her thigh and fancied that the mark there was fading, too.

Edward Falcon had given them all news of Ben Fiske.

"I had a full report from the Lord Chief Justice yesterday—most civil of him, but he knows my interest in the affair. The verdict brought in was guilty, of course. However, due to the excellent account I gave of Fiske's previous good character, the death sentence was commuted to transportation for thirty years."

There had been no sound from any of them, and then Helen had turned her ruined face to her father.

"How very kind of you to bring us London gossip," she said.

The portrait was varnished, framed, and hung with the other portraits at the back of the gallery. Apple often looked at them, her eyes moving from one face to the next, her mind seeking the weakness and strength of each one. It was possible, as she saw her family more clearly, to trace in their living features shadowed attributes of their forebears.

Her father's smile was the same smile that his grandfather wore, and the eyes of Edward Falcon had the unrelenting intensity of that same grandfather, Charles Falcon, who was the bastard of a King and about whom tales were still told in the village. Her mother, born a Fleet, bore the same anxious, lined look as Lady Alys Falcon. Lady Alys had been a Prescott before her marriage, but the Fleets were descended from the Astons and the Prescotts, and both Joanna and the long-dead Alys had the same worried eyes.

Her brother Prescott was no more than a tracing of Edward Falcon, and Weston's plump mouth held the exact weakness that showed all-too-clearly in the handsome features of Sir Hal Falcon who had fought for the Royalists in the Civil War. Eliza had the blonde beauty of Hal's wife, Marie, who before her marriage had also been a Fleet, and something about the way the very first Harry Falcon carried his head reminded her of Nat. Poor Helen was the witch-girl, Catrin, whose perfect face stared out of its canvas with the dreaming gaze that Helen used to have.

Time and again Apple went back to look at the portrait of her great-great-grandmother. Regina Falcon had been Hal's daughter and mistress of a King. Aunt Rosemary had been reared by her and had spoken of her often.

"A beautiful woman, even when she was old and fat and painted too heavily. She was always greedy for life, but she gave more than she received, and she had more courage than anyone I ever knew."

I wish I had her beauty and courage, Apple thought, gazing at the portrait, unaware that the painted green eyes and her own hazel ones held the same sweet sanity.

Preparations were in hand for Prescott's marriage to Blanche Fairfax.

"The end of July would suit us all very well," Edward Falcon had said. "We are usually certain of a spell of fine weather round about that time. A country wedding can look very charming. We will hold the reception here. The manor is too small for the occasion, and Mistress Fairfax will be happy to have the arrangements taken out of her hands."

Eliza and Apple were to be bridesmaids and Weston would stand as his brother's best man. A bridal cake was being brought from Maidstone, and girls from the village were being hired as extra servants for the day. To all of this, Blanche had docilely agreed. Their tenant's daughter had lost weight and grown pale this past year. Apple wondered sometimes if Nat's love had been entirely unreturned.

"I intend to come to the ceremony," Helen had said.

Her father, raising well-marked brows, had answered, "I never thought for one moment that you would not, my dear."

The story of Helen's violent outburst had gone round the village, carried by the listening servants, losing nothing in the telling. Geraint Price had the general opinion expressed to him by the local innkeeper.

"A crying scandal, I call it, for the maid to mark herself in such a way! Poor Lord Falcon, with an undutiful son and a bad-balanced daughter! The pair of them ought to be grateful for what they have, not go falling in love where they've no business."

That was the opinion shared by most. Edward Falcon was a respected man, though it was admitted that he was not sociable.

"But a man has the right to keep himself to himself. And milord doesn't spend his time drinking and gaming in London as so many do. He stays home and takes care of his property," the innkeeper had said.

Ben Fiske was also discussed, some being of the opinion that the young bailiff had stolen the cup on impulse, others declaring that a man as clever as Master Fiske was bound to have a streak of dishonesty.

"Always did fancy himself a cut above the rest of us," the innkeeper confided. "Never mixed much, even as a lad. And to cast his eyes at a lord's daughter, and the two of them so sly about it! I tell you, sir, there's no wonder trouble's broken out in the colonies when there's so many folk at home seeking to ape their betters."

Geraint had drunk his ale and listened silently. He had, after all, no right to argue, for by not warning Ben or Helen about Edward Falcon's spying, he was as guilty as any of preventing the elopement.

He had seen Helen many times in the past months, and been astonished by the violence of feeling that gripped him when he looked at her scarred cheek. She was no longer a dream in his mind, but a living and passionate being whom he desired and had not the right to approach.

He had painted a picture for his own pleasure, not of

Helen, but of the cottage. A small picture of the white-washed building in the sun-dappled clearing. A figure was needed to bring humanity into the subject, and he had started out consciously to paint Apple.

But the young girl with long black hair and slanting yellow eyes who took shape under his brush bore no resemblance either to Apple or to anybody else he had seen in Marie Regina. When the picture was dry he put it away, feeling a need to keep it, though he could not understand it.

Apple was often in his mind. She was, he thought, like the little sister he had never had. His childhood, which had seemed happy, appeared in retrospect to have been a lonely one. His father had been immersed in the life of an actor, and had not tried to conceal his disappointment at his son's lack of interest in greasepaint and buskins. With conscious self-pity, Geraint remembered himself as a thin, dark child, crouched in the wicker basket that held the props, and drawing swiftly the lineaments of the faces on stage and in the audience. All his life he had moved about from place to place, never staying long, recording the life of a district without ever becoming part of that life, until he had ridden to Marie Regina and been caught in the toils of an unfinished spell.

"You will, of course, come to the wedding breakfast, Master Price?" Edward Falcon had said. "We regard you now almost as one of the family."

He had bowed and accepted, and made up his mind that when the marriage was over he would pack his few belongings and move on. He had more than two hundred guineas left of the money he had received for the portraits, sufficient to keep him in moderate comfort for a considerable time. If he stayed he would inevitably lose not only his freedom, but also the need of it.

The morning of the wedding dawned as bright and clear as the rest of the month had been. Apple was the first to wake, and lay for a few moments still half-wrapped in sleep. She had been dreaming, and snatches of the dream still hovered in her mind. Prescott and Blanche had been in an open carriage of some sort, with Prescott holding the reins. Her brother had been asking a question. She could not recall what it was, but she had heard Blanche cry out: "Yes, yes, yes! I loved him, loved him, loved him." And then Blanche had taken the reins and lashed the horses and the scene had split into fragments of snorting heads and pounding hoofs and crunching wheels.

Apple sat up, shaking her red braids, clearing the last remnants of nightmare from her consciousness. On this day it was positive *duty* to be happy. The optimism which never ran very far below the surface of her nature bubbled up. The sun was shining, she had a new pearl-shaded gown and a fresh curled wig to conceal her violent hair, and Geraint Price would be a guest and see her in her finery.

By mid-morning they were all ready. Standing on unfamiliar high heels that made her the same height as Eliza, Apple watched the rest of her family as they assembled. Prescott looked handsome and nervous, his hands sweating as he drank a last tot of rum.

"Nothing like rum to steady a bridegroom's nerves," Edward was assuring him.

"Perhaps I had better have a teeny libation myself," Weston hinted. "One may as well practice."

"Stick to sherry and wine," his father advised. "With your habits you are never likely to need rum."

The remark puzzled Apple, but it evidently meant something to her brother because he flushed deeply and fiddled with his embroidered cuff.

"And what do you think of our children, my dear?" Edward turned to Joanna. "Barring poor Helen, who must forever remain a blot on the landscape, are they not handsome?"

"I wish Nat could have been here," Joanna said.

Glancing at her mother Apple thought, with a little, cold chill, But there is something very wrong with Mother!

Joanna looked ten years older than her sixty years. Under the wig with its towering, plumed headdress, her face was so drawn that the lines of her skull could be discerned under the tight skin, and the paint on her cheeks stood out garishly. Her hands twisted and untwisted the ends of her silken girdle.

Her remark went unheeded. Few people took the trouble to pay much attention to what Lady Falcon said. Eliza had wandered away to look at the table with its burden of aspic salmon, honeyed hams, and syllabub.

"We will have a good meal later," she remarked, her beautiful mouth curving into a pleased smile.

"That sounds like Jem with the horses," Edward Falcon said, setting down his glass. "Prescott, you and Weston ought to be starting for the church. It would never do to have the bride arrive first!"

It was not Jem with the horses, but a solitary rider in the dress of a groom. For the rest of her life when Apple thought of that scene it split into fragments, as her dream had done. The groom dismounting and handing her father a letter. Edward breaking the seal with a little snap and reading the message. Prescott asking, "What is it, Father?" Edward answering, his voice cold and flat, "It's Nat. He was killed about seven weeks ago, at a place called Bunker Hill."

"Oh, dear God," Eliza said and sat down abruptly.

"Nat killed? But you said—it was an expeditionary force," Prescott said.

"The colonists seek independence," Weston said in a high, excited voice. "I read about it in a newspaper recently."

"But Nat can't be dead," Apple heard herself say. "He's only eighteen years old."

"Killed in action, fighting gallantly," Edward said.

"Then Nat won't be coming home?" questioned Joanna. Her mouth was working oddly and her eyes had a glazed, unfocused look.

"I'm truly sorry," Edward said. "This is the very last thing I wanted to happen. Nat was a disappointment in many respects, but he was a Falcon."

"He was my son," Joanna said. "He was my youngest son."

"He died, fighting gallantly," Edward reminded her. "We can be proud of that."

"Proud?" she echoed drearily. "Proud to have sent a boy into a strange land? Proud to have stood by and done nothing, said nothing, while you got rid of a child whom you never truly loved?"

"You are speaking wildly," Edward said.

"Never truly loved!" Joanna repeated. "I remember when he was born and you came in to look at him. And you said then, 'He's well enough. Let us pray he doesn't grow up to be a drain on the estate.'"

"That was a jest," Edward said. "I cannot understand how a woman will persist in remembering one sentence and holding it against a man for the rest of his life! I intended to buy Nat out of the regiment in a year or two, settle him with an heiress. There are some still in the county apart from Blanche, you know."

"I will have to ride over and tell the Fairfaxes the wedding is postponed," Prescott said.

"My dear boy, what possible reason can you have for doing that?" Edward exclaimed.

"Nat is dead," Prescott said blankly.

"And postponing the wedding will not change that melancholy fact," Edward said. "Nat has been dead for nearly two months. That didn't prevent any of us from enjoying our meals."

"But we didn't know about it then," Eliza said.

"And if this letter had arrived tomorrow—it is from his commanding officer, by-the-bye—we would have spent a perfectly happy day," Edward returned. "We really must be sensible and not permit our very natural grief to overwhelm us. Now, let me think for a moment. I am quite discomposed myself."

He paused, tapping his thumbnail against his strong, white teeth.

"We will continue as if nothing had happened," he said at last. "The messenger was riding back at once, so there is no danger of his stopping in the village to gossip. I shall depend upon all of you to say nothing, especially to Blanche."

"Why not to Blanche?" Prescott asked sharply.

"Because on her happiest day a bride does not wish to be troubled by bad news," his father said. "We will break the tidings later today. I will choose the most suitable moment."

"I don't think I can possibly do it," said Weston. He sounded upset and shocked. "I was never close to Nat, Lord knows! He was always a graceless young scamp, if you ask me. But to pretend that nothing has happened—"

"It would be extremely selfish and ill-bred to allow our personal grief to spoil an important social occasion," Edward interrupted. "Helen! have you nothing better to do than stand staring at me? Help your mother into the carriage. Prescott, be on your way now! You, too, Weston! We must all of us stand together as a family."

"I am not coming to the service," Joanna said.

"Not coming to your son's wedding! Don't be ridiculous, my dear."

"I am not coming," Joanna said again. "I will *not* come."

"You will do as I bid you, my dear," her husband said smoothly.

"Edward, I never disobeyed you," Joanna said, twisting and untwisting her girdle. "I never disobeyed you in my life, until now. All these years, watching you clutch and hold at this estate, watching you treat your own children as if you owned them! But Nat was my youngest son and I'll not be cheated of my grief. I won't come to the wedding."

"Under the circumstances, perhaps it would be best if you stayed at home," Edward said at last. "I forget sometimes that you were not born a Falcon, and so cannot rise to events as we can."

"I will go to my room," Joanna said, and she began to nod her head up and down as if she were agreeing with herself. "I will go to my room and say a prayer for Nat. I used to know some pretty prayers."

"I will let it be known that you are unwell," Edward told her, "and didn't feel yourself capable of making the drive to the village. You may expect us back in an hour. By that time you will, I sincerely trust, have composed yourself sufficiently to receive the guests with a little dignity. I have no intention of allowing you to disgrace us with your lack of courage. Eliza! Helen! Apple! We will leave for the church."

The carriage was bedecked with white ribbons, the windows rolled down. Edward mounted his own black stallion, and as his daughters settled themselves on the cushions, he signalled to Jem to drive on.

For years afterward folk in Marie Regina talked about the day that Prescott Falcon married Blanche Fairfax. It was discussed openly, whispered about in chimney corners, remembered on winter evenings.

Nobody remembered exactly what the bride had worn. White, no doubt, with a high bonnet and a lace veil. She had been very quiet and still, and made her responses prettily, and that was all one expected of a bride. Prescott had looked gravely handsome at her side. It was a pity, everybody said, that Weston had fumbled and fidgeted. It was noted also that the two bridesmaids were both weeping quietly.

"Lady Falcon is not at all well," Edward said quietly to the parson as he met them at the church door. "She hopes to be well enough to play her part at the reception, but I advised her to rest."

The service seemed long to Blanche Fairfax, and the church was cold. Stone pressed in about her, and Prescott was more like his father than she had ever realized. She had shed many bitter tears since the day she had met Geraint Price on the road from Maidstone. If Nat had only written to her once she would have found the courage to tell her parents the truth and break off her engagement to Prescott, but Nat had never written, and as the months went by it became harder and harder to remember his face.

Now, feeling the gold ring as cold as iron about her finger, a curious kind of relief swept over her. It was done, and even if Nat walked through the door this minute, nothing could change her from Blanche Falcon into Blanche Fairfax again.

They came out into the sunshine and the chattering of the small crowd around the door. Some children were throwing flower petals, and somebody gave her a silver horseshoe. She lifted her head and smiled, noticing out of the corner of her eye that Helen was staring at her with a blank, closed expression on her face. Poor Helen! she must have truly loved Ben Fiske to have mutilated herself in such a fashion!

They were helping her into the coach; the panniers of her gown tilted as she negotiated the step. They were all making the short drive back to *Kingsmead* for the reception, after which she and Prescott would drive to Maidstone where they were to stay at Paget Place for a few days.

"It's fortunate you're not going far away," her mother had said. "We will be able to visit often."

Other girls had come from the manor to marry Falcon men. Their names passed through her mind—Marie Fleet, who had never borne a child and had died of the plague; Temple Fleet, who had died in childbirth; Joanna Fleet, who wandered about with anxious eyes.

"I hope your mother's illness is not serious," Blanche said now timidly to Prescott.

He had not spoken to her since they had left the church. "She has no physical ailment," he said shortly. "It is simply that—Blanche, did you ever guess that Nat was in love with you?"

Her heart thudded under the tightly laced bodice of her gown, but she answered as lightly as she could. "Why, sir, what a question to put to a girl on her wedding day!"

"Did you guess?" he persisted.

"I thought him very fond of me," she said slowly, and in her own ears her breathing sounded loud and uneven.

"And you? Were you fond of him?"

"Why, of—of course I am fond of him," she stammered. "I am exceedingly fond of all your family. Helen, Eliza, Apple ..."

"Were you in love with him?" he said loudly. "I found out today that Nat loved you. Did you return his affections? Did you, Blanche?"

"Why, of course not—he's a boy, younger than I am. Today! You said—is Nat come home?"

"Nat is dead, killed in the colonies," Prescott said.

Her first thought was, But he is cruel to tell me in this fashion! How can I weep when all the other guests are driving behind us, when we are turning in at the gates of *Kingsmead* on our way to my wedding breakfast?

In a small, prim voice, the thorns of the roses in her wedding bouquet pricking her hands, she said, "I am so very sorry to hear it."

"My mother was quite overcome," Prescott said. "He was only eighteen, and that is young to die."

And now I will forget his face very swiftly, forget his boy's eager embrace and how we sat in the woods weaving dreams. I am Prescott's wife, and I will live at *Kingsmead* with all the other Falcons and bear a son to carry on the name. And all my young summer is fled!

The carriage stopped so abruptly that she was jolted forward. Through the open window she could see the luck-tree, its branches spread out, weighed down by a panniered figure that sagged among the rust-red leaves. Joanna Falcon's girdle was tightly around her neck, and her restless hands were quiet at last.

CHAPTER EIGHT

There was a new inscription at the back of the Falcon tomb. Enrolled in gold on the dark stone were the words:

MASTER NATHANIEL FALCON.
BORN 1757.
DIED BUNKER HILL, 1775

Edward Falcon had gone to great trouble to ensure that the lettering was perfect.

"To have one's father and one's son die for King and country is something of which to be truly proud," he had said.

What he meant was that it compensated in some degree for the shame of having one's wife kill herself on the day of an important social occasion. Nothing would ever eradicate the stigma of it in his mind, though his bearing had excited admiration from the villagers.

"A terrible thing to happen! To lose one's wife and

hear about the death of one's son on the same day. How many men could endure that?"

He had not only endured, but surmounted it. On the very day of the inquest he had ridden back into the village to make arrangements for a tombstone for his wife, accepting muttered expressions of sympathy with a grave inclination of the head.

"There was never a Falcon who committed suicide before," the innkeeper said, when milord was out of earshot. "There've been Falcons drowned and kicked by horses and died in childbirth, but never one committed suicide."

"While the balance of her mind was disturbed," a customer remarked. "Lord Falcon told us what the coroner said."

"There was never a Falcon actually went crazy, that I ever heard about," the innkeeper said.

"Lady Falcon was a Fleet anyway," another reminded them.

"She had Falcon blood," the innkeeper said. "There's bad blood in that family. Look at that poor Helen, forgetting her station in life to lust after a working man, and then spoiling her pretty face! That was enough to break poor Lord Falcon's heart, but he didn't allow it to happen."

They had nodded at that and called for an extra round of drinks on the strength of it. Then the talk switched to Nat Falcon who, it was generally agreed, had had a look of early death about him since childhood.

"Born to suffer," the innkeeper said wisely. "Born to suffer."

And I, thought Geraint Price, putting down his empty tankard and walking out into the street again, have no

part in that suffering. It's not my affair. It never was my
affair.

He crossed the road and glanced through the railings
into the churchyard. The Falcon tomb was high up on
the slope, facing down the hill toward the village.
Joanna Falcon had been interred outside the low wall
that bounded the cemetery, near to the witch-girl Catrin. He had been up once in the month since her death
and seen that the stone was already in place, its wording
contemptuously precise.

LADY JOANNA FALCON, *née* FLEET.
BORN 1715. DIED BY HER OWN HAND 1775

There had been some flowers on the mounded soil. He
guessed that Apple had put them there.

The cottage had been cleaned and swept. There was a
sad pleasure for him in making everything neat and
shining. At least Apple would return to her refuge to
find it unchanged. And he knew, even as he scrubbed
paintmarks from the floor, that everything was changed,
that nothing could ever be quite the same. In the year
and a half he had lived in Marie Regina the world had
tilted and he would never look at it in the same way
again.

As he approached the clearing Apple came out to
meet him. Her hair was hidden under a wide Leghorn
hat, and for an instant the slender grace of her figure de-
ceived him into thinking that it was Helen who stood
there. There was the taste of sour disappointment in his
mouth as he slipped to the ground and bowed.

"You are going away," Apple said breathlessly. "Eliza
said that you had been up to the house to say good-bye.
I was in the north pasture gathering colt's-foot. Was Father very angry?"

"He said very little," Geraint said.

Milord Falcon had, in fact, glanced up and said, indifferently, "Go if you choose. The portrait is completed and satisfies me very well."

"I have ceased to amuse him," Geraint said now. "He made no difficulties."

"So you're leaving." Her voice was dull, her face so pale that her freckles stood out clearly across the bridge of her nose.

"It's time to move on. I left everything . . . as it was. It's all clean, tidy, the linen folded. It will need to be washed."

"Eliza will see to that. She's seen to everything since—Eliza has been very good."

"She's a very sensible young lady," Geraint said.

"Yes. Yes, she's—Master Price, would you take me with you? I mean—would you allow me to come with you?"

"With me?" He looked at her stupidly.

Apple put both hands behind her back and spoke rapidly and nervously.

"We have not talked, not since that day when you—we had no opportunity, and I know I'm not pretty. I never was very pretty, I'm afraid. My hair—it's red. You probably noticed. And my mouth is too big. And you may think that I am very young, but this month I will be seventeen and I'm old enough to wed. Of course, my being a witch may discourage you. I can't blame you for that. But I was never very good at casting spells. I was always afraid they might go wrong and hurt people. It's not—not very comfortable at home these days. It's lonely, you see. Helen is so silent, as if she were locked up inside herself, and my father is—he watches. He watches all the time. I would be most grateful if you would take me with you and marry me."

He went on looking at her in silence, seeing not the slim, freckled girl but Helen, unblemished, her loops of amber hair pale against the green of her cloak, seeing not the wide, hazel eyes of a living Falcon, but the dead ones of Lady Joanna as she swung gently from the branches of the luck-tree.

"I would be glad to marry you, mistress," he said at last. "I would be very glad indeed, but your father—"

"Can do nothing. Father can do nothing. We can ride far away very quickly. We can go anywhere at all. I don't need anything, you know."

"I have some money still. It will serve for two of us, for a while."

There was a sudden lightening of his spirits as if something gay had sprung into the clearing where they stood. This marriage could be in some measure an atonement for that evening when he had crouched behind a wall and watched Edward Falcon smile up into the moonlight.

"The old will!" Apple exclaimed. "The document you read out to me, Master Price, would prove that I had a claim to the farm in Wales."

"It would prove that the woman called Margred had a claim."

"And she left that place to Regina Falcon and Regina left it to Aunt Rosemary and Aunt Rosemary left it to me. Those wills are all in the lawyer's chambers at Maidstone, but the Welsh one would show that somebody owned that land, wouldn't it?"

"Is that what you want to do? Go to that place that your aunt left to you? I thought nobody had ever been there since the woman left Wales two hundred years ago! It will have gone back to wasteland by now, or somebody else will be on it."

"It's my land," Apple said stubbornly. "It's my own

land to live on as I please. I've left a letter for Eliza, telling her that she may have this cottage. I put the letter at the bottom of her linen chest. 'Twill be a month or more before she finds it. But the land in Wales is mine. We could go there."

He was an artist, not a farmer, a man born to travel from place to place, not to spend his whole life on a small farm in the midst of rain and mountains. But Apple loved him very much, and he could never leave her here to be destroyed.

"We'd better start if we're to make good time along the London road," he said, and bent his head to kiss her, stifling the weeping in his heart.

At *Kingsmead* the family was gathered for supper, waiting for Edward Falcon to join them and begin the carving of the meat. They sat in silence, eyes downcast, minds occupied with their own thoughts.

Prescott, glancing down at Blanche, thought, as he thought every moment of every waking day, Did she ever feel anything for Nat? They were together a great deal, a very great deal. I was occupied with the management of the estate. Perhaps I ought to have paid more attention to her, but she was always meant for me, and Nat was much younger.

Blanche, holding back nausea, thought, If he asks me once more how I felt about Nat I will lose my mind. Over and over, when he makes love to me, the same question. Over and over and over.

Eliza thought, I hope Apple comes in before Father gets back! He expects us to be waiting for him at meal times. And Father is late. The pudding will spoil.

Weston thought, I wish somebody would say something amusing. Mother and Nat are dead. There's no use in our sitting here with long faces, no use at all.

Helen sat without thought, one hand stroking the livid

scar that dragged down the corner of her eye and lifted the edge of her lip.

"Perhaps we had better begin," Blanche said in a high, desperate little voice.

Nobody answered her. Their heads turned as if drawn by the same invisible cord toward the door as it opened and Edward Falcon came in. His face was so dark that Prescott sprang to his feet.

"Father? Father, what is it?"

"Your sister has ridden off with that artist," Edward said starkly.

"Ridden where?" Prescott queried.

"Who knows? London, probably. They were seen riding out of the village. I was on my way back from Wittle Farm when Master Stone hailed me."

"Apple eloped!" Weston clapped both hands to his mouth in excited pleasure.

"She will be brought back," Edward assured him. "They will both be brought back. The abduction of a minor is a capital offense."

"They will not be brought back," Helen said, clearly and softly. "I'll not have it."

"You'll not have it?" Her father echoed the words.

"Let Apple alone, Father," Helen said. "Let her ride away."

"With a no-account artist who can give her nothing?" Edward asked in astonishment.

"He can love her," Helen said. "He can love her, give her a new life away from here."

"Apple is a Falcon and her place is at *Kingsmead*," Edward said coldly. "Eliza, you may have the meal served. I intend to eat swiftly and then ride after them. Prescott, you had best come with me. I want this unpleasant affair settled as quietly as possible. The new bailiff is settling down well in the farm, incidentally. He seems a capable young man, and his being already married is a burden lifted from my mind. At least Helen will not be casting her eyes in that direction."

"You will not ride after them," Helen said. "You will leave Apple alone, Father. You will leave both of them alone, Father. If you do not—"

"Yes, madam! What will you do, pray?"

He stood at the head of the table, his face set in grimly unrelenting lines. Helen had risen from her place, and her scar throbbed as she turned her face toward him.

"I will hang myself," she said calmly. "I will hang myself from the luck-tree. That is one scandal you will never be able to overcome. I will hang myself, as my mother did. People will say there is madness in the Falcons and shrink away if any of us venture near. I will hang myself, Father."

"You are right when you speak of madness," Edward said, his face contorting. "You are crazy as a Bedlamite!"

"I am dead," Helen said softly. "As dead as Nat and Mother, though I still move and speak. There was so much love in me, Father, and you took it all away, and now I lack even the hope of love. I am already dead, Father, and my hanging will be a very little thing."

"You are insane," he whispered, but she shook her head, the ghost of a smile on her pale lips.

"I am perfectly rational," she said gently. "I'm sorry, Father, but you have no choice. You must accept my terms, because I will do exactly as I have said if you try to bring Apple back."

"They will pity me for having a crazy child. There will be no scandal, only sorrow for my misfortune," Edward said chokingly.

From her place at the table Eliza said loudly, "I will

make absolutely certain that everybody knows exactly why Helen was driven to such a terrible thing."

"I do not recall inviting you to speak, Eliza," Edward said.

"If you bring Apple back," Eliza continued firmly, "Helen will do as she has said. You know she will. And I will tell everybody why she did it. I will tell them how all our lives you have thought of nothing but the estate. I will tell them how you drove Nat away—"

"Nat took the King's shilling," Prescott said.

"He was tricked into it. Father could have bought him out of the regiment, but he did nothing. He wanted Nat out of the way until Prescott and Blanche were safely married. And when Helen fell in love, why, Ben Fiske was very quickly found to be a thief, wasn't he? But Apple must have her chance, Father, or I'll cry scandal through every house in the district."

"So you also are undutiful," her father said slowly. "Nat was always wild and undisciplined, a foolish schoolboy! Helen is a romantic fool, like her mother. But I am disappointed in you, Eliza. I had thought you a sensible young woman, but I fear you're as stupid as the rest. No doubt you're about to inform me that you're madly in love with one of my ploughboys?"

"I'd not marry any man at all," Eliza said. "A husband is nothing to crave, not with the example that I've had before me all my life! But Apple must have her chance. You have the rest of us, and you must let Apple go!"

"So dramatic! I really cannot understand why females find it necessary to make a drama out of every situation," Edward said, unclenching his fists quite deliberately. "You speak as if I were a monster, my dear. If Apple is foolish enough to—well, no matter! I certainly don't intend to render myself open to public ridicule by having my two remaining daughters make spectacles of themselves. We will eat now, I think."

Helen sat down again, her scar still throbbing. Weston was shaking with hysterical mirth.

"Are we not to go after them?" Prescott said.

"We will bow to the superior wisdom of Helen and Eliza," Edward said with a slight bow as he sat down at the head of the table. "Eliza! Your moment of grandeur is over. Would you have the kindness to have the meat brought on? By now it will be completely ruined."

Blanche suddenly burst into noisy and uncontrollable tears.

"My dear, what in the world ails you?" Edward exclaimed. "You really must not allow our family troubles to cause you to lose your sense of dignity."

"I wish to be excused," Blanche said tremblingly.

"I prefer you to remain at the table," Edward said genially.

"I am not hungry," Blanche gasped. "Please, I wish to—"

"Blanche is pregnant," Eliza said.

"Pregnant? But it's only a month since the wedding! She cannot be," Prescott said blankly.

"I've seen mares in foal," Eliza said coarsely. "I always guess before the stallion finds out. Blanche is pregnant. I'd lay a wager on it."

"Pregnant! A grandson!" Edward's face had changed, his dark eyes gleaming. "A grandson! It's what I hoped for, of course, but I must confess that this has occurred sooner than I expected. Let me see! the child will be born at the end of April or the beginning of May. We will have to consider a name. It would be a pleasant compliment to your parents, my dear, if the boy were named Fairfax."

"I have always liked the name James," Blanche sobbed.

"James is not a family name," Edward said. "Fairfax is not in our family, either, I know, but it does have a certain ring to it, and a little novelty doesn't come amiss from time to time."

"It may be a daughter," Weston said maliciously.

"Don't be ridiculous," Edward said mildly. "Blanche knows her duty."

"Oh, please, *please* may I be excused?" Blanche said faintly.

"I'll take her upstairs and rejoin you later," Prescott offered.

"By all means," Edward smiled, geniality restored. "We must take good care of you from now on, my dear. You carry my grandson. Eliza, you must prepare a tray for Blanche later. Some white meat, a piece of pudding, a glass of wine. Wine strengthens the blood. Well, we must take a little wine ourselves, I think. We must drink a toast to Fairfax Falcon."

"A future milord," Helen said wryly.

"A fortunate child. Born into a wealthy, respected family, with two doting aunts and an indulgent uncle," Edward said.

"Three aunts," Eliza said. "You forgot Apple, Father."

"Apple does not exist," Edward said calmly. "I have two surviving sons and two daughters. Apple does not exist, and that name will not be mentioned again in this household. We will drink to my grandson, to the future master of *Kingsmead.*"

Up in the two rooms that served them as dressing-room and bedroom, Blanche and Prescott stared at each other in silence. Occasional sobs racked her, but her eyes were dry again. She fixed them now on her husband.

"I am not well, Prescott. Could I go home, do you think, for a little visit?"

"But this is your home," he told her.

"I know. I meant—to the manor house. To stay with—my parents for a while. A girl in my condition—and I am certain Eliza guessed aright—I would like to see my mother."

"My dear, your parents are welcome to visit here at any time they choose," Prescott said. "The manor is scarcely a three-mile ride, shorter if one cuts across the fields. You speak as if they live in the colonies."

"No. Nat and Ben Fiske are there," she said.

"And what is that remark supposed to mean?" he queried sharply.

"Nothing, nothing. It just came into my mind."

"Because Nat is in your mind?" He seized her arm, holding it tightly. "Is that why you wept? Because Nat is dead? Because you wish that the child you carry had Nat for a father?"

"I told you that Nat was a friend, your brother."

"You tell me too often," he said grimly.

"And you ask me too often!" she cried. "Over and over and over, like a drum beating in my head! I married you, Prescott, and I will bear your son; but I'll not be questioned over and over."

"Then you did love him?"

"I was fond of him," she said wearily. "He made me laugh, and he had a kind heart. But he was your brother."

"Long ago," Prescott said, "one of the Falcons seduced his brother's wife. Did Nat ever—"

"I was a virgin when we wed. You know that."

"But girls sometimes allow familiarities. Did he ever attempt anything of that nature?"

"No, no!"

She wrenched her arm free and went over to the window, leaning her burning cheek against the cool pane.

"Did you ever wish that he would?" Prescott followed and stood behind her. "Did you ever want him to kiss you? To touch you?"

"You are tormenting yourself for no reason," Blanche said. "I am your wife, and there is no other man."

His hand reached out and patted her shoulder. "Forgive me, but sometimes I cannot help wondering," he said awkwardly.

"You have no cause," she said, and turned to face him, her lip trembling.

"And you are not well," he said contritely. "I'm sorry, my dear. These sad events have unsettled me, unsettled us all. I'll go down and get some wine for you, and we'll not mention Nat again."

"I don't want anything," she said.

"Wine is good for you, good for the child," Prescott said. "My father will be very anxious in the coming months about your health."

Always Edward Falcon! When Prescott had left the room, she sat down limply on the bed and stared at her hands in a stupor of misery. They would never be free of the man who ruled *Kingsmead* as if he were its monarch. As a child she had seen her parents' landlord as a vague, benevolent figure who visited her father from time to time and smiled at her when she met him.

Her parents had married late in life, and as an only child Blanche had sometimes envied the Falcons. Now, remembering that past envy, she wanted to weep again. Edward Falcon, seen through the eyes of her own experience, was a frightening figure. She had never known a man so coldly ruthless, so certain of his own perfections. Yet his son was dead, his wife had perished by her own hand, one daughter was scarred for life, another

fled. He had shrugged them off as if they had never existed, and turned his attention to the grandson he desired.

"Fairfax Falcon," Blanche said aloud.

Useless to think of James. James was not a family
name, and was therefore not acceptable. "But it's my
child," Blanche whispered.

"I brought some wine. Eliza is keeping my meal hot."
Prescott came in, set down a tray, and unstoppered the
decanter of dark port.

"What did you say as I entered? I didn't catch it."

"I want to name the child James."

"Father said Fairfax would be a pleasant compliment
to your parents," he reminded her. "He has not, after all
insisted that it be named after him. I suppose two Edward Falcons would lead to some confusion."

"Oh, I think one Edward Falcon is sufficient," Blanche
said, and taking the glass, felt hysterical mirth splinter
painfully within her.

"I wish you would tell me," Prescott said. "I would not
be angry, but I have the right to know. You and Nat—
was there truly never anything between you?"

1804

CHAPTER NINE

Huldah Clegg was in her favorite place. Perched on a section of crumbling grey wall, her father's spyglass in her hand, she could, simply by turning her head, survey her entire world. On her right the hill sloped down toward the slate-roofed house in its huddle of barns and sheds where she had lived ever since she was born.

Her father, Samuel Clegg, was bailiff for Lord Falcon, and though Wittle Farm was Falcon property she had known no other home. Its low-ceilinged rooms, its narrow corridors, the smoke-blackened walls were part of the fabric of her life. Indeed, she never thought of Wittle Farm at all, save as the background to her own existence.

On her left the orchards filled up the green space as far as the river, on the other side of which the houses of Marie Regina were dotted like toy buildings in the valley that sloped up again behind the church toward the highway. If she leaned forward, craning her neck, she could see past the bridge toward the estate itself, its fields of corn rippling like waves, its trees heavy with fruit, its gardens fragrant with herbs. From where she sat the high roof of *Kingsmead* was barely visible through the trees. The manor house was screened from view by its attendant oaks and elms, and the tiny cottage down by the river was completely hidden. It was enough to know that all those things were there, that if she went away they would still be there upon her return.

In that fact lay the two conflicting sides of Huldah's nature. Part of her clung to the safe, secure world of childhood, accepting the changing seasons without question. Another part of her longed for adventure and travel, longed above all to sail in a white ship to lands whose names she had traced in her geography book. That book and the spyglass were all that remained of the years her father had spent at sea, until a fall from the rigging had confined him to the land.

He had entered farming with the same determination as he had once gone to sea, had married a girl from his native town of Portsmouth, and never talked again of his first love. After nearly thirty years in Marie Regina he was beginning to be accepted as a member of the community, and only the spyglass and the old book were left to fill his daughter's head with dreams.

If I had been a boy, Huldah thought wistfully, I could have gone to sea. I could have climbed the rigging and swabbed the decks and drunk grog.

Her ideas about life at sea were culled from the adventurous tales she borrowed from the circulating library at Maidstone. Since her mother's death five years before, Huldah had had a great deal of time in which to read and dream. Jane Clegg had tried very hard to turn her daughter into a neat and frugal housewife, but Huldah had been an unwilling pupil.

After Jane's death Samuel Clegg, having endured six weeks of his daughter's cooking, installed a housekeeper and turned his attention back to the land. At twenty, Huldah was as wild as a young colt, her wheat-yellow hair tossed like a mane over her small, well-shaped head, her long legs striding across the fields, her clear whistle summoning her dog Beau.

Now, perched astride on the ivied wall, she imagined herself high in the rigging of a ship, watching the ebb and flow of the white-crowned waves, straining her eyes toward the first glimpse of land. A solitary figure rode into her imagination and she was back on the wall, her legs dangling, her hands gripping the stone.

The man riding toward her was bareheaded, the sun glinting on his fair hair, striking sparks from the silver-mounted harness of his mare. Huldah stifled a small regret and waved her hand cheerfully.

"Master James! Are you coming to call on me?" she demanded.

James's fair skin flushed with a mixture of pleasure and embarrassment.

He had loved Huldah Clegg for five years, ever since he had seen her at her mother's funeral. Before that he had thought of her only as the daughter of his grandfather's bailiff, but on that day she had been crying and drew his eyes. He had never seen her gentle again, but he carried the image of her in his mind, and saw her always as she might have been, with a dreaming look in her eyes and a sweetness about her mouth.

"I'm riding over to see your father, mistress," he said, dropping to the ground and leading his mare toward the wall.

"Is your grandfather sick?" she enquired.

"Grandfather is never sick," James assured her. "He's wonderful for his age, don't you think? Eighty-eight years old, and he still rides out every day. But he's been persuaded to rest this afternoon."

"You worry about him, don't you?" Huldah said curiously.

"I worry about all of them," James said, laughing a little. "Grandfather, and Uncle Weston, and the aunts. They brought Fairfax and me up after our parents were killed."

"Yes, I know." She looked down at him, remembering what her mother had said.

"We hadn't been here very long when it happened. The Falcon boys were scarce a year old, and Master Prescott had taken Mistress Blanche for a drive in the new phaeton. The horses must have bolted because the phaeton overturned and they were both killed. It was a great tragedy for Lord Falcon, but he stood up to it like a great gentleman. Nothing has been too good for those twins. A private tutor, fencing and French, the Grand Tour—nothing has been too good for them."

"Are you going to sit up on the wall, or are you coming down?" he enquired.

"I'll come down."

As she scrambled to the ground, her narrow skirt ripped to her thigh exposing a long length of slender, honey-tanned leg. Unabashed, she inspected the damage and cursed softly.

"You ought not to climb walls," James said, amused.

"I ought to wear breeches," she said ruefully. "I wish that I could, but the village is already shocked that my father allows me to run about like a boy. If I dressed like a boy, too, they would be absolutely scandalized."

"My aunt thinks you're a splendid young woman," James said earnestly. "She has said over and over that you would make a beautiful wife."

"I'm scarce twenty," she said airily. "You're twenty-eight, Master James, and should be thinking of taking a wife yourself."

"I wish you would call me James," he said impulsively.

"It wouldn't be fitting," she said, shy suddenly at the look in his candid eyes. "Your grandfather wouldn't like it."

"My grandfather thinks a great deal of your father," James protested. "He trusts him absolutely."

"As a bailiff. I don't think he's ever invited my father in for a glass of brandy," Huldah said wryly.

"We never did entertain very much," James said. "You must not take it as anything personal."

Huldah looked at him kindly. She liked James Falcon and considered it a great pity that his elder twin would inherit title and land. Fairfax had no interest in either, but James was proud of his family and of his home. Indeed, he loved them deeply, with an affection that had in it no breath of criticism. To James, the white-haired old man with the piercing eyes who ruled his family with a rod of iron was the beloved grandfather who had reared him.

"I'd better ride on," James said. "Your father wants me to go over some accounts with him. Are you riding back with me, mistress?"

"I'll come later. When my father starts adding up figures he becomes exceedingly crotchety."

"What were you thinking about," he asked, "up on the wall?"

"I was imagining it was a ship," she said promptly. "A great ship, high above the waves. I would like to travel on a ship!"

"It is worth nothing at all," he said. "I was so sick when we first crossed the Channel that I spent my entire tour dreading having to make the return trip."

"But they say that Lord Nelson himself is often seasick," Huldah said.

"Then I pity him," James said feelingly.

"Pity him! But he has earned the love and respect of the entire country," Huldah said, her shyness vanishing as her enthusiasm mounted. "If nobody in England stood up against Bonaparte except Nelson we would still be able to rest easy in our beds."

"You're an admirer of Lord Nelson, I can see," James said, watching with pleasure as the color mounted in her face. There was strength in her thin features, a strength that appealed to something lonely in him that he scarcely realized himself.

"I would give the whole world," she said, "to sail with Nelson."

"I wish I could grant your desire," James said, "but there seems no way in which I could."

He wished, as he watched her, that he could grant all her desires, save her desire to leave Marie Regina.

"Tell my father I went for a walk," Huldah said, growing a little uneasy under his continuing regard. "And don't tell him that I tore my skirt! On accounting days he is apt to expect me to behave like a lady!"

She dropped a swift curtsey and set off down the hill, her hair bobbing around her shoulders, her skirt flapping ragged about her ankles. At the bottom of the hill she paused and whistled, and her little golden hound ran from the cover of some bushes and walked sedately at her heels.

James remounted and rode slowly across the level ground between the ruined walls and broken arches toward the path that wound down into the farmyard. He enjoyed his visits to the bailiff, finding in Samuel Clegg a thoughtful man whose temperament was similar to his own. Huldah appeared to both men as some exotic, untamed creature landed unexpectedly in the quiet village.

Samuel was in the small parlor at the side of the

kitchen. It was not the most comfortable room in the farmhouse, but it had the virtue of privacy. The accounts were spread out on the table and the bailiff was checking over the figures. An unlit pipe dangled from his mouth. Jane Clegg had confined her husband's tobacco smoking to the outhouse during her lifetime, and he still felt twinges of guilt if he lit up within doors.

He greeted the younger Falcon with a neat mixture of deference and friendliness, and within a few moments they were engrossed in facts and figures relating to crops and stock.

Finally, closing the last book with a little snap, the bailiff said, "And that's the position, Master James. Nothing for milord to fret about."

"Grandfather will be relieved to hear that all's well." James leaned back in his chair and stretched aching muscles. "I have sometimes wondered if it might not be wiser to concentrate on one crop, and not spread our interests too widely, but if the market's down in one direction it's comfortable to tide over in other ways. And the estate's not large."

"One thousand two hundred acres, including Wittle land. It's a tidy piece."

"But you and I between us will manage it."

"Aye, sir."

Obedient to their usual ritual, Samuel poured a measure of cider for them both and sat down. As he drank he observed the younger man covertly. James Falcon looked the typical gentleman farmer that he was, with nothing of the rake or dandy in his attire. Broadshouldered, fresh-complexioned, with his dead mother's fair hair and blue eyes, James was a throwback to those early Tudor squires who had first farmed Falcon land. There was nothing in him of his grandfather's brooding quality, nor of his elder twin's nervous, darting energy.

Thinking of Fairfax, Samuel Clegg frowned slightly. There was no denying that the heir of *Kingsmead* had great charm. His lazy smile and deep voice, red-gold hair and brilliant grey eyes had ensnared female hearts for miles around. There was, the bailiff thought, no evil in the young man, but there were disquieting shifts of mood from the wildest hilarity to the most abysmal despair. And there was a weakness in him that Samuel had already seen displayed: Fairfax shrank from blame or responsibility.

The bailiff remembered having seen Fairfax, years before, riding his mare furiously across the meadows. The older man had called out in warning, knowing the mare to be in foal, but the lad had ignored him and galloped on, his face full of the excitement of the moment.

That night the mare had miscarried, and Samuel remembered the evasive look in Fairfax's eyes, the quick, pleading glance toward James, and the younger brother's swift remark.

"I'm sorry, grandfather. I must have ridden her too hard."

He had received a flogging for that, Edward Falcon bringing down the crop over and over until he drew blood. Samuel had left the barn and passed Fairfax, who was being violently sick into a clump of grass.

"You're very silent," James said chaffingly now.

"I was wondering where Huldah had gone," Samuel said hastily. "I worry about the girl."

"I met her among the ruins. Sitting on top of them, to be more exact," James said. "She asked me to tell you that she's gone walking."

"I'm too indulgent with her," Samuel said sadly. "Her mother was stricter, but since Jane died—how can a man deal with a growing girl? Not that she's a bad girl, Master James. I'd not have you think that! Sweet as a nut is Huldah, but wild in her ways. She wants settling."

"Mistress Huldah is very comely," James said.

"Aye, she's handsome," Samuel admitted.

"I have been thinking," James plunged on, "of taking a wife. I have been thinking about it a great deal these past weeks. At twenty-eight a man likes to look to the future."

"Aye, that's so," Samuel put his glass down carefully and gave James an oblique, slanting look.

"I have admired Mistress Huldah for a long time," James said. "I did wonder—if you would have any objection to my paying my respects to your daughter? I mean, would you object to my asking for her hand?"

Samuel reached for lucifers and flint and carefully lit his pipe, puffing and sucking with an appearance of great concentration. When the bowl glowed scarlet, he said, "Have you spoken to Lord Falcon about this matter?"

"Not yet, but he'll not object," James said eagerly. "He'll be glad I've chosen a local girl—after all, if I'm to manage the estate it will be the best possible thing for me to wed Mistress Huldah who was born here and knows the land."

"I'm not denying she'll have a good dowry," Samuel said. "I've saved carefully ever since I came to Marie Regina, and Huldah won't go empty to her bridegroom. And I'm not questioning your own prospects."

"My grandfather pays me a high wage for the work I do," James said. "He knows that I give him good value for it, and Fairfax will be pleased to have me manage when he comes into the property."

"You wouldn't live at *Kingsmead*?" Samuel questioned anxiously.

"I think it better if we have a place of our own,"

James said. "My brother will marry one day, and I think he'll want his own wife to be sole mistress."

"It's natural," Samuel said, drawing smoke into his lungs and exhaling it with sensuous pleasure.

"I thought we'd live at the manor house," James said. "It's been empty since old Grandpa Fairfax died, and Grandfather's not put in another tenant. It's not as large as *Kingsmead*, but it's well-built and in good repair. It would make a comfortable home."

"Huldah's not much on cooking and such," Samuel warned.

"I'm not marrying her for her kitchen skills," James said, a smile lifting his mouth. "I can afford a cook and servants, you know."

"And I'm not denying it."

"And I'd be a good husband. I'd take care of her."

"I've no doubt you would."

"Then you'd look favorably on the idea?"

Samuel puffed again at his pipe. There was certainly no denying that the match would be a good one from a social standpoint. And James Falcon would make a kind, steady husband. But the bailiff had not lived for nearly thirty years in the district without learning something of his employer's family.

"A fair man," the villagers said, "as keeps himself to himself, and asks for no sympathy."

True enough, and perhaps Lord Falcon deserved sympathy, having lost his youngest son in action and his wife by suicide. But there was Mistress Helen with the dreadful scar on her face, and the former bailiff who'd been transported. Samuel had inherited the account books kept by his predecessor and had seen the lists of carefully worked additions, and wondered how a man who had kept count so meticulously could have risked

SEASON OF THE FALCON

almost certain arrest in order to steal an easily identifiable cup.

"It's the difference in station," he said. "Now, I'm not shamed of my family. My father was a North countryman who went to sea as a lad and wed a girl from Portsmouth, as I did. And I sailed before the mast myself until an accident stiffened my leg for good. We're hardworking, decent folk and owe no man a penny. And Huldah's been educated. She had three years at the Dame School in Maidstone and writes a good hand. Reads, too, very prettily. But when all's said she's not of the quality, not even from the merchant classes. Lord Falcon will want his grandsons to marry well."

"I do not propose to allow my grandfather to choose my bride for me," James said simply. "It is not as if I am to inherit either the title or the estate. Those will go to Fairfax. I will be plain Master Falcon, manager, to the end of my days, so Mistress Huldah is not getting such a prize catch."

"If she'll have you," Samuel warned, "for I'll not force her. She has a mind and a will of her own."

"But she seems to look kindly on me?" James said anxiously.

"Aye. She speaks well of you, but—"

"But?"

"Huldah has a restlessness in her," Samuel said slowly. "I blame myself in some measure, for in my heart I always hoped for a son. Well, we only had the one, and now I'd not change her for a lad, but when she was little I talked to her about the sea and the tall ships. Jane put a stop to it, for she was wise enough to know there's no sense in filling a maid's head with things that can never be. And it was doing me no good, working the land with my ears tuned to the waves. So I left off, and I reckon Huldah forgot the tales, but something stayed with her all the same. She's forever looking beyond, in a manner of speaking, and I wonder if she'll ever truly settle."

"But you would not oppose our marriage?"

"If it set well with Huldah and your grandfather, I'd say nothing but God bless the union."

"I'll speak to my grandfather," James promised. "He'll say nothing against it, I know. And I'll choose my time to ask Mistress Huldah."

"I'll say nothing," Samuel affirmed. "Another drop of cider, Master James?"

"Nothing more. I have to be riding back." James rose, motioning the other to remain seated.

In the yard he mounted again and rode down the track, bypassing the ruin-crowned hill and making for the main highway which sloped down toward the bridge. As he rode he looked about him with conscious pleasure.

James Falcon loved every inch of the land, and there was in that love no tinge of possessiveness, just as in his affection for his brother there was no hint of envy. That the span of ten minutes divided him from a peerage and a prosperous estate was a simple fact of life and not something to be regretted or resented. It was sufficient that the land was there and that he lived upon it.

The two years he had spent on the Continent had merely convinced him that Marie Regina was the most beautiful place on earth and *Kingsmead* the only estate he could imagine as home.

Instead of riding on to the main house he cantered up the winding drive toward the manor house. It was a small, comfortable building, the main hall rising up through two storeys in the old fashion, with a parlor to the left and a kitchen to the right. There were two bedrooms above and a tiny apartment between them. Nobody had lived there since Grandpa Fairfax's death the previous year, and the roses in the garden scattered pet-als onto the unclipped grass.

It had been, in the old days, almost a habit for Falcon men to wed women from the manor. His ancestor, Sir Hal Falcon, had wed Marie Fleet and been unfaithful to her, if rumor were true and Charles Falcon had mar-ried Temple Fleet and lost her in childbed. Even his own mother had come from the manor to be wed to his father.

Soon, if all his hopes were realized, he would reverse the habit. A Falcon would bring a wife to the manor. He intended to make it so beautiful that Huldah would never wish to leave. Not that he wanted to change the house. James had grown up with the strong conviction that most changes were of very little value. But he would have the floors carpeted and buy new hangings for the walls. It was unfashionable to have wall-hangings, but James had little interest in fashion, and suspected that Huldah had less.

He sat for a long time, surveying the ivied façade of the manor, the diamond-paned windows set deep in the mullions. In his mind Huldah Clegg came to the door and held out her hand to welcome him. Her golden hair would swing loosely about her face, for he disliked the curled fringes and high chignons that were now in style. On her finger would be the gold ring he had placed there in the village church, and she would not be Hul-dah Clegg but Huldah Falcon.

"Hey! James!"

His twin's voice broke the dream, as Fairfax rode around the side of the manor. His brother's face wore its usual expression of cheerful devilment, his smile widen-ing as he saw the other's startled jump.

"The garden needs pruning," James said hastily, forestalling questions.

"Aye, it does." Fairfax slashed idly at a truant rambler.

"Leave it. No point in bruising the stems," James said.

It worried him to see grass or flowers torn up. In an ideal garden he was quite certain that even weeds had their place.

"I've been over to the heath. The gypsies are back," Fairfax said.

"We'd best check the livestock," James said.

The gypsies had been coming every summer for as long as he could remember, and he rather liked them than otherwise, for they were part of the landscape. But it was common sense to take precautions.

Fairfax, his mind filled with thoughts of a young lady in Maidstone who was proving difficult to seduce, grinned affectionately at his twin. Poor old James was a dull dog, but he kept the estate running and the profits increasing despite the war with France.

CHAPTER TEN

The Falcons still ate supper together in the great hall, a practice of which the tradition-loving James approved, though it irritated Fairfax, who was often absent from table. This evening, when the young men entered, they found their elders already assembled.

Their grandfather, upright despite his eighty-eight years, was in his usual seat at the head of the long table. He still wore the brocade coats of his youth, and behind thick-rimmed spectacles his dark eyes gleamed with much of their former vitality.

Uncle Weston was still by the fire, sipping the last of a glass of port and warming his white-breeched legs. His plump face wore its habitual frown of solemn concentration which made people regard him as "deep," but he was, in fact, debating with himself whether or not to risk a little of the goose.

The aunts, Helen and Eliza, sat at table, their sacque dresses echoing the styles of thirty years before. Eliza's blonde hair had darkened to steel grey, but she had retained her figure and high coloring, and middle age had given her a dignity of bearing that swept away the last traces of youthful hoydenishness.

James, with whom she shared a passion for the land, bent to kiss her cheek, while Fairfax embraced Aunt Helen, whose favorite he was. Time had dealt gently with Helen Falcon, laying delicate shadows under the high cheekbones, whitening one wing of the looped amber hair. The scar ran in a puckered purple line from eye to mouth. The reason for it was never discussed in the family, both the twins being under the vague impression that an accident years before had caused the scar.

"You are early for once," Edward Falcon observed. "It is not the month for good resolutions, is it?"

"I went over to see Samuel Clegg, Grandfather," James reminded him. "The books are all in order."

"Good. He's a reliable man." Edward Falcon nodded his permission to Eliza to have the meat brought in and raised his voice to his son.

"Weston! you need not pretend you have any intention of not eating the goose! An inch more on your waistline will make no difference at all. Indeed, it looks very much as if you and the Prince Regent have entered into a competition as to who requires the larger corset."

"A morsel won't hurt me," Weston decided, joining the others.

Supper continued along the usual lines. Fairfax, his mind on the unwilling lady in Maidstone, ate heartily. Nothing disturbed Fairfax's appetite, though the elegance of his figure would have led many people to suppose that he ate very little. James ate more slowly, savouring the taste, thinking of Huldah. When they were settled in the manor he would invite the old people for supper. He thought of them as old, though his aunts had about them an illusion of youth.

"You're very silent this evening," Edward said, sharply, pointing his knife at James. "Is something wrong? Something you're not telling me about? I shall require to examine those books myself at the end of the month, mind!"

"Nothing's wrong, Grandfather. The books are in order, sir," James said patiently.

"So you say. I shall know if they are not. Too much fat on this meat, Eliza! You had best leave the carving of it to me in future. Weston does not carve. He teases the bird until it falls apart out of sheer exasperation."

"I never did enjoy butchering a joint," Uncle Weston said.

"Your delicate feelings don't prevent your eating more than your share, I notice," his father said sourly.

"And what have you been doing today?" Helen addressed herself to Fairfax, her white face gentle. She had always been fond of her elder nephew, finding in him an echo of a gaiety she had once known in her own heart.

"Precisely nothing, Aunt. I rode over to the heath. There are gypsies there, by-the-bye, Grandfather. You will have to look to your stock. I met up with James at the manor house."

"The manor? What were you doing there?" Edward demanded.

"Staring at it as if it had just sprung out of the ground," Fairfax said. "You never saw a man so startled when I rode around the corner. I was taking a short-cut—to avoid being late for supper."

"You're a liar, but a charming one," Edward said placidly. "What are you doing, James? Choking on this indifferently cooked goose or trying to attract my attention?"

"I'd be grateful for a private word with you, Grandfather," James said.

"You may have one immediately." Edward scraped back his chair, reaching for the stick which was his only concession to age.

"Father, you haven't finished your meal!" Weston exclaimed.

"Curiosity has killed my appetite," Edward said. "It is a great pity that you cannot develop a little curiosity about something, Weston. James, you had best come into the solar. We shall be private there."

James, following his grandfather through the parlor into the solar, admired the old man's bearing. There was, he thought, a magnificence about his grandfather, a pride which had its roots deep in family loyalties. As a child he had listened eagerly to Edward's stories of bygone Falcons, of Hal Falcon wounded during the Civil War, of his own father killed at Preston Pans while fighting against the Jacobite rebels. Yet his main reaction had been one of pity for these ancestors who had been forced to leave the security of *Kingsmead*.

"Close the door," Edward ordered. "Now, what is so important that I am dragged away from my food to hear it?" He lowered himself into a chair and settled his wig more comfortably.

"I was at the manor house today," James began. "It has been empty since Grandpa Fairfax died."

"If you're thinking of tenants," Edward interrupted, "you may save your breath. In my old age I want no strangers on Falcon land."

"You have tenants in Paget Place," James said.

"That's different. I don't fall over the wretched people every time I step outside my front door!"

"It's not a question of strangers anyway," James said. "I thought of living there myself."

"Living at the manor? Leaving *Kingsmead*? And what, pray, has crept into your mind now?"

"I'm of a mind to wed," James said bluntly.

"To wed! You've not spoken of marriage before," Edward said.

"I've not loved before," James said simply.

"Ah! you're in love! A common ailment."

"Not with me, sir," James said earnestly. "Oh, I'll not deny I've cast my eyes at girls before this, but I've never seriously considered marriage until now. This is no green fancy, sir, for I'm only two years short of thirty and a man of good sense."

"So I've always said. Don't prove me wrong."

"I'll not do that, sir. I know the great store you lay upon the family name. I like to think that I place great value upon it myself. And I think you know that I would choose a bride carefully, but you need have no fear of Huldah's being an embarrassment to the family."

"Huldah?" Edward leaned back, his face carefully composed.

"It is Huldah Clegg, Grandfather. A fine girl, healthy and comely and intelligent. You like Mistress Huldah, don't you?"

"I like her well enough," said Edward.

"I talked to her father today, to Samuel Clegg," James said eagerly. "I asked him for permission to address her, and he gave it, on condition that I spoke to you first. He seemed anxious, most anxious, that it should not appear as if his daughter were marrying out of her class. But the Cleggs are solid, respectable folk, Grandfather, and it is not as if I am to inherit title or land."

"If I were to refuse," Edward said slowly, "what would you say?"

"Grandfather, I am of full age," James said. "In law I may marry where I choose. It would pain me to go against your wishes, but I have the right to wed."

"Nobody would deny that," Edward said. "A man has

the right to take a wife, and the right to choose that wife for himself. I am an old man now and don't propose to stand in your way, though I confess I had hoped you might marry well. However—it is not for me to judge. Mistress Huldah has, no doubt, charms to which I am insensible. I will ask one favor—unless you have already spoken to the girl."

"I have said nothing yet. And her father will not."

"Delay for a month or two, until after harvest. It would please me if your betrothal were to be announced then. An old man's whim!"

"Gladly, Grandfather." But the young man's face had dropped.

"Speak to her in a month or two. You could clean out the manor, have it refurnished a little, as if we were going to install new tenants," Edward said. "Then take her there and ask her to be your wife. It was at the manor house that I proposed to your dear grandmother. I plucked some cowslips and made them into a ball. You did not think me capable of so much romantic feeling, did you?"

"I will be happy to please you in the matter," James said at once.

"Then we will keep this to ourselves until harvest time, eh?" Edward held out a veined old hand and gripped his grandson's arm. "Now go and tell that idle brother of yours I'll be glad of a few minutes of his company when he has finished his meal. I'd not have him jealous of the time we spend together."

"I am very grateful to you," James said. "You will grow fond of Mistress Huldah, I promise."

"No doubt I shall." Edward leaned back, adjusting his wig again, a smile on his lips.

The smile lingered as his grandson left the room, then froze into a broader grimace.

The thought that James might choose to marry had never seriously entered his head. He had believed the young fool to be devoted to the land, to the upkeep of the estate, to the interests of his elder twin. One day, of course, Fairfax would settle down and take a bride, to bear a son for *Kingsmead*.

I have been remiss, Edward decided, in not having arranged a marriage sooner, but I left the lad to go his own way. I spoiled him. And now James will marry a bailiff's brat, and if Fairfax is not careful, the estate will not pass to his child, but to a nephew.

He clenched his hand about the ivory knob of his stick and fixed his mind upon his land. It was not, he supposed, enormous as estates went, but every inch of it was profitable, every inch of it belonged to him, to be held in trust for Fairfax and for Fairfax's son. The long years of responsibility had taken their toll. There were days now when he felt weary, so weary that it was an effort to rise, an effort to think clearly. Now, because of his indolence, James, on whom he depended, would wed and fill *Kingsmead* with children who would require to be fed and clothed. Little by little the profits of the land would be drained away.

He knew Huldah Clegg and shuddered inwardly at the thought of that tall, wide-shouldered girl as James's wife. The wife he had chosen for himself had been a kinswoman. Prescott's wife had not been a lady, but her parents had been wealthy and respected, their trade origins discreetly forgotten. Samuel Clegg was no more than a highly paid servant, and now it seemed that he had ideas above his station.

"James said you wanted to see me, Grandfather." Fairfax was standing in the doorway, his handsome face alert with curiosity.

"Close the door and sit down. It hurts my neck to have to look up at you," Edward said sharply.

"Is something wrong, Grandfather?" Closing the door, Fairfax came over and took the chair opposite the old man.

Instead of answering, Edward propped his chin on his hands and stared at his grandson.

The elder twin was certainly handsome, with the virile, lively aspect of a young man in love with life. But there was a faint weakness about the well-shaped mouth, a hint of indecision in the bright grey eyes. It was a pity that he had never taken an interest in the estate as James had done.

"Have you any thoughts in your head of females? Of marriage?" Edward enquired abruptly.

"Females, yes. Marriage, no."

"James has been talking to me."

"Of my marriage?"

"Of his own. The fool intends to take a wife."

"Good luck to him! Where's the harm?"

"The harm?" Edward echoed. "The wife he has in mind is Huldah Clegg."

"The bailiff's daughter?"

"Do you know her?" Edward asked.

"Of course I do. She's a ripe piece, but not, I'd have thought, in my brother's line."

"That's why I wanted to talk to you," Edward said. "God knows I've never stood in your or his way, and I've a fancy for great-grandchildren, but I've no mind to see my own bailiff as a member of the family."

"I don't think that's so important these days," Fairfax said carelessly.

"Do you not? Perhaps so, but I am old-fashioned in my ways. I was brought up to believe the lower classes should be kept in their place."

"But if James loves her," Fairfax argued, "and she makes him a good wife—"

"Ah, but would she? That's the heart of my problem. They tell me this Huldah Clegg is wild and undisciplined."

"More like a boy than a girl," Fairfax grinned, "but handsome."

"Such women are often easy in their morals," Edward frowned. "I wonder if James would satisfy such a girl. Now, don't misunderstand me! You and I are fond of the boy, very fond indeed, as is natural, but there's no denying he's set in his ways. A dear boy, but not, I'd wager, the most exciting lover in the world, eh?"

"He's shy with women," Fairfax said.

"That's exactly my point! Shy with the females and apt to be bamboozled by a cunning one. Now, I may be wrong, but I've not lived nearly ninety years for nothing."

"I've not heard any gossip of Huldah Clegg, save that she's wild in her ways," Fairfax said.

"And James might not learn the truth until after he's wed."

"The truth, Grandfather?"

"About Huldah Clegg. A wild wench makes a wild wife. You don't believe a quiet fellow like James will bridle such a filly?"

"Have you discussed this with him?" Fairfax asked.

"Discussed such a delicate matter with a man in love? Great good that would do! No, in his present mood, James wouldn't listen to a word of doubt concerning the girl, but he's my grandson and I cannot sit idly by and wait for him to be hurt."

"And she may prove faithful."

"Aye, there's the chance that she might," Edward agreed. "If we could only make test of her virtue . . ."

"How?"

"If you were to make certain advances to Mistress Huldah yourself, hint that you intended marriage at the end of it? That would serve our purpose."

"Cut James out of the running! But that would be—"

"The only sure way of finding out if the girl is honest, if she has a true affection for James or merely a hankering after money. If she thinks well of him, she'll turn you down, and there's nothing lost. Indeed, it would gain me great peace of mind. If she flirts and flushes and lifts her skirt for you, better for James to learn it now than have his heart broken after they're wed."

"I could do it, I suppose," Fairfax said uncomfortably, "but I was never one for meddling."

"Neither was I," Edward said sadly, "and I tell you there are times now when I wish I had meddled. You know, my children have been the joys of my life, and its curses. I wanted the boys to marry well, but only Prescott married. Your uncle Weston—he's not interested in females. It happens sometimes; nobody's fault. And Nat, my youngest boy—nothing would please him but to join the regiment. He was killed at eighteen, you know. I've blamed myself for that, for not preventing him from leaving."

"You cannot feel guilty for letting people do what they wish to do," Fairfax protested.

"And your aunts," Edward said. "I won't deny that I was against their marrying at all. They had a beautiful home, a kind family, and there was no need for them to seek husbands. Eliza never gave me any trouble, but poor Helen—she fell in love, an unsuitable man. I warned her but she wouldn't listen, and I was proved right. The man turned out to be a thief. Poor Helen! And Apple—"

"The one we never mention?" Fairfax looked up with sharp interest.

"She married an artist, Spanish or Welsh or some such country. I let her have her way. She was a mere child, a month short of seventeen, but I'd spoilt her. Apple had a way with her and she was my youngest, so I let her go. In thirty years she's never written, never come back once for a visit. I leave her name unspoken. It is too painful for me to remember."

"I'm so sorry, Grandfather."

"Ah, I've lived a long time, and it's to be expected that an old man should have known sorrow," Edward said. "But it would grieve me more to have James hurt. If we can guard against that ... Could you help me?"

"I'll do it," Fairfax said slowly. "I'll make up to Huldah Clegg, and find out what kind of wife brother James has picked out for himself. She may slap my face and tell me to mind my manners, of course."

"I'd be the happiest man in the district to be proved wrong," Edward said. "The happiest man!"

"I'll see to it," Fairfax promised.

"It'll be our secret," his grandfather said.

It was, he thought, a credit to his upbringing that neither of his grandsons harbored a suspicious thought or an ungenerous impulse. Once James had discovered his goddess to have feet of clay, he'd quickly recover from his infatuation and settle down. And then there would be the business of finding a wife for Fairfax. It was high time that the heir of *Kingsmead* begot a son. Edward sighed. At nearly ninety, a man had surely earned the right to a little peace, but it was not easy to lay down the reins of responsibility.

In the courtyard, Helen Falcon leaned against the archway and gazed down the darkening drive. She usually came out for a few minutes after supper to stand beneath the branches of the luck-tree. Anybody seeing her there, her narrow hands folded like petals, might have supposed her to be praying for her dead mother, but it was years since Helen had prayed. Her eyes were fixed on the the winding track that led between the oaks and elms toward the main gates.

There was a slight rustle as a figure moved across the cobbles and joined her. Without turning her head, Helen said, "I'll be there in a moment, Eliza."

"There's nothing to be done. Weston is playing cards with James, and Father is having a nightcap with Fairfax. It's cooler tonight."

"Summer will soon be over," Helen said.

"Funny, but when I was a girl the summers went on forever," Eliza mused. "These days, come July, and I can smell that snow. It's a sign of old age, and yet I don't feel old. I was thinking only the other day that I'm forty-eight years old, and it seems it was only yesterday that I was eighteen."

"It's a hundred years since I was eighteen," Helen said. "A hundred years."

"No sign of anyone?" Eliza too directed her gaze along the track.

"Not tonight."

"There's always tomorrow," Eliza said.

"Is there? Is there, Eliza?" Helen turned and faced her sister. "It's nearly thirty years. That's a long time."

"He'll come," Eliza said.

"I'd not speak to him," Helen said, "nor let him see me. He'd not know me anyway, not after all these years. But to see him—you think there's a chance he might still be alive? Very few ever return after transportation."

"Of course he's alive! Kentish men don't die so easily."

"If he is alive he'll be wed by now. There'll be children perhaps."

"There'd be nobody to wed in the Penal Settlement," Eliza said. "And he'd not marry one even if there were."

"He liked children," Helen said softly. "We talked sometimes—no matter! It was a long time ago."

"But he'll come," Eliza said.

"Yes. One evening," Helen nodded, her eyes wide with remembering.

"We'd best go indoors," Eliza said.

"In a moment. You go and I'll come after you."

Eliza touched her sister on the arm and went back across the cobbles. At the top step she paused and glanced back, but Helen was part of the shadows. A brief moment of thankfulness shook her.

She had never been in love, never met the man for whom she would have given up an hour's sleep. She had never felt the lack of children, either, having reared both Fairfax and James after the deaths of their parents. She was proud of both her nephews, though she loved James the most. A strong current of sympathy ran between aunt and nephew, fostered by their love of the land.

Her life had been, she decided, both full and rich, because she had never made the mistake of depending on people for affection. People died or went away; horses and dogs were easier to love, because even when they died they left no legacy of bitterness.

Under the luck-tree Helen was remembering. Memory had once brought pain, but she had been dead for a long time and even the remembrance of anguish was beginning to fade. One day, soon, she would no longer come out after supper to wait and watch, and on that day she would know herself to be truly dead.

If he comes in the next few minutes, she told herself, I will move deeper into the shadow. He will have forgotten me, of course. Men do not remember as women do.

But he will ride up and look through the archway, and some feather of feeling will touch him, and then he will ride away because there is nothing here that he craves.

It was a game. She knew well as Eliza did that Ben Fiske would never return to Marie Regina, that he had died years before, but the game was all that she had left.

I'll close my eyes and count to one hundred, she told herself, and if he's not come by then I'll go in.

He would not come. She knew that, but she closed her eyes tightly and stood, very still, among the rust leaves of the tree. There was no sound of hoofbeats and the drive remained empty; but she went on counting.

CHAPTER ELEVEN

Huldah was trespassing. It was not, strictly speaking, trespass at all to go to the little cottage down by the river because it was part of the estate, although nobody bothered very much about the place. It had been empty for as long as the girl could remember, with the woods grown up about the small building and the windows obscured by long trails of creeper. But nobody went to the cottage, and on the rare occasions that Huldah had ventured there, something in the silence of the place had repelled her. Even Beau had drawn back, whimpering a little.

However, the cottage fascinated her, and when any problem of great importance faced her she went as close as she dared, and sat down on a fallen log to think out some conclusion. She had gone there after her mother had died, because she was ashamed of having wept publicly, and after an hour or two the pain had begun to die.

This problem had nothing to do with death. It was a problem of living, and for the first time she was not certain how to deal with her own life. In one week that life had changed, become blurred around the edges.

It had begun only three days before when she had

gone down into the village to buy sugar and tea, and come out of the store to find Fairfax Falcon bending and talking to Beau.

"This is a one-woman dog!" he exclaimed. "He's ignoring me!"

"He has bad manners, I'm afraid," she said.

"But his mistress is almost as bad," Fairfax said, "for she never raises her head to greet me when I ride past the farm."

"You ought not to ride past," Huldah said. "Master James always comes in."

"To see your father and sit stewing over the account books! I would find a better way of spending my time if I came calling."

"In teaching Beau better manners?"

"In telling his mistress what beautiful hair she has."

Color flamed into the girl's face. Huldah was still, while not ignorant, completely innocent. Her position as bailiff's daughter, her schooling in Maidstone, her own boyish independence of manner, had shielded her from the haystack fumblings of the village lads. She was unused to even the mildest compliment, and to have Master Fairfax smiling at her and saying she had beautiful hair was so unusual that she stood, blushing furiously, and completely tongue-tied.

"I've offended you," Fairfax said quickly.

"No, Master Fairfax." She ducked her head and began to walk back along the street.

"My name is Fairfax." His long legs kept pace with her easily.

"But you will be Lord Falcon one day, when your grandfather dies," she said simply.

"And am I to lose all my friends because of that." he asked lightly. "You are my friend, aren't you, Mistress Huldah?"

"If you wish it," she said breathlessly and began to scramble up the path toward the highway.

"I do wish it," he said, and the scarlet glowed in her cheeks again at the meaning in his voice.

She had gone home then, clutching the packet of tea and the loaf of sugar so tightly to her that a ridge cut into the thin cotton of her high-waisted gown.

The very next afternoon she had looked up from feeding the chickens and seen him at the other side of the wall, pulling a piece of grass between his teeth and gazing at her.

"Good afternoon, sir." She had bobbed a hasty curtsey and wished passionately that her apron was cleaner.

"Fairfax," he corrected. "And I shall call you Huldah. That's a pretty name, you know."

"Huldah? It was my grandmother's name, she who married the sailor. It means "weasel," my father says."

"And I am a Falcon. Do falcons prey on little, bright-eyed weasels, do you think?"

"Weasels might run and hide," she said.

"But not if the falcon was tender?" He leaped over the low barricade between them and imprisoned her hand between his palms.

"You are mocking me," she said uncertainly.

"No, my young weasel. I am admiring you. That is something to which you must grow accustomed if we are to keep company."

His eyes and hair were brilliant in the sunshine, and his voice made strange patterns in her mind. She moved abruptly away.

"I always wished to be a boy, you know, and go to sea like my father and grandfather. I used to dream of swarming up the rigging, high to the crows'-nest, and see the world dip away to the furthest end of the horizon. I have a book with all the countries of the world in it, in different colors, with the names in strange printing. I read it over and over, and dream of leaving the village and travelling thousands of miles."

The idea of going to sea had never entered the young man's head, but fired by her enthusiasm he exclaimed, "But that has always been my dream, too! You cannot imagine how confined and tame *Kingsmead* seems to me!"

"You are a man. You may do anything you please," Huldah said.

"And if you were me," he enquired, amused, "what would you do?"

"I'd sail with Lord Nelson," she said promptly, "and drive old Boney back to France and make him stay there."

"You're a fierce weasel!" he cried, laughing, and pressed her hand to his lips.

And then he had jumped back over the wall, and she was left among the chickens as they squawked and pecked and fluttered about her ankles.

"Have you ever thought of what you'll do in the future?" her father asked that night.

"The future? No, I never have." She looked at him in surprise.

"I'll not be here forever," he said. "I was close on thirty when I wed, and it was ten years before you were born. We'd about given up hope. And in the winter now, when it rains, my leg stiffens up cruelly."

"But Lord Falcon won't dismiss you," she said quickly.

"Even if he did I've enough set by, enough for you, too, if you'd a mind to marry."

He glanced up at her through the smoke from his pipe. Smoking was out of fashion, but Samuel Clegg, like his daughter, had little interest in fashion.

"I've no mind to take a husband," she said.

"And I'd not force you to it, but if you took a liking to some man, I'd never stand in your way," he said.

"I've plenty of time," Huldah said lightly, and bent over the fire to hide the color in her face.

Now, picking her way along the old bridle path, she thought again of those two brief meetings. In essence they had meant everything and nothing, because so much had been left unsaid, because she was not certain of her own feelings and was even less certain of Fairfax.

She pushed past a clump of brambles and stood in the green-lit clearing. The grass was knee high, scratching her legs through the thin stuff of her gown. Overhead the branches laced and entwined, dappled with sunlight.

She sat down, leaning her head against the trunk of a tree, while images of Fairfax and tall ships and white sails rushed through her mind. She had never been in love, and she was not sure if she was in love now, but she wanted to see Fairfax again, to hear his voice and have him touch her hand.

There were noises in the trees behind her. Although she was not nervous when she was alone, her muscles tensed slightly. Beau, who had been scrabbling in the undergrowth, ran out barking, his tail wagging furiously. The branches behind her parted, and Fairfax stepped through.

"You choose odd places for your rambles, young weasel," he said.

"I wanted to be alone," she said.

"Are you telling me to leave you?" he enquired.

"I couldn't do that, even if I wished it," she said. "This is Falcon land."

"This part belonged to my Aunt Apple," Fairfax told her.

"Apple? That's a strange name. As strange as Huldah."

"It was really Abigail, but she called herself Apple."

"Did she die?" Huldah asked with interest.

"She went away and married a Spaniard or something," Fairfax told her. "Before she went she gave the place to my Aunt Eliza, but nobody comes here now."

"Except weasels?" She gave him a quick, slanting look.

"And falcons." He sat down beside her and laid his hands one at each side of her face. "Golden-haired weasels with dreams of the sea in their eyes."

Huldah began to tremble, but her mouth was imprisoned beneath his, and he was urging her down into the long grass at the side of the log. For a moment she resisted, and then a long shudder ran through her limbs and she was hungry for his hands and mouth, and all the little secret desires ran together in her mind and body like waves crashing against some half-imagined shore.

She came back into the world slowly, opening her eyes as if she had slept, seeing the arched trees overhead, the elegant figure turned away to adjust his attire, the small cottage shimmering in the dappled light.

"I did not know," she said, "that it was like that."

"Nor I." He came back to her and knelt down, brushing leaves from her hair.

"It was . . . better than dreaming," she said, and curved her hands as if she held something precious.

"Much better," Fairfax said.

There was a mixture of tenderness and regret in his face. Seeing it, she said earnestly, "You must not blame yourself, for it was my wish, too. And we are both human."

"You were a virgin," he said slowly.

"Of course. After all, I have never loved before, and I could not give myself where I did not love," she said simply.

"We will meet again?" His voice was anxious.

"Whenever you please. But for a little while, may we keep it to ourselves?"

"Lord, yes!" He looked at her in sudden alarm.

"There are things I must turn over in my mind," she said shyly.

"Yes, of course."

"I wonder," she mused, sitting up and clasping her hands about her knees, "how many people have come here through all the centuries and loved one another under the trees."

"Dozens, I suppose, but they're dead now, anyway."

"Poor things!" Huldah exclaimed, and threw back her head, laughing for sheer joy because she was alive.

"Won't they be missing you at the farm?" he asked.

"Who? The cows and chickens? My father's away to market."

"Yes, I know." He had made certain of that before he followed her down the bridle path.

"Once, when I was very young," she confided, "I came down here to play. I glanced toward the cottage and I saw a face looking out at me. A girl with long, black hair. I thought she might come out to join me, and I went closer and waved, but there was nothing there."

"It was imagination," Fairfax said.

"No, I saw her," Huldah said. "I saw her quite clearly."

"Then whoever it was went away from the window. Did you go in and see?"

"I've never been in," Huldah confessed. "They say the cottage was owned by a witch once."

"And all the Falcons are descended from a witch! I've been reared on such tales."

"And you don't believe them?"

"Not a word," Fairfax said cheerfully. "My grandfather half-imagines them to be true, but he's lived nearly a century and can remember times when folk believed all manner of marvels. Come! I'll show you the cottage. You'd not be afraid with me beside you?"

"No, of course not." She took his hand trustfully as they pushed their way through the bracken.

"I wonder if it's locked," he said, pitting his weight against the door.

It groaned inward, revealing a long, low apartment out of which narrow wooden stairs spiralled. On the right another door stood open, leading into a smaller room lined with shelves and cupboards.

"It's years since anybody has been here!"

He brushed away a cloud of cobweb and went through into the cupboard-lined room. Huldah followed more cautiously, her eyes piercing the dust-laden gloom.

"The place needs a good clean-up!" he exclaimed, looking with disgust at the grime-encrusted jars and bottles that littered the shelves and the table.

"It was from this window that she looked out at me," Huldah said.

"Then you certainly imagined it. These windows are black!"

"It's cold here," Huldah said, and shivered.

"Probably damp. It's fairly near to the river."

Fairfax came over to her and took her hands again, smiling into her eyes. "You see, my young weasel, there is nobody here except you and me."

"The bottles and jars?"

"Are probably old herbal remedies and such like. My grandfather's aunt lived here, years and years ago. I think there was a tenant here, too, before I was born. Someone who painted the likenesses of the family before anyone got married. It would be interesting to delve into the contents of these jars, wouldn't it?"

"No!" Huldah spoke sharply, her tanned face paling. "I don't like it here. This place wasn't meant for us."

"Then we'll go outside," he said patiently. "But don't

you want to look upstairs? There are two bedrooms, if I remember right, and some old tapestries."

"I don't like closed-in places," Huldah said breathlessly, and fled through the door.

Fairfax shrugged and followed her, his hands reaching out to grasp her shoulders.

"You're not running away from me?" he questioned.

"No, oh no!" She flung her arms about his neck, and the trembling flowed through her limbs and possessed them both.

"Not here! Not within sight of the cottage!" she whispered.

He put his arm about her waist and hurried her deeper into the wood, until the creeper-clad building was hidden from view, and there were only ferns, and pale willows, and the rippling of the river.

"I must go home," she said, and wondered how it could be that the blue twilight had enfolded every leaf when she could not remember any time having passed at all.

"And so must I." He rose and stretched, white teeth gleaming as he smiled down at her. Even with her hair tousled and her gown crumpled, she was still desirable.

"You do not think badly of me?" she asked shyly.

"No. No, I think . . . most highly of you," he said.

Beau trotted up to them, his tail waving, nose and ears alert for rabbits. Fairfax patted him absently and held aside a branch for Huldah to pass ahead of him toward the main bridle path. When they reached the highway they parted without further words, Fairfax mounting the stallion he had left tethered by the bridge, Huldah striding in the opposite direction toward the farm.

At the gates of *Kingsmead* Fairfax met James, who came striding down the winding track, a rifle over his shoulder and three hares dangling from his hand.

"Aunt Eliza has been agitating for jugged hare these

past two weeks," he remarked by way of greeting. "These will serve to content her."

"You've not been down in the woods?"

"Over to the north pasture. Jasper strained a foreleg, so I sent Jem back to the stables and walked down to see if you were on your way back."

"With your trophies displayed for my admiration?"

"Lord, I forgot to give them to Jem to give to Aunt Eliza!" James looked at them ruefully and grinned.

"Why were you looking for me?" Fairfax enquired, swinging himself to the ground and beginning to walk in step with his brother toward the courtyard.

"Grandfather has been fretting the entire day, wanting to know why you haven't been to see him."

"Been to see him! We live in the same house!"

"He says that you don't talk to him these says. He's showing his age, I think."

"Well, he can't last forever," Fairfax said.

"He could live another ten years," James said quickly. The thought of change disturbed him. In his mind Grandfather and Uncle Weston and the aunts went on forever, without dying.

"He's marvelous for his age," Fairfax said.

"And one day, you'll be Lord Falcon," James said slowly.

"Don't fear I'll start interfering in the estate," Fairfax said. "I never could pretend to take any interest in the price of grain or the ailments of dogs and horses. I'll gladly leave it to your management, and enjoy the fruits of your labor! You know, I think it surprises people that we never quarrel!"

"Why should we?" James asked in surprise.

"Brothers are supposed to quarrel. Think of the Bible."

"I don't very often," James said.

"At least none of us are religious!" Fairfax said thankfully.

"You'd better have a word with Grandfather," James advised. "He's in the solar, I think. At least he was there when I went out, drumming his fingers on the table and declaring that nobody ever tells him anything!"

"I'll see him." Fairfax tossed the reins of his horse over to James and strode into the house.

Edward Falcon had slipped into one of the dozes which occasionally overcame him, but he was jerked awake by his grandson's cheerful voice.

"James says you wished to see me, sir."

"Close the door," Edward ordered. "It is a week since our last conversation. Have you made any progress?"

"In one week? You must allow me more time."

"Time indeed! At your age I'd have tumbled the wench by the end of the evening! You've spoken to her?"

"Briefly. One has to be subtle."

"You need not preach subtlety to me," Edward said. "You have not begun to learn the meaning of the word. Did she welcome your speaking?"

"As far as I could tell."

"Good. Play her like a fish and then draw her up slowly. But don't let her wriggle off your hook. James will thank you for it one day."

"Yes, Grandfather."

Fairfax rested his hand briefly on the old man's shoulder. Grandfather was right, of course. James would be a fool to wed Huldah Clegg. Better for him to realize that she was not a fit mate.

But not yet, Fairfax thought. She is too sweet a mouthful to taste only twice. A month or two's dalliance won't make any difference. And I want to see her again. I want to hold her in my arms and hear her talk of the sea.

At the same moment Huldah stood at the window of

her own room and gazed out over the darkening fields toward the ruins on the hill. She had gone to the woods to resolve a problem, but now it had grown as large as the hill that blocked her view of *Kingsmead*.

He knows that I am no light girl, she thought, so he will, sooner or later, ask my father if we can wed.

It would cause something of a sensation locally if the heir of *Kingsmead* married the bailiff's daughter. From her reading in the circulating library at Maidstone, Huldah knew very well that such things did happen. And it seemed now that this was happening to her.

She clasped her hands tightly and leaned her forehead against the pane. To be Lady Falcon was, she supposed, an honor that would be coveted by many girls, but to be Lady Falcon meant also that for the rest of her life she would have to live in *Kingsmead*, and that life would be bounded by Marie Regina, with an occasional trip to Maidstone, the furthest she would ever travel. Her dreams of far countries would be no more than dreams. But they were muddled in her mind now with brilliant hair and eyes, a deep voice that called her "young weasel," hands that stroked her limbs into a frenzy of desire.

"I am in love with him, Beau," she said softly. "I gave myself to him and now we are bound together, Beau. And I cannot tell if it is sufficient for me."

The dog bounded up, scrabbling with his feathery paws at her skirt. She bent and hugged him, and thought again of Fairfax. She had not really believed that love could spring up so rapidly, though she had read of such things.

"But it happened to me," she told Beau. "It really happened to me."

It would have been so pleasant, she thought wistfully,

if Master James had been the elder twin. Then he could have inherited land and title, and she and Fairfax could have made a life for themselves away from the confines of Marie Regina.

In the kitchen at *Kingsmead* Eliza hovered over the cooking range, alert for any hint of burning. She was trying her hand at a new sauce which required constant watching if the spices were to be blended to that pitch of perfection the dish required. Cook had retired to the fireplace, to warm her knees and pass approving murmurs on the smell wafting to her nostrils. The hares were hung, ready for skinning, and Becky knelt at the table cutting out pastry shapes.

This was the time of day that Eliza enjoyed. Supper was over, and she had an hour to herself in which to experiment in the kitchen. When the sauce was ready and sealed into the cooking jar, she would slip out to the stables to check on Jasper's leg. Jem's eyes were not as clear as they had been in his youth, though he would have died rather than admit it, and Eliza liked to keep some measure of supervision.

It was, she thought, a pity that everybody could not be as content as she was. Helen's tranquillity was no more than a shield against the years of bitter loneliness, and Weston's selfish light-heartedness was no more than the stupidity of a child afraid to grow up. Even her nephews had seemed immersed in their own thoughts at supper. Fairfax had eaten less than usual, and James had seemed constantly on the verge of telling them all something and then of checking his impulse.

Life, Eliza thought as she tasted the sauce, could be so simple if only folk made the best of what they had and ceased fretting for the moon.

CHAPTER TWELVE

Harvest had come and gone in a blaze of gold, green, and scarlet. An early frost whitened the ground and the holly berries glowed like rubies against the dark emerald of their spiked leaves.

James had dressed more carefully than usual, sleeking down his fair hair, tying his cravat with more artistry than he generally employed. He had decided that it was pointless to wait any longer before speaking to Huldah. He had fully intended to propose after the last of the crops had been gathered in, but his grandfather had asked him to wait yet a little longer.

"The girl will accept you," Edward had said. "I've no doubts on that score. To tell you the truth I'd planned to give a dinner party when you announced your betrothal, but it will take some time to arrange, and I have not felt well recently. I shall be better when the cooler weather comes. Heat exhausts me."

He had indeed looked tired, and for the first time his hand trembled as he laid it over his grandson's.

"Wait another month or two," he advised. "To please

me, eh? It will give you more time in which to make the manor house ready. You've hired women to do the cleaning?"

"And ordered new hangings from Maidstone. I gave out that we were expecting new tenants."

"Good! You don't want the entire neighborhood to know about your future plans."

But not even Mistress Huldah knows of them, James thought.

He had seen very little of Huldah in the past weeks. The gathering in of the harvest and the refurbishing of the manor had occupied much of his own time, and on the rare occasions he had seen the bailiff's daughter she had ducked her head and scurried away shyly. He hoped that this new shyness meant she was becoming aware of him as a person and not as the boy she had known all her life.

He had intended to ride to the farm and speak to her there, but good fortune was evidently with him for as he approached the bridge he saw her striding toward him with Beau trotting at her heels. Her cheeks were flushed with health and the cold, and her eyes sparkled with sheer joy of living.

"Mistress Huldah! It's a pleasure to see you," he exclaimed. "I was on my way to the farm."

"Father is at Maidstone," she said brightly.

"It was you I wanted to see," he said quickly before she could walk on. "I wish you to come with me to the manor house."

"To see the new hangings? I heard down in the village there were to be new tenants at the manor."

"Will you ride with me there now?" he asked.

"I was going for a walk," she said doubtfully.

"Ride double with me. It won't take very long."

"Very well."

She gave a long, frowning look past him as if she expected somebody else to be there, and then put her foot to the stirrup and sprang up lightly behind him.

As they trotted up the drive to the manor, James had a sense of homecoming. In years to come he would ride home from the village with Huldah perched at his back and Beau scampering ahead. And later still he would ride up alone and Huldah would run out to greet him with a child at her skirts and another in her arms.

"Come inside," he invited when they stood at the front door. "I want to hear your opinion."

"I cannot think why," she said frankly, "for I know little of women's matters. My mother despaired of ever teaching me anything about cooking or sewing. Oh! but this is a pretty room."

He had opened the front door and ushered her into the hall. More modestly proportioned than the hall at *Kingsmead*, with a staircase of wood instead of stone, its hangings of brown and green and gold echoes the colors of the rugs on the floor, and the few pieces of furniture were polished to burnished perfection.

"I had the fires lit to take the chill out of the rooms," he said.

"The whole house feels warm. I was never inside this manor before," Huldah said, wandering around with engaged curiosity in her face.

"It's as old as *Kingsmead*, and was in my grandmother's family for generations," James told her. "My mother's parents were tenants here before she was wed to my father."

"Yes. I remember Master Fairfax," she said, and a wave of color suffused her face. He wondered what had caused it, but she had darted across to an inner door and was looking inside the parlor.

"This is pleasant, too," she said approvingly.

"It would be comfortable to sit here in an evening," James said. "With the fire blazing and the shutters closed against the wind—"

"I *like* wind!" Huldah interrupted. "I like to be out in the wind, with rain driving across the fields. That's even better than sitting indoors, toasting your toes."

"Oh, that too!" he agreed. "But the manor pleases you?"

"Yes, Master James." She gave him a faintly bewildered look.

"We have known each other for years," he protested, "and you still refuse to employ my Christian name."

"Your grandfather might not approve," she said.

"My grandfather thinks of you most kindly," James said.

"Oh?" Huldah gave him another bewildered look.

"Indeed, I was talking of you to him recently," James said, "in connection with this house. You do like it?"

"Yes, but I've no liking for housekeeping," she said, "so if it's a question of my working for the new tenants—"

"There are none."

"But you said. In the village they said . . . the new hangings everywhere."

"For you," James said.

"For me? I don't need to rent a house," she said, amused.

"For both of us. Mistress Huldah, it would make me very happy if you would consent to become my wife," James said in a rush.

"Your wife? You want me to be your wife?" she said blankly.

"If you could find it in your heart to take me," James said, "I'd do my best to make you happy."

"But you're Lord Falcon's grandson!" she said.

"And not due to inherit either the title or one foot of

the land," he reminded her. "But I manage the estate and I'm paid well for doing it. This manor will suit us well, and my grandfather is willing to rent it to us."

"You've talked to him?"

"To him and to your own father," James said. "They both counselled patience."

"Did you—have you talked about this with anyone else?" she asked slowly.

"Of course not. I wished only to be certain there would be no objections from Grandfather or Master Clegg. This manor—I've had it cleaned and refurbished for you. You do like it?"

"I said I liked it," Huldah said a little desperately.

"And you are kindly disposed toward me?"

"Yes. Yes, of course."

"Then you will consider my proposal?" he asked eagerly.

"It's impossible," she said bluntly.

"Impossible?" His face dropped as he stared at her. "Have I been too hasty, presumed too far? I would not willingly offend you."

"Oh no, of course not. I am—" She cast about for something to say, and dredged up out of her memory a sentence she had read in a novel. "I am deeply honored by your proposal, sir, but you must give me time to search my own feelings."

"You are offended," James said.

"No. Truly . . . James." Scarlet with embarrassment, Huldah put out her hand toward him. "I am most flattered. Any girl would be pleased to have Lord Falcon's grandson propose marriage."

"But you don't favor me, do you?"

"It's that we wouldn't suit," she said. "You'd grow tired of me. I know you would, because I'd not be content to stay at home all day and keep house."

"We'd have servants," he protested. "You speak as if I expected you to get down on your knees and scrub the floors!"

"No, not that," she said. "But where would I go and what would I do while the servants were cleaning the floor?"

"You could ride with me," he said. "If you wished we could go to Maidstone on market day."

She gazed at him thoughtfully, watching the eagerness grow in his face. This was the worst thing that had ever happened to her. That James Falcon should fall in love with her was an event that had never entered her head.

"It wouldn't do," she said harshly. "It really wouldn't do. I'm not the wife you need and you're—I'm so sorry!"

The eagerness had faded in his face and his eyes were clouded as he looked at her. "You are attached to somebody else, aren't you?" he said. "I was a fool not to have realized that a beautiful girl of twenty would not be without suitors. I rushed ahead like a bull at a gate, and never thought for a moment my proposal was unwelcome. I hope he will make you happy, truly I do."

"I am so sorry," she said again, and spread out her hands piteously.

"I've been stupid," he said. "So stupid that I wish I could make time run backward so that I could arrange everything in a different way."

"It would have come to the same in the end." she said in a low voice, and hurried past him into the hall, her head bent and tears scalding her cheeks.

"Mistress, please wait! It's a long walk back to the farm," James called out, but she had slammed the front door and it echoed in his ears above the barking of the little dog.

Huldah sobbed in a mixture of anger and pity as she zigzagged down the path. The anger was for herself because she could not love a man who had offered her honorable marriage. The pity was for James Falcon, who had built a nest and been scorned by the mate he had chosen.

She slowed down as she neared the gate and glanced back, fearful that he might have followed her, but there was no sound except the crackling of frost under her shoes. The highway was deserted, and she paused for a moment, drawing deep gulps of cold air into her lungs. If she went to the farm now her father might have returned and he would be anxious to see her upset.

She turned instead toward the river, hurrying across the bridge, plunging without heed down the slippery bridle path. Fairfax would be waiting for her. She had been on her way to meet him when James had asked her to go to the manor. Now she hurried as fast as she could, swerving between the trees until she glimpsed her lover's form just ahead of her and flung herself into his arms, sobbing as she clung to him.

"Huldah, what in the world ails you?" Fairfax exclaimed. "Has something frightened you, young weasel? Are you hurt?"

"Your brother," she gasped out.

"James? Surely James hasn't frightened you?"

She shook her head, rubbing her wet eyelids childishly. "No, he has—he has proposed marriage to me!" she cried dolefully.

Fairfax gave a long, low whistle. Now he would have to let his grandfather know that he had succeeded in seducing the girl. If he had made it known earlier James would never have proposed, but he had delayed because each meeting with Huldah had increased his desire for her. And he had not dreamed that his brother would ask the girl until he had consulted again with Lord Falcon.

"He has been getting the manor ready for me," Huldah

was saying. "I thought new tenants were to rent the house, but he has prepared it for me, for himself and for me. He says he has spoken to Lord Falcon and to my own father, and they both approve."

"What did you answer him?" he asked sharply.

"I said I could not wed him." She drew away, a trifle hurt at his tone. "I could never marry where I did not love."

"You told him about us?"

"No, although he guessed there was another man. But you asked me to keep our meetings secret, and I have told nobody."

"Secret love is more romantic, you said," he reminded her.

"I know." She bit her lip and shook her head a little in puzzlement. "But we will have to announce our own betrothal very soon."

"Our own betrothal?"

"I know you wished to wait," she said innocently, "but we cannot wait now, not if our child is to be born in wedlock."

"Our child?" He seemed fated to go on repeating what she said as if he had no words of his own.

"I have been going to tell you," she said nervously, "but I wanted to choose the right moment. I am with child, nearly three months gone."

"Are you certain?" he asked.

"Yes, quite certain. My courses have stopped and—"

"There is no need to go into female details!" he snapped.

"I'm sorry, but I thought . . . I am quite certain."

"Couldn't you—there are ways in which a birth may be prevented."

"I know of none," she said simply, "and I could not use them even if I did. It is your child."

"Can you be certain of that?" he enquired.

"Of course I can be certain," she said. "You are the only man I love. How could it be anyone else's child?"

"Forgive me, mistress." He took her hand, pressing it absently. "I have no right to condemn you."

"Condemn me?" Now she was fated to be his echo.

"We will have to think carefully. My grandfather will make ample provision for the babe; he is a generous man. And if you leave Marie Regina fairly soon, you will be able to return later when a foster-mother has been found. We could give it out that you had gone to visit an aunt."

"I have no aunts."

"An uncle then! Some relative. The important thing is to avoid scandal."

"The important thing," Huldah said slowly, "is that I am with child and we must wed."

"I never promised marriage," he said.

"We needed no words. I would not have given myself to you if I had not believed that you loved me!"

"I did love you," he said swiftly. "I do love you."

"When two people fall in love they marry," Huldah said.

"I am not ready for a wife."

"Not ready!" Anger bubbled up in her. "You are nearly thirty years old, and most men are wed by that age. You cannot spend the rest of your life in hunting and gambling and enjoying yourself. You must think of marriage, and would it not be good sense to wed a bailiff's daughter who loves you rather than a fine lady who only craves your estate?"

"I do love you," he said again, "but I never spoke of marriage, never promised you that."

"Then why did you make love to me?" she whispered.

"You knew I am a respectable girl. You must have known that. So, why?"

He stared at her in an agony of indecision. To tell her that he had seduced her on his grandfather's instructions in order to blacken her in the eyes of his brother now seemed quite impossible. It would not only destroy her, it would destroy his own credit with her, and Fairfax could not bear to have anyone think badly of him.

"I do love you," he said.

"Then wed me! Wed me as I believed you would! I'd be no burden! I'd not clip your freedom nor expect you to sit at home night after night. You would be free to go where you choose."

"I'll not be forced into marriage," Fairfax said sulkily.

Huldah began to cry again, softly and hopelessly, the tears sliding down her face onto her cold hands.

"You've said many times that you'd like to be free yourself," he reminded her.

"But where is the freedom in bearing a bastard?" she cried.

"I've told you, you can go away for a while, have the babe fostered."

"I'll not give away my child!" she said fiercely. "If you won't wed me then I'll bear it out of wedlock, and let everybody in the village know the name of the father. Your grandfather would hate that. He loathes the whole idea of scandal, doesn't he? The high-and-mighty Falcons must always be better than anybody else. They must be richer, more powerful, own more land! But I'll create a scandal. It will shame me, but it will shame you more. I'll say you forced me to it."

"Your father will lose the farm."

"He has saved sufficient to live on, and he's a proud man. As proud as any Falcon! He may even call you out.

You're a better shot than he is, I suppose, but if you killed or wounded him then you'd go to prison."

She was talking wildly, her words tumbling out incoherently, her fists beating the air. In panic Fairfax drew her to him.

"No need to become hysterical! I'll think of something," he said desperately. "You must give me time to think."

"One week! I will give you one week, and then I'll come to *Kingsmead* and tell your grandfather. I'll tell everybody!"

She meant exactly what she said. He sensed the determination in her and saw the defiant jut of her chin. In one week she would arrive at *Kingsmead* and all hell would break loose. His grandfather had wished the girl to be disgraced, but to abandon her when she was with child would be to disgrace his own reputation.

In Marie Regina a stern distinction was drawn between young men who enjoyed the favors of light women and those who seduced and then abandoned respectable local girls.

James, with his slow smile and candid eyes, came into Fairfax's mind. He had always felt a deep affection for his younger brother, had relied on him more than he was willing to admit. James loved the girl and had proposed marriage. He would regard Fairfax as a monster of treachery. And Aunt Helen would look at her elder nephew with cold disbelief.

"One week!" Huldah said, and looked at him with a fierce, bright passion that was midway between love and hate.

"I do love you!" he said, not able to bear the thought that he was diminished in her regard. "I love you most dearly, but you must give me a little time."

Even if he married her he would lose his twin's affection. James would not be likely to wish to remain as manager of the estate. Fairfax himself might have to take over the running of it, and that would tie him to the land for the rest of his life.

"I must go. They are expecting me at home," he said.

"And you may expect me there in one week," she returned steadily. "I mean exactly what I say. If you do not announce our betrothal to Lord Falcon I will come to *Kingsmead* and tell him how you betrayed me."

Because she feared that if she stayed longer she would begin to weep again, she turned and walked rapidly away deeper into the wood. The temptation to run back and tell him that she loved him beyond all reason was so strong that she dug her nails into the palms of her hands.

Fairfax stared after her, his hands clenched in rage and impotent desire. It was madness, but to have taken her once more would have satisfied him beyond reason. She was unlike any young woman he had ever known. There was a sweet wildness in Huldah Clegg which struck an answering chord in his own restless nature. If he had been of a marrying mind he could have done worse than choose her.

But marriage and a child would tie him down, bind him more closely to the estate. And James loved her, had asked her to be his wife. She must have given the younger twin some encouragement, for James was shy with girls. If Huldah could give herself to one man she could give herself to another. Fairfax unclenched his hands and drew a shuddering breath, driving desire out of his heart.

Huldah had reached the clearing and stood for a moment staring at the little house as if it held some unexplained fascination on her. Frost had whitened the windows and no face was framed in them. Nobody ever came here now, not even Eliza Falcon who owned it. Frost and silence covered it.

She pulled a corner of her shawl and rubbed her eyes. Their lids felt heavy and sore as if she had been weeping for a long time, and her breasts ached. In a little while her pregnancy would become apparent to everybody. She wanted to carry the child with pride, to wear a wedding ring on her finger. And at the same time she longed to be free of the burden of her female nature, to wear breeches and climb the rigging of a tall ship.

After a few moments she turned and walked away slowly, her head bent, her long legs moving tiredly over the frozen ground.

Within the cottage a big, bearded man crouched close to the fire he was trying to kindle. He was taking a risk that the smoke might be glimpsed through the bare trees, but he was cold, and though the years had changed him he had not wished to invite possible recognition by taking a bed at the inn or lodging at Maidstone.

He would wait for a day or two, cramming the hours with memories of the long, bitter years, and then he would go up to *Kingsmead*. Lord Falcon was still alive. That much he had ascertained from the stagecoach driver.

"Close on ninety and flourishing like a green bay!" the fellow had exclaimed.

Of the rest of the family he had no idea. Alive or dead, single or married, they had ceased to be important save as reasons for his revenge, for they too must have suffered at the hands of Edward Falcon, and in killing the old man he would be avenging them all.

He stretched calloused hands, flexing his fingers before the tiny flame that had sprung up. The backs of his hands were scarred and sunburnt, the nails broken after years of unrelenting toil. His mouth hardened into a grim line as he looked at them. Strong hands. Hands innocent of theft, but very fit for the killing of a Falcon.

CHAPTER THIRTEEN

"You look a mite peaked, Huldah," Samuel Clegg said, glancing at his daughter.

"It's cold." Her voice was listless as her shoulders, and Beau, curled at her side, shivered as if to give point to her words.

"Too cold for snow."

Never analytical, Samuel applied himself to his cold bacon and hot tea with the relish of a man who takes life as it comes.

Huldah drooped closer to the fire, her eyes seeking pictures in the reluctant flames, but there were no red ships nor glowing orange sails. Across her mind her pregnancy was scored in dark, dying letters like the epitaph of her lost virginity. On her fingers she counted the three days that remained until the end of the week.

Every impulse urged her toward *Kingsmead*, but she had given Fairfax seven days and would keep her word. Better for him to come seeking her before the week was up, rather than for her to go with tattered pride along the frost-rimed road.

191

"Someone's coming." Her father was out of his chair and peering through the window before her own ears had caught the clop-clop of hoofs in the yard.

So Fairfax was come. Triumph rose up in her and was flavored with guilt. Perhaps she should have given him a month in which to announce their betrothal and make his peace with his grandfather. But that he had come meant surely that his need was as great for her as hers for him.

Her fingers went to her hair, patting it into place. She had slept little for nights and had woken weeping from some dream she could not remember. She had never thought much about her appearance before, but suddenly she wanted to be beautiful.

"It's Master James!" Samuel exclaimed, going to the door. "I wonder what he's wanting at this hour!"

Disappointment and relief mingled in her, to be replaced as he entered by a feeling of guilt. James had been so good, so eager to please. When she thought of the manor house, newly polished and refurbished, she wanted to weep.

"Samuel. Mistress Huldah." His nod was curt, almost unfriendly.

"It's a bad night to be out," Samuel said. "There's nothing wrong up at *Kingsmead* I hope? Your grandfather isn't sick?"

"Only with temper," James said, coming over to the fire and kneeling to warm his hands.

"Why, what's amiss?" Samuel reached for his pipe.

"My brother has taken himself off to the French wars," James told them. "He rode off yesterday morning, declaring he would sign with Collingwood and hope to transfer under Nelson's command when the fleet docks at Portsmouth next year. My grandfather is furious, but Fairfax never cared much for other people's opinions."

He was talking swiftly and smoothly, not looking at

Huldah, but she was conscious of his hand, reddened by the fire, spread out near to her. She had not realized before that his hand was beautifully shaped, with strength and comfort in the hard palm and long fingers. She went on staring at it as if it were some magical talisman against hurt.

"But what in the world possessed him to do such a thing?" Samuel was asking.

"Restlessness, a craving for adventure, a longing to be away from the village. Fairfax always wanted to travel."

"Aye, it's understandable in a young man. I was like that myself," Samuel said. "Huldah, if she'd been a lad, would have been the same, I reckon."

"But Fairfax will inherit the land one day and my grandfather feels that he should stay home," James said. "I pointed out to him that I can manage everything as I usually do, until my brother comes back, but he doesn't listen."

"He's getting old," Samuel excused.

"Perhaps." James frowned slightly, disliking the notion.

"You'll take something to warm you?" Samuel remembered. "Huldah girl, where are your manners?"

She was so cold that her legs shook beneath her as she stood up, yet her cheeks were brilliant from the heat of the fire. She willed her hands to be steady as she poured whisky, but something about her made Samuel add an invitation.

"And take a drop yourself. You look a mite feverish."

"I'm fine," she said through stiff lips. "I must get Beau his supper."

"That dog is overfed," Samuel began, but she had gone out into the pantry.

Beyond the pantry the yard was black and silent under a heavy sky. She opened the outer door and let the icy air fan upon her face. There was a soft whinny from

James's horse and she went over to it, burying her fingers in the thick mane, forcing back the long shudders that gripped her.

Fairfax had ridden away, leaving her to face ridicule and shame alone. He had not stayed either to confirm or to deny any tale she might tell. He had not loved her after all, and she had been a fool to listen to his soft whisper or heed his yearning fingers.

"Mistress Huldah?" James spoke into the darkness, his voice gentle.

She leaned her head against the horse's side and tried to answer, but a sob broke in her throat.

"Don't cry, mistress," James said, and coming to her laid his hand on her shoulder. "It was my brother whom you loved, wasn't it? He told me before he went that he feared you'd taken his little flatteries too seriously."

"Little flatteries!" The sob was turned to bitter mirth.

"I'm sorry," James said. "I'm sorry if you ever thought him serious. Fairfax means no harm by his gallantries. He has a way with women, that's all."

"I was very foolish," she said in a low voice.

"No more foolish than I was," James said ruefully. "To think of my asking you to wed me! Of my thinking myself good enough."

"You are a great deal too good," she interrupted. "You are a very fine man, Master James."

"James. I wish you would call me James."

"James, then." She turned and looked at him gratefully.

In the uncertain light he was very like Fairfax. Her cold hand strayed briefly to his cheek.

"This is not the time perhaps," he was saying jerkily, "but I have to ask you. I have to ask you again if you'd ever consider taking me as husband. I know now I'd be second-best, but I love you, mistress. I have loved you for a long time, and you might come to care for me."

"I care now," she said, and a kind of desperation seized her as if everything she valued were slipping away from her. "I have always cared for you."

"Then you would consider—"

"If we could be married quickly," she said. "I would like to be married as soon as possible."

"I haven't the right," he began.

"You have every right. Fairfax was—I took him too seriously, that's all. It was only a summer-liking."

"Then you'll take me? Live at the manor?"

"Yes," she said, and was quite calm and still as if the saying of one word had destroyed all passion in her.

As he kissed her the thought of the coming child swept over her. James would know that it could not possibly be his, might guess when he learned of its existence that Fairfax had actually seduced her, but he would accept the babe as his own for her protection.

"Will you come back to *Kingsmead* tonight with me?" he was asking.

"Tonight!" She looked at him in surprise.

"It's not late, and I'd have you home by midnight. I want my family to know tonight. I want them to know that you've accepted me."

A sensation of being trapped gripped her. Once the announcement had been made she would be committed.

"I'll tell my father," she said, and something within her ceased to struggle.

Samuel Clegg was embarked upon a second whisky when his daughter came in and folded her hands in a prim manner quite unlike herself.

"Master James has asked me to wed him, and I've accepted."

"I'd a notion that was in the wind," Samuel said dryly.

"I did speak to you of the matter," James said, following Huldah through the door.

"I remember it, and I remember saying that it was fine with me if it sat well with your grandfather."

"He gave his approval," James said.

"Then I'll add my own, if you're both sure of your minds."

Samuel glanced between them with a slight frown. Master James was a fine, upstanding man and Huldah a comely girl. They made a handsome couple, yet there was some tension in the room which nagged at him because there seemed no reason for it.

"With your permission I'd like to take Huldah over to *Kingsmead* to tell my family," James said.

"We can be back by midnight," Huldah put in.

She had a mulish expression on her face that reminded Samuel of the time years before when she'd had an aching tooth. He'd offered to take her to the tooth-drawer at Maidstone.

"There's a fair on the common and a tooth-drawer there. Let's get it over with quickly."

"You'll bring her back safe." It was a statement, not a question. Master James would always keep safe that which he loved.

Events had become dreamlike for Huldah. The dark landscape was flat as a painting, and the horse beneath her had no reality. The clip-clop of its hooves along the hard road carried the refrain "Fairfax is gone. Fairfax is gone."

James was kind. He would be kind when, after the marriage, she confessed her pregnancy. And Fairfax would lose all claim to his child. She hoped that he would feel some pain about that, some echo of the dumb misery that hung about her.

"You will never regret it," she heard him say as they

turned in at the gates of *Kingsmead*, and she nodded, stretching her lips into a smile that he could barely glimpse through the darkness.

The luck-tree was silvered by the emerging moon as they rode into the courtyard. James leaned from the saddle and plucked a spray of the leaves and handed it to her.

"For a pledge," she heard him say, and somewhere an owl sent its mournful, questing cry through the bitter night.

Huldah had been to *Kingsmead* occasionally during her childhood. She had come with her mother to receive the Christmas box meted out to the employees of the Falcons, and a tall, slim lady with a scarred face had given her some gingerbread. Then, they had gone round to the kitchen door. Now they went through the great main door which yielded to James's touch with a slow creaking of ancient oak.

Fires blazed in the twin fireplaces at each side of the staircase and the hall blazed with candles. Yet the shifting tapestries, the bare stone floor, the massive dresser towering to the rafters conveyed a sense of chill which had nothing to do with the season of the year.

There were three people gathered about one of the hearths. They sat in high-backed chairs, their heads leaning together, as if they watched for some message in the leaping flames.

Huldah was reminded of a story of three sisters who sat weaving threads of destiny for each human soul. Then James banged shut the heavy door, and the three figures turned in their chairs, resolving themselves into Lord Falcon, his son, and his daughter.

"Grandfather, Huldah has agreed to wed me," James said.

He sounded excited, like a schoolboy just passed an

important examination. His arm around Huldah's waist he was urging her forward.

"Wed! My dear boy, I couldn't be more pleased," Weston was exclaiming. His chins bulged over his cravat. The hand which he extended was white and soft, the fingers dimpled.

"At last, a piece of good news!" Eliza said fervently, coming to kiss James. Her handsome, high-colored face glowed with pleasure.

The old man in the chair had not risen, but now he came to his feet slowly, his veined hand gripping the carved arm of the chair. His face had grown more hawklike under the full-bottomed wig. Light from the candles gleamed on his spectacles.

"Huldah agreed tonight to wed me," James said triumphantly.

"Did she so?" Edward turned a beaky profile toward her. Behind the twin suns of his lenses his eyes were hidden.

"I mean to make him a good wife," Huldah said. In her own ears her voice sounded loud.

"We mean to be married soon, before Christmas," James told them. "Her father approves the match and we'll live at the manor."

"You will let me design a pretty dress for you?" Weston begged. "My sisters will tell you that I have an eye for color and materials."

"The manor house will suit you splendidly," Eliza said. "Is that why you've been refurbishing it? Not for new tenants, but for yourself? I never guessed you to be so sly, James!"

There was an undercurrent of hurt in her laughter, for James was her favorite and she had enjoyed his boyish confidences; sensitive to it, he put his other arm about her.

"I have been longing to tell you, Aunt, but I had to make certain she would accept me first."

"Helen must be told," Weston began. "She has been so miserable since Fairfax left that news of a wedding will cheer her immensely."

There was a little silence when he had spoken, as if the memory of an earlier wedding and its grotesque aftermath had briefly intruded. In the silence, the knocker on the front door was lifted and banged down three times, as if some ghost of the past sought to effect an entrance.

"Who in the world can it be at this hour?" Weston demanded.

"Open the door, James," Lord Falcon said.

For an instant Huldah wondered if it were Fairfax returned. In that instant her heart leaped with a mingling of joy and apprehension. Then James stepped to the door and opened it and a big, bearded man walked in and stared at them all out of sun-furrowed eyes.

"You'll not remember me," he said. "It's been a long while and you'll not remember."

"Ben Fiske?" Edward Falcon was peering at the newcomer. "I know the voice, though you have grown older."

"After thirty years a man grows older," said Ben Fiske.

"I thought you dead," the old man said heavily. "I thought you dead and buried."

"You hoped me dead," Ben corrected. "You hoped that the convict ship had taken me away forever, away from Marie Regina and *Kingsmead*."

"I don't understand," James said in bewilderment. "Grandfather, who is this man?"

"I was bailiff at Wittle Farm thirty years back," Ben said.

"The one who stole the cup? I heard about that. You were transported."

"I stole nothing," Ben said. "I fell in love with Helen

Falcon, and that was considered a kind of theft. But there had to be a reason for getting rid of me, didn't there? A man cannot be transported for falling in love. An excuse had to be thought up. I was brought here on an excuse and bidden take the christening cup to Maidstone for re-chasing—another excuse so that the cup would be found in my saddle bags. And Lord Falcon was an important man, a peer of the realm whose statement was accepted without question. He even pleaded for leniency for me, and so instead of being hanged I was transported. For thirty years, Master—Falcon, is it?"

"My son Prescott and his wife had twin sons. James is the younger," Edward said. "How long have you been back?"

"A few days. I stayed at the Dower Cottage lest anyone in the district remembered me. I wanted to think, you see. I wanted to think about what happened in the place where it happened."

"And where did your thinking lead you?" Edward enquired.

"To the conclusion that a man like you would be better dead. By all the laws of nature you should be dead already. But you live on, don't you? You live on while the world crumbles and dies around you."

"You have no right to talk to my grandfather like that," James said, flushing angrily.

"Be quiet!" Edward said sharply. "This goes back to before you were born and you have no part in it. Now, Ben Fiske, what other conclusions have you reached, save the one that I have lived too long?"

"That it is my right to kill you," Ben Fiske said.

Weston made an odd, squeaking noise and Huldah put a hand over her own mouth to prevent a similar sound escaping herself.

"So you are come back to kill me, are you?" Edward

observed. His voice was lazily amused. "I saved you from the gallows once, but I'd not be able to do that again, not if I were dead. And this time there are witnesses."

"The pleasure will outweigh the consequences," Ben said.

James had stepped back a pace and was measuring the other with his eyes.

Without turning his head Ben said, "You are young and strong, but I'm bigger and heavier than you, with thirty years hatred to give me strength. So don't do anything to make me hurt you."

"You're a fool." Eliza, who had stood silent, spoke passionately. Her face had flushed scarlet and her iron-grey curls were ruffled wildly about her head. "You're a fool to think that killing him will solve anything. We are as we are, Ben Fiske. My father's death will alter nothing except your own ending. And how will my sister feel when she learns that you died at the end of a rope after all?"

"Your sister?" His attention was caught. "Is Helen still—I had imagined her dead. I could not bear, I suppose, to think of her alive in a place where I could not come."

"Prescott and Blanche were killed," Eliza said tensely. "After the twins were born, they were killed in a carriage accident. Nat was killed in the American Revolt and on the day we heard the news my mother hanged herself from the luck-tree. They are all dead but Helen—"

"Helen is dead, too," a voice said from the top of the stairs.

Helen stood there, her loose gown outlining her slender form, her hair a curtain of white silk obscuring her face. Her voice was very clear and sweet, and it rang through the silent group below like a chime of bells.

"Helen died thirty years ago," she said, "when her lover was found guilty of theft and sent away. But she always believed that he would come back one day. Not to her, but to the place where she had lived. She waited night after night, not meaning to speak, not meaning to let him see her. Ghosts can love the living, but the living would be very foolish to love the dead."

"Helen?" His voice had changed, becoming deeper and softer.

She came down the staircase very slowly, her skirts whispering over the stone. On the lowest step, under the glare of the candles, she paused, raised her arms and pulled her hair back from her face. The livid scar that ran from eye to mouth sprang into cruel prominence.

Ben Fiske walked to where she stood and put out his hand toward her.

"Helen, my lovely girl," he said simply, and something young and gay and undying sprang between them.

"No need to kill," Eliza said. "Take her far from here, Ben Fiske. Marry her. That's why you survived, that's why you came back here."

"Not with my permission," Edward said. "She'll not wed with my consent."

His voice quavered suddenly, for his daughter had taken Ben's hand and was walking with him down the long hall, without turning her head. The door opened and closed behind them.

"She will marry him!" Weston cried on a high, thin note of hysterical mirth. "She will go away from here and wed him, as Apple did all those years ago!"

"I have only one daughter," Edward said. "Those other names will not be mentioned in this house again. I have only one daughter."

"And I am not about to run off to find a husband," Eliza said cheerfully. "James, you chose an inopportune time in which to announce your own betrothal. Poor Huldah will think us all savages."

"I would like to go home now," Huldah said in a small, polite voice. "I would like James to take me home."

"I'll come tomorrow, to measure your finger for a ring," James said.

His face was troubled, for the scene he had just witnessed raised questions in his mind to which there seemed no answer. It was perhaps best not to ask them.

"You seem in a tremendous hurry," his grandfather said sourly.

"A man must seize his happiness where he can," James said.

"I would like to go home," Huldah said again.

Her lower lip trembled as if she were a scolded child. In the faces of the three who confronted her she seemed to see traces of dark centuries stretching back through generations of Falcons. And she had promised to become a part of that family.

"It will snow tomorrow," James said as they remounted.

There was a certain safety in the uttering of banal phrases. In the space of a few days his ordered world had begun to disintegrate. The sudden departure of his brother, the appearance of Ben Fiske with his accusations, the behavior of Aunt Helen, all upset the careful balance of his universe. He did not even want to think too deeply about everything that had happened.

"We can be wed at the end of the month," he called above the rising wind. "I'll make you happy. I promise it."

There was no doubt in her mind that he would be a gentle and considerate husband, but there would never leap between them the fierce joy that had leapt between Helen Falcon and the man returned from transportation.

Huldah's lips moved silently, shaping the thought that had come into her mind.

No more dreams of tall ships and tossing waves and lands with strange names.

Her hand tightened upon the rein. She glanced down and saw, clenched still in her fingers, the spray of leaves from the luck-tree. They were crushed and bruised now, but their fragrance haunted the air she breathed.

CHAPTER FOURTEEN

"But we must all die some time," Apple told her daughter. "Dying is nothing to be feared."

"Not when one is old," Mair said passionately, "but you are not old!"

"I am nearly forty-seven," Apple said, amused. "That is past middle age, sweetheart."

"If only we could winter in the sun," Mair yearned, "your cough would get better. I know it would."

"Aye. Doctor Parry Edwards has said a warm climate would improve me," Apple admitted.

Against the pillow her red hair fanned out brilliantly with no trace of grey, but her face was white and shrunken like the face of a wax doll. Her hands spread on the counterpane looked brittle as twigs, the ring on her wedding finger so loose that she had secured it with a bit of cotton.

"If we could only afford a trip," Mair said wistfully. "Mam, couldn't we sell something?"

"There's nothing to sell, except the land and the house," Apple said, "and those are yours when I am gone. I wish you could have seen this place when your father and I came here thirty years back. Nettle and thistle and scrub, and the old farm a heap of stones with the roof fallen in. Your father and I rebuilt the house with our own hands from the original stones."

She talked as if Ty Saron was a mansion instead of a one-storey building with a living room that ran from front to back with a bedroom at each side. The floors had been laid with slabs of blue-veined slate from the local quarries and wooden shutters protected the small, uncurtained windows.

"If your father had lived," Apple was saying, "he could have taken up his painting again and made a name for himself. But there was so much to be done, and we had no sons to help him."

Her eyes were soft with yearning when she spoke of him. He had been a good husband, working hard to make a living for them on the land, and in the end the land itself had killed him. He had straightened up from digging one afternoon five years before, put his hand to his chest, and sagged slowly to his knees.

Mair also was remembering that day. She had been fourteen then and had run across the field as her father collapsed. He had looked up at her with faint surprise on his face and then said questioningly, "Helen?" and not spoken again.

Mair had never told her mother about that. Neither had she ever told her about the finding of the graves. Hidden under a tangle of rust-leaved foliage in a part of the meadow which had not been reclaimed, they had come to light by accident, when her father had decided to scythe that portion of the land. Her mother had been away at the market, and Mair had gone out to help with the scything.

She had seen her father frown down at the reddish, purple-veined leaves and then begin to tug at the sprawling roots and branches. The graves had lain beneath, all tumbled together now with bits of broken headstone and a few decaying bones that might have been human.

But a little further on, where the leaves grew most thickly, they had uncovered a complete skeleton. A woman with strands of hair still clinging to the almost fleshless skull, and on one thighbone a dark purple stain like the crescent moon Mair had on her own leg.

Her father had gathered the bones together and taken them to the river and set fire to the leaves and branches that had hidden them. But Mair had saved a few pieces of the leafy twigs and planted them by an old, dried-up well further along the twisting road. The well was concealed by fern and elm and pine, and the twigs had taken root quickly and were grown into a small tree. Mair went to the old well to think and dream sometimes, and she usually plucked a few leaves and crushed them between her fingers to inhale the vinegary fragrance.

She was usually a practical, level-headed girl who enjoyed housework and gardening and cooking, but there were times when a kind of dream enveloped her mind, and at such times she needed to be alone, to sit in a quiet place while strange and violent images chased through her imagination. She dreamed of red-tailed foxes then, and a rushing river over which dark shapes hovered and skimmed and darted.

But her mother's illness had, in recent months, made it impossible for her to slip away for more than a few minutes at a time. Occasionally one of the local farm wives would call in to sit for an hour, but these people of the hills were slow to accept strangers, and after thirty years Apple was still considered a foreigner. And the farm itself was shunned by many for no reason they could explain, save that it was believed a witch had once lived there. Mair wondered if the skeleton that she and her father had discovered had been that of the witch, and if in life as well as death she had borne the dark stain of a crescent moon upon her thigh.

"It is so cold in the winters here," Apple said now. "Perhaps it's because I'm getting older, but it seems to me the weather was much warmer when I was a girl at *Kingsmead.*"

"Tell me about it," Mair said. Her mother spoke seldom of her own childhood, but since her illness had begun she had seemed more inclined to talk of her old home and of the family from whom she had run away to be wed.

"The land around us sloped to the river," she said dreamily, "and along the edge of the river rushes grow very thickly and mingle with the trees. My cottage is down there—it is Eliza's now, for I gave it to her when I left. I wonder if she ever goes there."

"Tell me about your sisters."

"They were very beautiful," Apple said. "Helen was gentle and pure of face, and Eliza had hair so gold it looked as if she carried sunshine on her head. My father never wished any of us to leave home or to marry. We were part of the estate, you see." But she spoke without bitterness, and her drawn face was lit by a smile.

"They never came after you when you ran away?"

"Not one word have I heard of them from that day to this one," Apple said. "When your father was alive, we had each other, and we had you, and we worked the land. That was sufficient then. But there are moments now when I think of Marie Regina, and wish I could go back to see them all. If my father is still alive he'll be near ninety. His pride might stop him from finding out where I am or what happened to me."

"And you?" Mair asked.

"Oh, I have pride, too," Apple said ruefully. "When I was a little girl I was exceedingly proud of having the witch mark on my leg. I thought it made me special. Not that I ever worked any spells, none that were very successful, anyway!"

"I bear the mark, too," Mair reminded her.

"I know." A faint frown shadowed Apple's brows. "And there are times when I wish it were not so. It is as if the past reached out and laid a finger on you even before you were born. And it means that I must tell you the curse."

"The one the Welshwoman laid upon the Falcons?"

"She was a witch, they say. A real one, whose daughter married into the Falcons. For some reason they offended the witch, so she planted a tree and cursed it. All those who bear the mark must hear the curse. At least that is what old Aunt Rosemary told me. But I wonder sometimes if it's right to pass on words of evil. Perhaps it's time to let it die for lack of repeating."

"So that I can spend the rest of my life worrying what it was?" Mair teased. "If you promised—"

"Ah, time enough for the telling. I'm not dead yet," Apple coughed suddenly and painfully. "I'll be better when spring comes and this east wind dies," she said. "I'll see another summer out, I daresay."

But the previous summer had been wet, with little sunshine to ripen the corn. And that was when her slow coughing had begun.

She had fallen into one of the brief sleeps that often overcame her of late. In the wide bed she seemed defenseless, like a doll that some thoughtless child had tossed down.

Mair stood looking at her for a moment, her thin face

unusually tender. It was as if Apple were becoming the child and her daughter were moving into motherhood.

Moving quietly, her red flannel skirt swaying above her ankles, the girl went through into the yard. Her hair, chestnut brown in color, bobbed in a thick braid on her shoulders. The brown eyes that were her chief beauty scanned the road that twisted between marshland and isolated farm toward Caernarvon.

Beyond the fields the mountains reared starkly into the sky, their heads swathed in mist. On the high ground the snow lay thickly, but here, where she stood, there was still black earth to be seen. The wind was bitter, cutting a swathe toward her, and her own breath made a white vapor cloud in the air.

In Kent she supposed it was winter, too, but she imagined a mild season with the trees still green and a pale sun sparkling on the river. If her mother could go there, to the big house where she had spent her childhood, she would surely get better.

She looked again toward the road. Gareth the Post rode this way perhaps two or three times a year when there was a letter to be delivered to one of the outlying farms. No letters had ever been received at Ty Saron, but Mair was waiting for one now.

It was more than a month since she had written in the careful, round script her mother had taught her. It had taken her the best part of a morning to compose the message, for she was not sure if the man to whom she wrote still lived, or how he would receive her news. In the end she had written very simply.

Dear Lord Falcon,

You do not know me, but my mother, Apple, is your daughter. She is a widow now and very sick, and it would give her much pleasure to see her family again and to visit her old home, /

where it is warmer and her cough would get better. I am sorry to trouble you in this fashion, and am

> your respectful grand-daughter
> Mair Price.

She had written her address neatly at the top of the page and walked down into town to have the letter franked. And since then she had waited more or less patiently.

If the old man was still alive he would be very old and eager for reconciliation. If he were dead then her letter would be opened by somebody else in the family, and they would surely send for Apple. Her mother had always spoken most lovingly of her brothers and sisters.

Mair hoped the journey south would not be too tiring. They would have to take it slowly in very easy stages.

Gareth the Post was riding up the road! Hat pulled over his ears, spindleshanks dangling at each side of his fat, brown pony, muffler tied tightly round his chin, he came on steadily, importance and curiosity mantling his bony shoulders.

She hurried to the low wall for fear that he would call out and disturb her mother's sleep.

"It's cold, mistress," he greeted her. "Very cold, even for the time of year."

"Indeed it is," she agreed.

"Hard for the sheep when the lambing begins. Trying to find some cover for their young. Diawl, but I'd not be a sheep!"

"Better to be a man," she nodded.

"Better to be a rich man!" He cackled at his own wit. "And how is your mam? Very poorly she looked when I saw her."

"She's resting now."

"Then I'll not come in. Daniel Morgan's wife had her baby, by the way. Nine months to the day since the

wedding! The providence of the Lord, I'd call it myself.
Winking His eternal eye at a bit of sinning. And Dan trying to tell us the baby was early, as if he and his woman
had spent their courting chipping slate out of the
quarry!"

"Did you have a letter for me?" Mair cut into the flow
of conversation.

"A letter? Aye, there's one for you, I'm thinking." He
looked about vaguely as if he expected it to float down
from the skies.

"Is it in your saddlebag?" she enquired.

"Now it might be there." He gazed at his saddlebag
with deep suspicion.

"Could you look?"

"I could indeed." Twisting in the saddle he rummaged
busily and came up with a letter, holding it delicately
between finger and thumb.

"It is sealed with a crest," he observed. "An important-
looking crest. Not a local family, I'd say. And something
inside it. Round and hard. It has your name on it."

"It was written to me," she said patiently.

"A letter with a crest on it," Gareth the Post handed it
over slowly. "I hope there's no trouble coming. It's the
first time there's been a letter for Ty Saron. Not bad
news, I hope, with your mam so poorly."

"I don't think so." She held the letter tightly, willing
him to go.

"Well, it's for me to get on, not stay here gossiping,"
he said at last, with a disappointed look. "You'll be going
over to see the Morgan baby, I suppose? Nine pounds it
weighed. Nine pounds, and Daniel trying to make out
that it came early!"

Mair waited until he had ridden on, and then went
back into the house. Her mother was evidently still
asleep, for only the ticking of the clock and the crackling
of the wood on the fire greeted her.

She went over to the fire, sat on the three-legged stool and slit open the letter with her nail. Two gold coins rolled out into her lap and winked up at her from the white linen of her apron.

The letter was written in a thin, spidery hand, as if a bird had dipped its beak into ink and trailed it across the thick, creamy paper.

Dear Madam,

I am not in the habit of replying to begging letters, nor do I consider myself responsible for you or your mother. However, in the hope that this communication will be the last that passes between us, I enclose the sum of two guineas toward any funeral expenses,

and remain,
Yours faithfully,
Lord Edward Falcon.

The crest was a falcon, wings spread, beak curved for the kill. She stared down at it numbly, while tears of rage gathered in her eyes and ran down onto her cheeks.

After a while she put the two coins into her pocket, and threw the crested letter deep into the heart of the fire. She was wiping the last traces of tears from her face when her mother's cough sounded from the bedroom.

Apple was sitting up, hunched over a red-stained handkerchief, her shoulders heaving. As Mair came in she lay back, gasping a little, her cheeks flushed scarlet, a blue tinge about her mouth.

"I'll get you some physic," Mair began, but Apple shook her head.

"Makes me feel sick," she said. "It's over now. Catches me between the shoulder blades while it lasts. It's gone for the moment."

But it would come back. Mair knew that, knew the slow, painful coughing which made the nights wakeful. And half the winter was left before they could look for the spring.

"Mam, that curse the old witch put on the Falcons," she said casually. "Won't you tell it to me? For interest's sake?"

"If you like." Apple looked doubtful. "But I'd not have you take it too seriously. Mind, when I was a girl, I used to wonder why so much tragedy happened in the Falcons, but then we're an old family and a large one, and seasons of light and dark come and go in every life."

"The curse?" Mair prompted.

"Old Aunt Rosemary gave it to me," Apple said, "just as she'd been given it by Regina Falcon. Regina was an ancestress of mine, one of the mistresses of Charles the Second. It went—let me get the words right—"

"Yes, Mam?" Mair leaned forward, her lips moving silently as her mother spoke slowly.

" 'Grow, little vinegar tree. Grow tall and strong and overshadow the house of Falcon. Let them taste the bitterness of your leaves, in season and out of season, by night and by day, in sun and rain, in wind and snow. Let them bleed from your branches and tangle their hearts in your roots, until Margred comes as a bride to Harry Falcon of Kingsmead.' "

"That's a terrible curse," Mair said with satisfaction.

"And you must try to forget it," Apple said. "I kept my promise to Aunt Rosemary and that's my conscience clear! No sense in passing on evil."

She began to cough again, her eyes closing wearily, her thin fingers clutching the edge of the quilt.

Later that day, when her mother was asleep again, Mair put her shawl over her head and went out. In her pocket was a flat tin box in which she had placed a piece of paper on which she had written out the curse. The words had stayed in her mind without difficulty as if they had been implanted there, printed there like the dark crescent moon on her thigh.

She walked briskly, her long legs moving effortlessly over the rough track that led to the old well. An early twilight had closed in, but she knew the way blindfolded, and anger pricked her on. The words in her grandfather's letter were blazoned on her mind as deeply as the words of the curse. She could scarcely believe that any man could be so cruel as to refuse a bequest for help from his own kin. But evidently a Falcon could behave in such a way.

And I am part Falcon, too, Mair thought fiercely, and can learn how to hate.

The trees arched over the stone parapet as if they sought to hide it from the lowering sky. The clouds were heavy with snow and the wind blowing down from the heights chafed her lips. She pushed her way through the trailing creeper and flung the tin box down into the depths of the dry well. It struck the bottom of the well and echoed sharply within the cavern of stone.

So now the curse was written down, not only handed on by word of mouth. When a thing was written it became more important. Mair knew. She gazed down into the darkness, sending hatred after the box, pouring bitter contempt upon the Falcons.

I am one with the witch, she told herself. I will plant the curse here and leave it as a long memory of revenge.

The tree she had planted bent its branches toward her, and beyond the clearing a fox barked suddenly.

Let it begin, Mair thought. Wherever a Falcon is, at this moment, let him or her know despair.

At *Kingsmead*, Edward Falcon dreamed of his estate, dreamed that his broad acres were being eaten away by tiny black ants, his houses crumbling into dust. He turned uneasily in the wide bed where he had once lain with Joanna and clenched his fists upon the covers as if he sought, even in sleep, to hold onto his possessions.

In the drawing room Eliza and Weston played cards together by the dying fire, and felt the silence of the great house close in about them like the bleakness of their own old ages.

In the bedroom of the low-raftered inn, Helen lay wakeful in the arms of her husband. On the next morning they would embark on the ship destined to carry them to a new life in America, but regrets for the wasted years, for the children she would never bear, hammered at her heart.

In his bunk, Fairfax thought of Huldah and of the child she was to bear. His child, if she had spoken the truth. Had he married her he would have been tied down forever to the land. A shiver of relief ran over him, and was followed by a burning sense of shame because, in running away, he had proved himself less than a man.

Huldah, saying goodnight to James, stepped out of the circle of his arms.

"I cannot do it," she cried. "I cannot wed you! I believed that I could go through with it and confess to you later, but it's no use."

"Confess?" He stared at her blankly.

"I'm carrying a child," Huldah said in a small, desperate voice. "Your brother is the father of it. That's why he left *Kingsmead*, because he could not face the responsibility. I would have told you after we were wed and begged you to be kind, but I cannot cheat you. I believed I could, but I cannot—"

"Fairfax? A child?" He was stammering, a childish habit he had long since outgrown.

"He was my lover," she said, and her voice was suddenly calm and sad. "I believed he loved me. I tried to force him into marriage with me, but he left *Kingsmead*. And when you asked me again—I am very fond of you, James, but that isn't enough."

"I love you," James said in a tired, bewildered way. "Even when I learned about the—I'd not have cast you off, Huldah. I'd have accepted the babe for your sake. I still will."

"It isn't enough," Huldah said again. "I'd try to be a good wife, but part of me would be crying after your brother. And in the end the child would stand between us."

"But why tell me now?" Out of all the questions in his mind he chose the simplest.

"I don't know. It's as if a wind blew into my heart," she said.

"After the babe is born, then perhaps?"

"It would do no good. I can see things too clear."

She drew from her finger the ring that he had brought from Maidstone, and pressed it into his shocked, reluctant hands.

"It would do no good," she repeated.

"Huldah!"

But she had turned and fled across the yard. The slamming of the farmhouse door was like the banging of prison doors about his heart.

Apple woke, coughing, the taste of blood in her mouth. The room was growing darker and she wished Mair would come to light the candles. At *Kingsmead* there had always been so many candles.

Mair drew back from the parapet of the well. The stone had scored weals on her hands, but their pain was muted by the dreary triumph that filled her.

"Let every Falcon suffer!" she said fiercely.

Somewhere, beyond the little tree, a fox barked again.

CHAPTER FIFTEEN

"My dear boy, I am shocked beyond measure," Edward Falcon said.

"Always did wonder why Fairfax took himself off to the wars in such a hurry," Weston said, giggling. "Cut you out with the girl, did he?"

"And she would have wed you and told you about the child after the ceremony, would she?" Edward asked angrily. "A bold-faced, saucy wench. I never liked her."

"I always liked her," Eliza said calmly. "I thought she'd make a good wife for you, James. I still think she would."

"The boy can't wed his brother's leavings," Edward said, shocked.

"She'd not take me," James told them. "She's too honest to pretend love where she feels none."

"First she won't, then she will, now she won't. Girl needs to make up her mind," Weston grumbled.

"My own mind is made up on one matter," Edward said. "I'll have the Cleggs out of this village before they're a week older!"

"Samuel Clegg is not to blame," James said.

"He's the girl's father, isn't he? He should have kept stricter control over her."

"You are Fairfax's grandfather," Eliza pointed out. "There are those who'd say you ought to have kept stricter control over him!"

"Fairfax was always restless," Edward said. "He had a lot of his mother in him. Blanche was a silly, fluttering creature."

"The land will still be his," Weston said with a touch of malice.

"When I am dead, sir." The old man banged his stick on the floor and glared at them. "And, God willing, I'll live a few years yet. Fairfax will come back to find his inheritance entire. He'll have to be looking about for a wife when he returns. A rich little wife will settle him."

"James ought to wed," Weston said.

"Not the Clegg girl, but a nice local woman."

"If James has any sense he'll take this lesson to heart and stay a bachelor," Edward said.

"I'll not marry now," James said.

"There's too much marrying in this family," Edward said sourly. "I'm not speaking of Prescott, mind. It was his duty to take a wife. But there was no call for anybody else to get the notion of wedding."

"I never had such a notion," Weston observed.

"No, sir, nor ever will until they make it legal to bed choirboys," his father said. "And Eliza there, thank the Lord, would never take a husband unless he had four legs and a saddle!"

"I never met a human being that could compare with a horse yet," Eliza said, unoffended. "But James is still young. He ought to wed, else the family will die out."

"That's for Fairfax to remedy," Edward said frowningly. "James will have enough to do with managing the estate. And I'll make certain my next bailiff is a widower, with sons!"

"Samuel Clegg will stay," James said. His eyes were kind but unflinching. "Clegg will stay on. I'll not have him or his daughter driven away because of what my brother did."

"*You'll* not have it! You talk as if the land were yours," Edward said, his eyes bulging.

"I manage the land," James said calmly. "You'd need to pay six men to take my place, and they'd not be family."

"You'll have your brother's by-blow walking about in the district for everyone to see."

"That will be my brother's affair, not mine."

"You still love the girl, don't you?" Eliza said.

"I don't know." Her nephew gave her the lost, bewildered look that was often on his face those days. "I was willing to marry her. Even when she told me about the child I still wanted to marry her. But as to love—loving kindness would describe it better now."

"You'll not hold it against your brother," Edward said sharply. "We cannot have quarrels in the family."

"I hold no grudges," his grandson said. "But to rely on the affections of other people, that's a mistake I'll not make again."

The bewilderment was back in his face, but Edward nodded as if he were satisfied.

In the farmhouse Huldah sat by her bedroom window, the old telescope in her hand. She had been watching the clouds, making shapes out of their white fleeces, pretending the bits of blue sky was a limitless ocean. In her mind her body was thin and hard again, and the bulge of pregnancy had never been. She seldom thought now of the coming child. It would be born, she supposed, and folk in the village would comment on its likeness to the Falcons. She did not expect to love it.

Her father was moving about in the kitchen below. He had listened to her tale in silence, then reached for his pipe, and sucked deeply on the bitten stem.

"Poor lass; poor little lass."

No word of bitterness or reproach, but since then he had moved heavily, with pain in his face.

She had not seen any of the Falcons for weeks. As winter crept into spring she had stayed close to the farm, ignoring Beau's pleas for a walk, studying the maps in the old book and watching the sky. She dwelt in a kind of limbo into which, from time to time, there pierced an anguish that was like hunger for the lover who had betrayed her, for the life of adventure which would never now be hers.

"Had you thought of going away for a few months?" her father had asked.

"Until after the babe is born?"

She had shaken her head. Pride would not allow her to hide away. Let the village women look down their noses at her, and the men lay bets on who was responsible for her condition. She would not run as Fairfax had run.

But with the coming of spring her loneliness grew intense, and the expected child was a tie binding her to the village. If she had not been pregnant she could have gone after Fairfax, dressed as a boy, smuggled aboard his ship—a dozen schemes ran through her head, and they were all worth nothing at all because she was anchored here with a bulging stomach.

"I could have married Master James," she told Beau. "He would have forgiven me and taken the babe as his own, but I like him too well to serve him such a trick. I tried to go through with it, but I couldn't."

The dog wagged a feathery tail and, head on forepaws, stared at her in sympathy.

Samuel Clegg had only talked once of her broken engagement.

"Master James is a fine man, and would have made you a good husband," he'd said reflectively, "but I'm not sorry that you changed your mind. They're a queer lot, the Falcons. Handsome, wealthy folk, I grant you, but with a doom on them, it seems to me. No, I'm not sorry to have you change your mind."

"I'm sorry to bring shame on you," she had said in a low voice.

"The shame is the young man's, too," Samuel had said. "You and I will weather this together, Huldah girl."

"Huldah girl" from her father. "Mistress Huldah" from the village women with their sidelong smiles. But never "young weasel" from Fairfax. Never "young weasel" again!

Spring lengthened into summer. The child was due early in June. She kept close to the house and yard, lethargy her constant companion. It would be a relief to be rid of her burden, to be able to run freely again with Beau at her heels.

At night, tossing and turning as she sought some comfortable position, she pictured Fairfax in some hammock in a strange ship on an ocean she could not reach. Perhaps he was regretting the impulse that had caused him to flee. Perhaps, somewhere, he too was picturing her, holding her in his mind as he had once held her in his arms.

The pain struck at her very early one morning, making her retch and gasp. She had not expected it to be so severe, and for an instant fear stilled her limbs. Then the wave of pain receded, and she reached for her dressing-gown, forcing herself to move quickly and calmly.

Mistress Slater, who delivered most of the children in Marie Regina, had agreed to help at the birthing.

"Though a fine, big girl like you should have no trouble at all," she'd said reassuringly, "and bastards usually come into the world very easily anyway, if you'll pardon the saying."

Hoping that Mistress Slater's opinion was to be trusted, Huldah made her way as quickly as she could to her father's room, banging on the door and gritting her teeth against another searing pain.

Huldah's daughter was born two hours later, and came into the world squealing lustily.

"Not a big babe," Mistress Slater said, looking at the child critically, "but a pretty one. Quite perfect, save for the mark on her thigh."

"A crescent moon," Huldah said weakly.

Fairfax had told her once something about certain women of his family bearing a mark upon the thigh. She could not recall the rest of the tale, but the mark might serve to prove the parentage of the babe.

"You will have to name the child," Mistress Slater said.

She had never even thought of a name for it. She had not even prepared any clothes. A basket containing some of her own old baby clothes had sufficed. The tiny garments were faintly yellowed and smelt of lavender.

"Babies ought to have a name," Mistress Slater said disapprovingly. "Even a fatherless child ought to have a name."

Huldah glanced down at the tiny, swaddled babe, its minute features screwed up in the faintly disgusted expression often worn by the newborn. Into her mind a stray line floated. It came from a poem she had read once at the school in Maidstone.

"Willow garlands 'bout the head," she said tiredly.

"What did you say?"

"A poem about false lovers that I read once at school. The girls they deserted put willow garlands about their heads. I'll call her Willow."

"That's not a decent, God-fearing Christian name," Mistress Slater objected.

"It's the baby's name," Huldah said firmly. "You may tell my father. I want to go to sleep now."

She closed her eyes and was instantly asleep, the fierce pain smoothed out of her young face.

"And not one word about the father of the babe," Mistress Slater said later on to her friend, Mistress Blake. "Not one single word, though we all know it's one of the young gentlemen from the big house, don't we? And the babe has a witch mark on her leg. Willow, indeed! Bastard or not, she deserves a decent, Christian name, poor little soul."

When Huldah woke the midday sun was pouring through the latticed window. She turned her head and looked down at the child swaddled tightly on the pillow beside her. The little face was pale, like a tiny moon, the eyes closed, a fluff of fair hair on the round skull.

"Willow," she said gently.

There was no warmth in her voice, nothing in her heart save an immense relief that it was over and she was rid of her unwanted burden.

"If Fairfax knew about you he would want to marry me," she said aloud. "I know it. But he doesn't know, and there is no way I can tell him. There is no way that I can reach him unless—"

Under the covers her body felt light and flat again, but when she tried to sit up her head swam dizzily. It would be at least a week before she was strong enough to travel. She lay back on the pillows and began to plan carefully.

"It's a girl," James told his grandfather. "Huldah bore a girl child."

"You've seen her?" Edward looked up sharply.

"Samuel Clegg told me. We should—some provision ought to be made for the baby."

"Provision? On what grounds?"

"Fairfax is the father," James said steadily. "Fairfax must maintain his own child."

"If it is his child—" Edward began, but something in the younger man's face made him pause.

"I was ready to make her my wife," James said. "The least we can do is ensure that the child is adequately maintained."

"And so advertize your brother's responsibility to the world? Perhaps you would like it announced in church."

"The child is a Falcon," James said unhappily.

"The child is a—! You can raise Clegg's wage if you've a mind. Not too high, though. I'm not a rich man, not since these French wars have shot prices up like rockets."

"We ought to write to Fairfax."

"To tell him the bailiff's wench claims her hedge-get is his? That's not the kind of news a man in the forefront of action wishes to receive."

"He's not been in action yet." James had a wry twist to his mouth.

The two brief letters that they had received from Fairfax had complained of boredom and a monotonous diet.

"But when the Fleet engages he will be in the forefront," Edward said. "He has a commission—"

"Which you bought for him."

"Would you have had the future Lord Falcon serve before the mast, like some monkey of a pressgang victim? Do you grudge your brother a uniform and a sword?"

"I grudge him nothing," James said.

He spoke truly, his old affection for his twin unabat-

ed, but his eyes were wistful. It sometimes seemed that
Fairfax took and undervalued everything which James
loved. The land whose acres he had nurtured would
pass to Fairfax who cared nothing for the estate. The
girl whom he loved and had wished to marry was now
the mother of Fairfax's bastard child.

My brother never really grew up, James thought with
a flash of insight. He was always indulged and spoilt,
never made to face up to his responsibilities.

He went over to the window and stood looking out at
the green lawns which sloped away toward the deer
park. He loved every inch of the land, knew it in every
season. To leave it would have been a kind of death for
him. Even without Huldah as his wife, *Kingsmead* conferred upon him a centuries' old tranquillity. It was a
substitute for the happiness he had expected to enjoy.

There was the sound of raised voices in the parlor, and
then the curtain across the entrance arch was swished
back and Samuel Clegg strode in, carrying something
bundled in a shawl.

"I'm very sorry, milord," a flustered servant was beginning, "but he pushed his way in."

"No matter. You may go." Edward waved an impatient
hand and fixed his eyes on Samuel Clegg.

"I'll not beg pardon for bursting in," the bailiff said
truculently, "for I reckon you Falcons have served my
daughter ill. And the time's past for politeness, for Huldah's gone, and if I'm to find her someone must care for
the babe."

"Gone? Gone where?" James asked blankly.

"Gone after that brother of yours, he who betrayed
you both. She must have ridden away last night after I
was abed. The babe's crying woke me. There was a note
pinned to the pillow."

He fumbled in his pocket and pulled out a piece of paper.

"Read it," he said and thrust it into James's hand.

> Dear father,
>   I am going to find Master Fairfax. Please take
> care of Willow.
>   Your obedient daughter,
>   Huldah Clegg

James finished reading and looked up, his face drawn.

"Obedient daughter! Your daughter has strange notions of obedience," Edward snorted.

"But where would she go? Fairfax is at sea," James asked.

"And she's not a week past her confinement," Samuel said. "But she'd an easy time of it and she's a strong girl. Her horse was missing from the stable, but whether she took the London road or went to the posting station at Maidstone I've no way of knowing."

"And you intend to follow her?" Edward raised his eyebrows.

"She's my only girl," Samuel said. "My one daughter. I'll follow her, and find her, and bring her back if she'll come. But somebody must care for the child until I return."

"And the farm must care for itself, I suppose," Edward said.

"Collins can tend the farm. He's a sound husbandman and will neglect nothing. But he cannot tend a babe."

"Give it to one of the village women. They have experience in these things," Weston said helpfully.

"The babe's part Falcon," Samuel said. "You must make shift for her here."

"At *Kingsmead*? In my house? You want me to bring a bastard into my home!"

"Your grandson's bastard, milord."

"So you say. There's only your daughter's word for it."

"The babe has a witch mark on her thigh. There's talk in the village that some of the Falcon women carry the same mark."

"Apple had it," Eliza said, "and before her, old Aunt Rosemary. A crescent moon."

"Even if the child is my grandson's," Edward said stiffly, "I see no reason why it should be left here. Surely some woman in the village can be trusted to care for it. Certainly we've neither the room nor inclination for a babe here."

"She named it Willow." Samuel Clegg looked down at the bundle in his arms. "Willow for false lovers."

"She's a pretty babe." Eliza crossed over and took the child, folding the shawl back from the sleeping face.

"It's out of the question for it to stay here. We know nothing of babies," Edward said.

"They cry a lot," Weston observed.

"It would only be for a short while, until I find my girl." Samuel addressed himself to Eliza.

"She wants a good whipping for abandoning her child," Edward said. "As for you, Eliza, pray don't make a spectacle of yourself by drooling over that infant!"

"I can take care of her," Eliza said.

"You! You've had nothing to do with babies," her father said.

"I reared Fairfax and James after Prescott and Blanche were killed," she said.

"That was thirty years back. You're an old woman now," Edward said.

"I can still remember how to rear a child," she said.

"But you'll not do it under my roof," Edward said.

"This is still my home. I may be near ninety, but I'm still master in this house."

"But not at the cottage," Eliza said. Her blue eyes blazed in her scarlet face and she clutched the babe tightly.

"And what is that meant to mean?" Edward demanded.

"The Dower Cottage is mine," Eliza said stubbornly. "When Apple ran away to be married she left a letter for me, giving me the cottage. That is my cottage now, not part of the main estate. I will take the child there."

"And who, pray, will see to the ordering of affairs in this house?" Weston asked in alarm.

"See to them yourself!" Eliza flamed. "You've sat here for years, waiting for your meals to be served, your cravats starched, your room swept. Do it yourself, or stand over the servants until they do it!"

"I forbid—" Edward began.

"Forbid? *You* forbid, Father? I'm a grown woman, an old woman if you like. I never had a husband. I never wanted one, not after watching you destroy Mother for years before she destroyed herself. I never had a child. You never wanted any of us to have children, did you? None of us, except Prescott, who *must* provide an heir." Her voice was full of bitter contempt. "But I'll have my child in spite of you all. I'll have this child, and keep her safe for a little or a long time."

"Take one step out of this house and you'll not enter it again!" Edward said. His eyes bulged behind his spectacles and the veins in his forehead were throbbing.

"Grandfather, you'll make yourself ill," James said.

"Be silent. I've a right to make myself ill if I choose!" Edward shouted.

Weston burst into hysterical mirth, his plump shoulders quivering.

"I'll not come back," Eliza said. "I'll not come into this house again until you are dead and buried, Father. I'll live at the Dower Cottage."

"And when the girl comes crawling back to claim her brat, you need not run home again," Edward said.

"I'll not!" Eliza said sharply. "You can leave the child with me, Master Clegg. I'll take good care of her."

"She never wanted the babe," Samuel said. "She named her Willow and gave her nothing else. She didn't even feed the child herself. She gave her cows' milk mixed with water, and said her own milk was dried up."

"Unnatural," Edward muttered.

"I'll see the babe is fed," Eliza said to the bailiff. "I'll take her down to the cottage."

"But it hasn't been lived in for years, Aunt."

James spoke in complete and utter disbelief. His world had shifted on its axis, and those he loved turned unfamiliar faces toward him. He kept his eyes averted from the baby. If he looked at it the image he had banished from his mind would come back. The image of Huldah clasped in his brother's arms, conceiving the child that might have been his.

"I'd be obliged to you," Samuel Clegg said. "I must seek my girl, you see. But I'd no mind to make you quarrel with your father."

"We have no father," Eliza said. "We have only the master of *Kingsmead* here, and the master of *Kingsmead* has no family. He has only property."

"You have no money. How do you propose to live?" Edward asked in triumph.

"You owe me an allowance for my years of slavery," Eliza said calmly. "You can spare a hundred pounds a year. If you cannot I'll hire myself out as a cook."

"I'll find my girl and bring her back," Samuel promised.

"Don't hurry," Eliza said. "I never had a home of my own before. Let me enjoy peace for a little while."

"And when winter comes and the roof leaks and the fire smokes, don't come whining to me," her father said.

"Did Helen come whining back?" Eliza asked. "Did Apple? They took their chance and left, as I am doing. And it will be as if a continent lay between this house and the cottage. And I'll not cross that continent, Father, not until you're dead and buried!"

CHAPTER SIXTEEN

They were steaming eastward toward Cadiz, steaming scarcely three knots an hour, for the weather was calm and sunny. The tall lad, a greased pigtail of blonde hair sticking out above the rolled neck of the blue and white striped jersey, leaned against the rail and watched the ripples of sunlight on the water.

Four months at sea had tanned Huldah's skin to bronze and taken from her face the last remnants of womanly softness. She had become so used to lowering and roughening her voice that she could speak now without thinking of the role she played, and her body under the loose garments was hard and lean.

Sometimes she forgot that she was a woman herself, so that it came as a shock when she saw her companions stripped to the waist and realized that she must continue to perform her own ablutions on the rare occasions when she had a few minutes' privacy.

Privacy was in short supply on the *Victory*. The decks were crammed with men at every hour of the day and night, and the watches were punctuated by the shouted

orders of tired and irritable officers. The stench from the
gun deck where all except the officers and midshipmen
slept had appalled her at first, but now she sank gratefully into the damp hammock and slept deeply for as
long as she was allowed.

It had been impossible for her to keep the secret of her
sex entirely to herself. One or two of the older sailors,
having made overtures to the pretty lad, and having
been indignantly repulsed, had eyed her more sharply
and arrived at the correct conclusion, but beyond a
good-humored nudge and a wink had done nothing.

There were several women on board the twenty-seven
ships of the line. Some were whores, one or two had been
smuggled aboard to join their husbands. If the officers
knew about it they said nothing.

Huldah had joined the *Victory* when she was anchored
at Portsmouth for three weeks the previous month. Before that she had been on a Channel frigate that ran the
blockade between Calais and Dover. It had been easier
than she could have hoped to ride to London, purchase
seaman's clothing with the egg money she had saved,
and loiter in the docks. A crowd of seamen had marched
back on board their vessel and she had insinuated herself
among them, given her name as Sam Piggott to the
boatswain, and settled down to the learning of a new
life.

It had not been easy but she had loved every moment
of it, loved it so much that sometimes she was in danger
of forgetting why she had run away from Marie Regina.
Fairfax had retreated into the storehouse of her memory,
and her present reality lay in heaving decks wet with
spray and the harshness of tarred rope between her calloused palms.

"The Admiral's on his way!" somebody hissed, and she
turned to watch the thin, slight figure, stars glittering on

the breast of his immaculate frock-coat. He was pausing here and there to exchange a word with a junior officer, a sailor pulling at a coil of rope, little Johnny from Edinburgh who was ten years old and whose first battle this was.

"Tie a kerchief over your head, lad, if you don't want to be deafened by blast," a big gunner advised as he passed.

She knotted her scarf about her ears, and the music from the band up on the poop was muted. The Admiral had moved away and stood talking to Dr. Scott. Nearby an assistant surgeon was sharpening the knives and saws that would be needed for emergency amputations. A small powder-monkey ran past on his way to the magazines.

"Hoping for prize-money?" One of the cooks had come up to her and leaned briefly against the rail.

"Hundreds of pounds!" Huldah said, cheerfully gruff.

"We'll be lucky to see ten," the cook said. "Still, that's nigh on a year's pay for some, but it's the captains who'll take the lion's share. Will you just look at that!" He nudged her and pointed out to sea. Other men were crowding to the rails, pointing and exclaiming.

The French and Spanish fleets that had been briefly glimpsed since dawn now spanned the horizon. Their sails were spread like wings against the blue sky.

"Three miles off, near as makes no odds." The cook squinted into the sunlight. "Would you fancy a bite of beef to settle your stomach?"

Huldah shook her head, but there was a queer, sick feeling inside her. The rippled water had murky depths and the sails spread against the sky were tinged with red.

They were hoisting a signal. Huldah screwed up her eyes to watch the flags being run up the mastheads and yards.

"'England expects that every man will do his duty,'" the cook translated gloomily. "Silly bloody signal, if you ask me. We know well enough what to do."

Thin cheers were ringing out from ship to ship. Behind the *Victory* the other vessels were closely crowded, their prows cutting a white wake through the turquoise ocean. She said some of their names under her breath. *Temeraire. Neptune. Conqueror. Leviathan. Britannia. Ajax.* And many more, and in one of them, somewhere, was the father of her child, the lover who would desire her again when he learned the dangers she had faced in order to follow him.

"Get a move on, boy. You're not paid to idle, and we're ordered to battle quarters," a junior boatswain said impatiently.

Men were hurrying to and fro, their expressions tensely expectant. The bandsmen, instruments under their arms, were climbing down the companionways toward the orlap deck.

"There's another signal going up." Huldah pointed.

"'Engage the enemy more closely,'" the boatswain read, "I never knew a man so addicted to sending signals."

He aimed an absent-minded foot at Huldah's backside and hurried off.

A burst of gunfire exploded across the water and black smoke puffed up into the clear air. Huldah, scrambling for the gun decks, heard the young boatswain exclaim.

"By God! the miserable French have dared to fire first!"

"The *Royal Sovereign* is firing back!" Huldah shouted.

"It's Collingwood's ship. The mizzen topmast is down!"

"But she's sailing on, into the midst of the Frenchies!"

"By Judas, she's locked on the lee side of the *Santa Ana!*" somebody called out.

The two ships were fading into the smoke and flame of their discharging guns.

"Get below!" someone yelled.

But she could not move. She could only stand, clinging to the rail, her eyes wide with excitement and fear. A shot whistled over her head, so close that she could feel the rush of air fluttering the ends of her kerchief.

Then she was running across the deck, her hands over her ears, her feet slithering on planks already slippery with blood. All around were the screams of wounded men, the yells of those who heaved rope and tackle, the curses of a big seaman who had begun to climb the rigging towards a shattered sail.

There was a shuddering crash as the ship rammed the port bow of a French vessel. The name *Redoubtable* loomed in painted letters before Huldah's eyes, and then the hulls were locked together and men were swarming over the upper decks.

Fire leapt in small explosions of orange across the planks and a sail hung tattered from its mast, the canvas riddled with bullet holes. Spent cartridges rolled underfoot, and a powder monkey knelt in the corner between two barrels of tar and cried for his mother.

"Nelson is down," somebody shouted in a panic of anguish.

She raised her head in order to see, but the clouds of black smoke that blew across the decks stung her eyes and made her cough.

"Our little admiral is dying!" somebody cried out, and then all the voices were lost in a renewal of cannon fire, and the sharp tingling of metal as hand-grenades flung at random landed on the boards and a moment later exploded.

"Clear the decks!"

The order was screamed out from somewhere on the

poop deck and Huldah was being thrust down the hatch-way into the dark, narrow confines of the gun deck.

Somebody at her feet was moaning. She looked down, peering through the gloom, and saw a young man crawling there. Half his face had been shot away, but what remained had an uncanny resemblance to Fairfax.

She closed her eyes briefly and groped her way be-tween the rows of sweating gunners. It was so dark down here that it was, she thought, like being in the bowels of the earth. It was like being dead and still aware of all earthly pain.

"Give me a hand, boy."

One of the surgeons was shaking her arm, indicating a twitching heap upon the deck. Huldah bent obediently, retching as the sweet, sickly odor of blood rose to her nostrils. She helped carry the man to one of the mess tables scrubbed ready for amputation cases.

"Is it true? Is our Nelson really hit?" somebody asked.

Time lost its meaning. She carried buckets, lifted men, rolled the dead in sheets of canvas, passed down water to sweating men who lifted begrimed faces from the black pit of the lower decks. Her shoulders and arms ached, the palms of her hands were rubbed raw, her feet were bruised. She no longer thought about Fairfax or remem-bered the green fastness of the woods beyond *Kingsmead.* Only death and blood and pain were left to make up a world that was more like hell than anything she had ever known.

"Boy! You there!" Somebody was calling her down the open hatchway.

She climbed up, her legs shaking with weariness, her face blackened with smoke. It was a surprise to see that it was still daylight, a daylight shot through with flame and cloud.

"I'm to take a message to the *Royal Sovereign*," the young officer who had hailed her was saying.

"A message?" She gaped at him stupidly.

"They're lowering a boat. Captain Hardy's orders. You can help to row."

She followed obediently, passing the littered dead and dying, climbing into the boat, her head ducked low over the oar. The green sea rose to meet them, its surface marred by the flotsam and jetsam of a battle at sea. Like green prehistoric monsters the ships circled warily, or were locked in combat.

"The *Royal Sovereign* is crippled!" one of the other men cried.

"The *Euryalus* has her in tow," another said.

"But she's still firing. And the Spanish ship is in worse shape."

"Hold your noise and row!" The young officer spoke sharply, his face tight with grief and importance.

The hull of the *Royal Sovereign* towered over them. She could see the black mouths of the guns and the tall masts tumbled amid billowing sails which rose and fell with the motion of the waves.

They were pulling themselves up the long ladder to the deck. Her head swam a little as she climbed, and her ears rang with the echoes of exploding cannon.

Her hands were gripped as somebody leaned to pull her aboard. She looked up to mutter her thanks and stared at Fairfax Falcon.

He had not changed in the months of their parting. Even if he had she would have known him, her heart recognizing him before her eyes could see him.

"Huldah! Huldah, what in hell are you doing here?" It was not the romantic salutation she had dreamed, but she flung herself into his arms.

"I came to seek you! Oh, Master Fairfax, I thought I would never find you again."

"*Mr.* Falcon, sir!" The outraged voice of a nearby officer penetrated the moment of reunion.

"Sir, this is a girl from home. Mistress Huldah Clegg." Fairfax made a brief, embarrassed introduction.

"A wench! You have no business to bring a female on board!" the officer exploded.

"I followed him," Huldah said. "I dressed as a boy and followed him, but he didn't know of it. He truly didn't know."

"Take her out of range of the guns, and then get back to your post," the officer said brusquely.

"I have to speak to you," Huldah said tensely to Fairfax.

"Not now. Later."

He would have gone, but she clutched at his arm.

"*Now*," she said. "Too much time has gone by and there are things to be said, matters to be settled."

"The child!" Remembering, he stared at her. "You were going to have a child, you said. Or was that a lie?"

"I never lied to you." In the grime of her face her eyes were clear and candid. "I never lied to you. The child was born in June. A girl. I named her Willow."

"Did the child live?"

"Your daughter is alive. I left her with my father and ran away."

"To find me?" He looked unwillingly flattered.

"I always wanted to go to sea. You know that. But it was to find you. Most of all, it was to find you."

"Why did you come aboard? Did you know I was here?"

"No. The boat came with a message. Admiral Nelson is wounded, shot. Captain Hardy wanted Admiral Collingwood to know as soon as possible."

"The admiral shot! Is it bad?"

"I think so. There are so many wounded, so many dead and dying." Without warning she began to sob, the horrors of the past hours crowding into her mind.

"Little weasel, don't cry!" He put his arm around her. "Don't cry!"

"I wanted you to marry me," she said shakily. "I meant to force you to marry me. It was stupid, very stupid. But being without you . . . I hungered for you so."

"I have to be free, not tied to the land, not tied to any one woman," Fairfax said. "I never wanted the things my grandfather valued. James should have been the elder. He loves *Kingsmead*, and he'd have made you a good husband."

It was true, but a lifetime with James was not worth these few minutes on a crowded, slippery deck with the man she loved.

Fairfax was smiling at her. Even when he was urging his brother's suit he was, half-consciously, charming his way more deeply into her affections. The approval and desire of others was always necessary to him.

"You made love to me," she said tremulously. "Didn't that show that you cared?"

His thoughts flashed back to his grandfather and to the old man's request. 'Seduce your brother's girl to prove her wanton.' He had succeeded all too well, and in so doing had been caught up himself in the enchantment of a brief affair.

It meant nothing now though he was pleased the child had been safely born. To have fathered a child proved his virility. But the girl he had held in his arms in the wood bore no resemblance to this grubby figure in loose jerkin and trousers with a kerchief knotted around her head.

"You did care, didn't you?" she said.

He took her face between his hands and smiled into her eyes, lying out of kindness and the need to have her think well of him.

"Little weasel, of course I cared! I still do," he said.

She closed her eyes in brief thankfulness and felt his breath on her cheek. It was her last conscious action before the grenade, flung from the crippled *Santa Ana*, exploded at their feet.

From hill to hill the beacons of victory were lighted and the bells rang out. The Fleet had triumphed and Napoleon, gathering together the remnants of his pride, had retreated to Boulogne for the winter. The threat of invasion had receded.

But there was grief amid the triumph. Grief for the admiral who had been loved so deeply, grief for the men who had been killed and maimed, grief for the proud ships that limped back to harbor in Cadiz and Gibraltar. Black crepe draped the flags of victory and the bells had a mournful toll.

"It was no use," Samuel Clegg told Eliza. "I've tramped the streets day after day, night after night, but there's no sign. And my money is running out."

He looked tired and defeated as he sat by the fire in the living room of the cottage. He had ridden straight there after his return and been relieved to see smoke curling up from the chimney.

Eliza, her hair pushed into a mob cap, an apron tied about her waist, had opened the door. Behind her the room glowed, warmly inviting. Roof and windows had been repaired and the walls replastered. There were braided rugs on the floors and covers on the chairs.

"James had it done for me," Eliza said, reading his glance. "You'd best come in and eat. Weather's turned stormy and cold."

She had brought hot, thick soup and new-baked bread

and some cold chicken. He ate greedily, his stiff leg stretched out to the fire.

"The babe?"

She nodded toward a wooden rocker in the corner, her lips curving into a smile.

"Willow is fine," she said. "Small, but thriving."

"Lord Falcon—"

"My father will not relent," she said shortly. "He will not allow me back over the threshold of the house, but it makes no odds to me. I'm comfortable here and I get an allowance, enough for the child and me."

"I'm obliged to you," he said. "If you hadn't stepped in to help—you know, I never thought that my Huldah would run off and leave her babe. When she comes back I'll have more than a word to say to her."

He broke off, seeing something of infinite sadness in her face, noticing for the first time that her dress was black.

"Huldah won't come back," Eliza said. "James told me about it yesterday. They received word up at *Kingsmead* and he rode down to tell me. Huldah and Fairfax won't come back. They were both killed at Trafalgar."

"Killed?"

The word sank like a stone between them and then there was only the ticking of the clock and the hissing of coals in the fire.

"My girl was at Trafalgar?" he said. "How could she? Did she really run away to sea? I made enquiry in the docks, but I had no joy of it. How could it be?"

"We have not had the full details," Eliza said. "It seems that she was on board the *Royal Sovereign* with Fairfax. They were killed together and buried at sea. We know nothing more than that."

"My poor girl." He passed his hand over his eyes and shivered.

"There is still the babe," Eliza said.

"Aye, my poor grandchild. No father, no mother. How will she fare?"

"Well enough, if I continue to rear her," Eliza said.

"You would be willing?"

"If you took her to the farm," Eliza said, "you would find it hard, even with your housekeeper to help."

"She left when I told her the child was coming. Fear of scandal," Samuel said wryly.

"Then you'd have to engage somebody else and she might not have any affection for the babe," Eliza said.

"And you would have that affection?"

"I love the babe," Eliza said simply. "The years have grown lonelier as one by one my sisters and brothers have died or left. Soon the loneliness will engulf me. But with a child, with Willow—oh! it is not only for my sake that I want her. It is for her sake, too. She must grow up in the knowledge that somebody loved and wanted her."

"Then I'll leave her with you." He stood up abruptly, his shoulders hunched.

"Will you stay on as bailiff?" she asked.

"Why not? There's nowhere else to go."

He went over to the cradle and peered down at the tiny flower face, the fingers of one small hand curled like petals against the white cheek.

"She bears the witch mark," he said uneasily.

"As my sister Apple did. I envied her that when we were young. But she has your daughter in her face."

"She looks all Falcon to me," Samuel Clegg said.

"We are not all bad," Eliza said lightly. "My sisters had great sweetness in them. And James is a fine young man."

"I'm grateful to you," he said again and passed out into the clearing.

Eliza stood at the door and watched him ride slowly toward the bridle path. She sensed that he had been relieved to have the problem of the babe taken out of his hands. Certainly the Falcons had dealt harshly with him and his.

Perhaps, after all, it had turned out for the best. Now James would inherit both peerage and land, and the restless charm of his elder brother was stilled forever under the wild breakers of the ocean.

James had told her that his grandfather had taken the news bravely, even with a certain pride. Fairfax was the third Falcon to die gallantly in battle. Now his name would join the others on the reverse side of the family tomb. She wondered if any monument would be raised to Huldah Clegg, who had translated her dream of adventure into reality and died in the doing of it.

The wind whipped across the clearing, bending the tops of the trees, ruffling the bushes into strange shapes. Eliza was conscious suddenly of the loneliness of the place. Even in winter the trees and bushes shut out the river and the long pasture which sloped up toward *Kingsmead*. She had brought her own roan mare down to the cottage, stabling her in a lean-to shed which James had erected against the main building. But she missed the horses in the stables with their undemanding affection and liquid, trustful eyes.

Something moved out of the trees toward her. For a moment she felt a ripple of alarm, but the newcomer paused in front of her, tail wagging.

"Beau! What are you doing here?"

She knelt to pat Huldah's dog. The animal had always been at the girl's heels. In the months since her departure Eliza had seen Beau several times, tail drooping, about the village.

The dog wagged his tail and licked her hand. Then he

went past her into the cottage. As Eliza turned to close the door she saw him, tail still moving, trot over to the cradle and settle down there, nose on paws, eyes fixed on the carved and painted wood.

"You know, don't you?" Eliza said. "You know that Huldah won't come home. Well, if you're going to stay, I'd best find you a bite to eat."

She was, all at once, ridiculously, irresistibly happy.

EPILOGUE

1806

Edward Falcon sat in the high-backed chair by the glowing fire. Although it was mid-May and warm for the time of year, he was cold. He was cold most of the time these days, cold and so weary that it was an effort to wake up in the morning, to dress himself, to go to bed again at night.

I am too old, he thought reluctantly. A man ought not to live too long, to find out that his family are not worthy of him.

None of them had measured up to his standards. *None of them!* They had all inherited weakness from their mother. He had been a fool to wed Joanna, even if the marriage had doubled his property. A stupid woman, he remembered, who had not even been desirable.

He recalled only too clearly her irritating mannerisms, her untidiness, her twitching fingers. She had spoilt the children, giving in to their whims, encouraging the girls to defy his authority. And they had all been disappointments. Even Prescott, whom he had shaped in his own image, had been fool enough to let the horses bolt, killing both himself and Blanche.

Weston was a twisted old maid of a man, all corsets and indigestion and embroidery. Nat had been headstrong, daring to fall in love with his brother's sweetheart. As for Helen, Eliza, and Apple! Much good their defiantly romantic notions had done them! Helen wed to a transported man, Apple run off with a vagabond artist and reduced to having her daughter write begging letters on her behalf, Eliza sulking her time away in that abominable cottage with someone else's bastard yet to rear.

He thought of his two grandsons, of Fairfax who had fled from the success of his own wooing and died in battle, of James who would now inherit. A good, steady man who loved the estate, but lacked that possessive adoration of it that Edward had tried to instill.

James would have to wed now, to ensure the continuation of the line. His infatuation for the Clegg wench would fade, and he would take a sensible wife, one with money.

When I feel a little better, when I am not so weary, I will look about and find a suitable bride, Edward thought.

A faint doubt stirred in him. James, for all his dutiful, affectionate ways, had a streak of obstinacy. He had set his face firmly against the dismissal of Samuel Clegg and he went down to see Eliza once or twice a month. He had even, to his grandfather's disgust, insisted upon contributing to a memorial stone for Huldah Clegg.

"She must have loved my brother dearly to follow him into battle," James had said, and his eyes had been wistful.

There had been, Edward considered sourly, too much loving in the family. His mother would not have approved.

"Land is the only thing that lasts," Fiona had

impressed upon him. "My parents loved each other, but their love brought them nothing. My mother dragged herself and me from town to town, following my father. No settled home, only a sergeant's pay on which to feed and clothe us. And I was foolish enough to fall in love with your father and wed him. But at least he had an estate, position, wealth."

And I, thought Edward, have added to that land, have increased that wealth. But James must add to the estate.

He mentally surveyed his possessions. There was *Kingsmead* itself, of course, and the manor house and the thousand acres that encompassed them. There was Wittle Farm and Paget Place in Maidstone, and the crops from the lands, the jewels passed down from Regina Falcon, the furniture and tapestries, silver plate, the gold christening cup, so many possessions, and each one a symbol of the power he had craved and the security for which he had longed.

Certainly James must marry, and soon. For I cannot, thought Edward, go down into the dark without ensuring that the estate will endure.

He rose stiffly, reaching for his stick, and went down the long hall toward the main door. To stand in the sunshine for a few minutes might warm him, might take away the heaviness that seemed to have settled about him. It was odd, but he had never been lonely before.

The courtyard was golden with sunshine, its cobbles mellow, its walls ivied. It lay before him, inviolate, and then a shadow stretched toward him.

A tall young woman stood in the archway and stared at him across the intervening space. Edward blinked, adjusting his spectacles, feeling cold again, for the girl was tall and broad-shouldered as Huldah Clegg had been.

Then she walked toward him, and he saw she was not like Huldah at all, but thin-faced with dark brown hair coiled about her ears and a shabby green dress under a tight-fitting jacket.

"Lord Falcon?" Her voice was deep with a lilting accent, as if she threw the last word of her sentence high into the air.

"I am Lord Falcon."

Without realizing it he had moved aside and without further words she walked past him into the hall and stood, calmly looking around.

"Who are you? What do you want?" he asked hoarsely, but even before she spoke he had begun to guess.

"I am Mair Price, Apple's daughter," she said.

"Apple—"

"Is dead," she told him. "She died a year ago, still talking of the summers in Kent. She never saw the summer again. She never came back to her family."

"My daughter made her choice a long time ago," he said harshly.

"She married the man she loved," Mair said passionately. "Is that so wrong? Is it so wrong to love?"

"I did not send after her to bring her back." He banged the door shut and glared at her.

"You did not send after her to find out how she did!" Mair flashed. "In all those years you never tried to discover if she was alive or dead, if she was sick or in want. You cut her off as if she had never been a part of you, never been your child. And it was the same with the others, wasn't it?"

"What do you know of my family?" he snapped.

"Enough! A little from my mother, though she spoke only of the happy days, for she was gentle and harbored no bitterness. Even when she lay dying, coughing her life away in a rainy spring, even then she had no bitterness. For her sake I delayed a whole year until I came, and when I travelled here I went first to the village."

"To listen to gossip?"

"To find out how you were regarded in the neighborhood, to find out if you had changed since you sent me two guineas for the burying of my mother!"

"The Falcons are respected," he began.

"And feared," she interrupted. "Feared for the witch blood in them, for the wealth that gives them power. The innkeeper talked of you. So many tragedies in one family, he said, as if God had forgotten you, or a witch's curse had grown stronger with the years. But the tragedy never touched you, did it? It touched only your children, and you never valued them. And in the end they too escaped in their own separate ways. But that didn't touch you either, because you never loved them. You are a man incapable of love."

"You have no right," he said shakily, "to speak to me in such a manner!"

"I am your grand-daughter!" Mair said fiercely. "I am a Falcon, and I too bear the mark. Look!"

She raised her narrow skirt, thrusting out a bare leg and he saw the purple crescent moon imprinted on her thigh.

"What do you want?" he asked.

"Everything," she said. "I want everything, Grandfather. All the things my mother was denied after she followed her heart. She had a hard life of it, she and my father. A little money might have lengthened both their lives, but you never sent to ask how they did. You never cared about anything except property, did you?"

Her fierce young face and torrent of whirling words were too powerful. It was as if all the ghosts of the past had come together in the person of this girl.

"I am old," he said faintly. "I am old and sick. It is not good for me to be bothered in this way."

"Then you had best sit down," she said, brisk and cool

again. "I left my bag at the inn and walked over from the
village. You will have to send a servant to pick it up."

"But you cannot possibly stay here!" Lowering himself
into a chair he stared up at her in alarm.

"Where else would I stay?" she enquired. "I am your
grand-daughter."

"You already have a home," he said. "There is the land
in Wales."

"It will stay until I return to it," Mair said. "But I am
come back to my mother's home. We will have a family
reunion."

"I forbid it!" He banged his stick upon the floor. "Old I
may be, but I am still master here. I will have you
thrown out unless you go of your own accord."

"James would not like it," Mair said.

"James? What do you know of James?"

"I know that he will inherit, now that his brother is
dead. The innkeeper told me that you have an affection
for him that is almost as great as the affection you have
for your property. The innkeeper said that he is a generous man, that he helps to maintain his brother's bastard.
And the innkeeper says that he is fond of you."

"So?"

"So, will he still be as fond of you if he learns that
when your own child was dying you refused to help her?
That when your legitimate grand-daughter came you
turned her out of doors?"

"You would not tell him," he said hoarsely.

But he knew that she would, and that the fatal flaw of
kindness in his grandson's nature would lead to a breach
between them which nothing could heal.

"You depend upon James, don't you?" Mair said,
watching his face. "In his eyes you see a reflection of
yourself as strong and proud. But it's not real, that affec-

tion. Inside you're mean and small and old. You don't want James to discover that, do you?"

She was saying terrible, wounding things, things that were not true. He was Lord Falcon, the master of *Kingsmead*. He was a man who had always stood alone, without the need for other human beings. But one by one they had left him, found him out and left him. He dare not let that happen with James, for if James went, who would manage the land and guard the inheritance?

"I'll not be a burden," Mair was saying. "I'm strong and capable, and will run your household well. We shall be exceedingly comfortable together."

Weakly he heard himself requesting her to call Thomas that her bag might be brought from the village.

James was on his way back from the cottage where he had been visiting Aunt Eliza. Her absence from *Kingsmead* was something to which he was not yet accustomed, for, having no memory of his parents, she had always represented for him the mother he had never known. There were moments when he was even tempted to regard his grandfather's attitude as harsh.

The child was, after all, a Falcon, and had to be gently reared. She was a pretty babe, too, already pulling herself up into a standing position. She and the dog Beau were inseparable; Beau sleeping by her crib, allowing her impatient starfish fingers to tug his silky coat.

"She will be a year old soon," Eliza said. "It will be interesting to watch her grow."

He had watched her himself, finding small resemblance to either Fairfax or Huldah in the tiny face.

When he thought of Huldah now it was with a gentle regret. He had loved her truly and that love would always be a part of him, but she had never been his, not even when she had promised to wed him. And, in the end, she and Fairfax had died together, bright-crested above the waves.

"You should take a wife," Eliza said gently.

His grandfather had been hinting much the same thing. It was, James supposed, his duty to beget an heir, but he could not bring himself to choose a wife as he would choose a mare or a cow.

"I'd like children," he admitted.

They might have been Huldah's children, but that was not to be, though he would always look kindly on Willow for the sake of those he had loved.

Riding home slowly across the fields he was conscious of a restless yearning quite foreign to his usually placid nature. He could go over to Maidstone, he supposed, and hire himself a wench. But he craved something deeper than a lustful coupling, something that was as clean and lasting as the earth he tended.

A young woman was standing by the archway that led into the courtyard. A tall young woman with chestnut hair coiled about her ears. As James dismounted she stepped toward him, her thin hand outstretched, glowing brown eyes raised to his face.

"Cousin James? I am Mair Price, Apple's daughter." Her voice was deep with a lilting accent.

"My aunt's daughter?"

"She and my father are dead now," Mair said. "I travelled down from Wales to seek my relatives, and Grandfather has invited me to make my home here, if you have no objection. I will do my part in helping about the house."

"Objection! I am truly delighted you are come." He wrung her hand warmly, all the cheerfulness in his nature rising to the surface.

"It was something of an ordeal, coming among

strangers," she confided. "I know my mother's marriage was a disappointment to her father."

"Grandfather is a trifle eccentric," James admitted, "and his standards of conduct are very high, often too high for other folk to reach. But he welcomed you?"

"Most hospitably," she said demurely, "once the first surprise was past."

"As I welcome you!" He shook hands again, his pleasant face glowing. "I never knew my aunt, for she left *Kingsmead* before I was born, but I've always suspected that Grandfather would have been glad of a reconciliation."

It was true, he was thinking, that life always had something new to offer. It had come now, in the shape of a brown-eyed girl with a warm voice.

"I think I will be happy here," she said wistfully.

"Happy? Of course you will be! There is so much to show you, so much we can do together. Do you ride?"

"Not well."

"Then we must find you a gentle mount. You haven't met Uncle Weston yet?"

Mair shook her head.

"He will be pleased to know you are here. Aunt Eliza, too, though there is a falling-out between her and Grandfather. But you will soon be at home here. There has been too much unhappiness, but I have a feeling your coming has altered that!"

As he took her arm and led her back into the courtyard the rust-colored leaves of the luck-tree quivered violently, as if someone somewhere shook with laughter.

THE END